WHAT READERS ARE SAYING

Lale Davidson's Beyond Sight is a deep exploration of college student Julie Sykes' journey to discover and embrace her origin story and the psychic gift that is her inheritance. Along the way, Davidson treats us to insights about fractals and quantum entanglement that deftly connect the dots between science, dreams, and psychic phenomena and give us a relatable way to enter Julie's visceral experiences of intuition and the supernatural. Set in Saratoga Springs during the beginning of the Trump era, the narrative reaches back in history to the murky circumstances of Julie's childhood and to some local capitalist corruption of the Victorian era. But the heart of this ghost story is the emotional growth that comes from facing our inner wounds and repairing the relationships that get damaged in the cauldron of child-parent relationships. This is a page-turner crafted by a master storyteller in graceful language that helps us unearth the magic of our own inner challenges and resources.

—Wendy Newton, yoga master, polarity therapist, and co-author of *Tantra of the Yoga Sutras*

A great ghost story for the Trump era, as we contend with the many ghosts that haunt the us, addiction, racism, capitalism, rage, and climate change.

–Peter Ferko, yoga master and author of *Incarnation* and *The Genius of Yoga*

A marvelous mystery wrapped around the beautiful and haunting city of Saratoga Springs, blending suspense with the paranormal.
  –Maeve Noonan, Northshire bookseller and Saratoga resident

Beyond Sight is a well-crafted story with the right mix of horror, intrigue, and the essence that one feels while reading the series Twilight.
  –Katherine Abraham, author of *Every Sunset Has a Story*

Lâle Davidson proves herself once more to be a master of the mystical and the beautiful. Rich characters, each speaking in compelling voices, lead us through life and death and life again, and lead the reader to continue reading, just to find out what will happen to them next.
  –B.A. Chepaitis, author of *The Fear Principle* series and *The Amber*

You don't have to believe in ghosts to love this great story full of Saratoga Springs settings and culture. But don't be surprised if you develop an appreciation of the energy and spirits that haunt our special city after reading Lâle Davidson's engaging book.
  Joe Haedrich, author of *Haunted Saratoga*

LÄLE DAVIDSON
BEYOND SIGHT

EMPEROR BOOKS

Beyond Sight

Copyright © 2023 by Lale Davidson

All rights reserved.

Published by Emperor Books

Bellerose Village, New York

ISBN

Print 978-1-63777-475-5, 978-1-63777-476-2

Digital 978-1-63777-474-8

No part of this book may be reproduced in any form or by any electronic or mechanical means, including information storage and retrieval systems, without written permission from the author, except for the use of brief quotations in a book review.

CONTENTS

Acknowledgments	vii
1. Out of Place	1
2. The Crackle	7
3. Meeting Damian	10
4. The Energy Thing	17
5. Geography of Nowhere	24
6. The Man With White Hair	28
7. Samantha's Problem	31
8. The Adirondacker	36
9. Confession	40
10. Falling Through	48
11. Haunted House	53
12. Jumbled Impressions	63
13. Mother-Daughter Dance	67
14. Anima Arcanum	72
15. Wilton Town Hall	75
16. Eminent Domain	81
17. A Plan Begins to Form	86
18. Séance	91
19. Forensics	106
20. Why No Pictures	112
21. Something's Off	118
22. Worlds Collide	122
23. Openings Without Close	127
24. Graves' Disease	133
25. A Question of Murder	138
26. Thanksgiving	146
27. Owning the Night	152
28. The Day After	158
29. Confrontation	162
30. Athena	168

31. Missing	173
32. Seer and Pusher	176
33. Meanwhile	184
34. At Jacob's House	191
35. Mistake	200
36. Emergency Room	207
37. Fathers	214
38. Athena Returns	218
39. The Nursing Home	223
40. At the Hospital	229
41. Revelation	235
42. At the Well	242
43. Pocketful of Dirt	254
Epilogue	265
Book Club Questions	269
About the Author	271

ACKNOWLEDGMENTS

I want to extend my profound thanks to my publisher Stephanie Larkin at Red Penguin Books. Before she appeared in my life like a fairy godmother, I felt like Cinderella toiling away alone at the hearth. Her constant enthusiasm and generosity are a wonder. I'd also like to thank my writing group SUAWP (Shut Up and Write Please), which consists of Jackie Goodwin, Anntonette Alberti, Elaine Handley, and now Ellen Santasiero for their insightful critiques. I'd like to thank my husband Charles Brown, my first reader and ever-loving cheerleader. Thanks also to other readers, Katie Bowen, Laura Albert, and Maeve Noonan. A big thank you goes to Rachel Person, the events manager at the Northshire Bookstore in Saratoga Springs, and to my adult child, Ex Davidson-Brown. I recently found an old draft of *Beyond Sight* in their room, with my name crossed out and the words, *Best Mother Ever* penciled in. Finally, thanks goes to the Saratoga Room at the Saratoga Springs Public Library for their help in researching Henry Hilton, one of the richest men in America during the Gilded Age. The true story of how he came into his fortune via his oddly close friendship with A.T. Stewart is detailed in many places, as well as how he created Woodlawn Park, part of which later became the Skidmore College campus. The details of Hilton's antisemitism, the fate of his mansions and fortune, as well as Stewart's body, are all true. All rest of the details in this story are a complete fabrication. All the names, characters, businesses, places, events, and incidents in this book are either the product of my imagination or used in a fictitious manner. Any resemblance to actual persons, living or dead, or actual events is purely coincidental. Also, no AI was used in the writing of this book (except Google searches). Viva the human imagination.

1
OUT OF PLACE

SEPTEMBER 2016

I blame my college English professor. She's the one who assigned us the autobiography. My father had died of an aneurysm when I was only four years old, or so I was told. As far as my mom was concerned, the topic was *verboten*. There were no pictures, no fond memories. Just. Don't. Ask. Not asking was part of my DNA. I was so used to obeying unspoken messages, I didn't even know I got them. I *did* look, though. When I Googled him, very little came up. On Facebook, Peran Sykes got no matches. None. And "Sykes" turned up a few different families, but it was impossible to tell if we were related, and I wasn't about to ask. It would have helped if I knew his birthday, or where he was born, but I didn't. And Skidmore College no longer listed him as faculty, of course. His absence was a palpable presence in my life.

I don't have weird extrasensory perception. I don't hear voices. I don't believe in ghosts, and God is not talking to me. I definitely *do not* see silver granules zooming into the black holes inside people. Not anymore, anyway. That was just a childhood fantasy, right? I'm

'Totally Normal' Julie Sykes. At least, that is what I used to tell myself in high school in an effort *not* to be an outcast. Totally normal, totally average Julie Sykes, average looks, average height, average intelligence—okay—maybe slightly above-average intelligence. It was the mantra that coursed through my veins. I thought I put on a believable act. I had just about convinced myself.

But my true self must have cracked that shiny veneer because only the *ab*normies were drawn to me. My best friend, Samantha, and her boyfriend, Jonathan, were excellent cases in point. Samantha was like an *extra* Snow White, with skin as white as snow and hair as black as coal, yadda, yadda, but comfortably overweight, excitable, and sassy. She dressed in black and wore such thick kohl eyeliner that it almost obscured her eyes. In high school, she'd been classified as an Emo, and maybe she was back then, but by college, she hummed with positive energy (a bit forced in my opinion), due to her Wicca practice, which I tolerated for her sake. She and Jonathan were practically married. They were an unlikely looking couple. Jonathan was quiet, uncannily smart, and looked like an undernourished hippie, but he listened to hardcore. His light brown hair hung in a lank ponytail over his shoulder, and he avoided eye contact. When on the rare occasion he made eye contact, his brown eyes were large and sorrowful. Yup. I liked the odd ones. It was the normies I found strange.

That said, I hadn't had any abnormal visions since junior high. By high school, I had mastered my "disability," as I thought of it, and by college, it was all but a distant memory.

So, I don't know, really, what triggered it. It could have been 2016. Talk about an extra abnormal year, with record-breaking floods, droughts, and heat waves all over the world. Since high school, I had diligently read the news, unlike most of my peers, but lately, I just couldn't. Instead of dealing with climate change, America was tangled in a live-action Punch and Judy show: the presidential race between Clinton and Trump. The more offensive he was, the more people loved him. Then there was the Zika virus, the mass shooting at the gay club in Orlando, and the crackdown on pipeline protesters at Standing Rock. It was starting to feel like a virus was infecting the country and driving everyone mad.

But the immediate catalyst for all the trouble that was to come was that darn autobiography assignment. It commanded us to find pictures, letters, and journals, or interview relatives. Since we never saw my Aunt Peggy anymore, that left Mom. And the more I thought about it, the lamer it seemed that I had accepted her status quo. What harm could there be in searching her room and the attic for pictures, letters— anything—while she was still at work? I'd lost my father. Didn't I have a right to his memory?

When I entered her bedroom, the word "trespass" flashed across my mind like an extreme weather banner. Her bed was neatly made, her clothes all hung up, and the scent of her skincare products hovered in the air. We had a decent relationship, I suppose, but she'd always had super-clear boundaries. I wasn't allowed in her room unless invited. The commandment was like a forcefield I had to press through just to approach her dresser. She'd artfully arranged a jewelry box, a wood-inlaid bowl for frequently changed rings and earrings, and a candle, all dust-free (unlike my cluttered room). I searched her glossy jewelry box and her folded underwear drawer (who folds underwear?), and I riffled the pages of her books. Nothing. Next, I climbed the narrow stairway to the attic.

We lived on Woodlawn Avenue in one of those huge Victorian mansions so common in Saratoga Springs, NY, not far from Skidmore College, where my mother taught anthropology and sociology. It used to be a one-family, but it was now divided into four apartments. We lived on the second floor, in the back apartment, with access via an external staircase to a balcony, replete with elaborate scrollwork. The third floor, where we stored things, had once been servants' quarters with smaller rooms and slanted ceilings. The staircase to it was steep and winding.

In the dim light of a round window, I searched through all the dusty boxes. Nada. Not one picture or sweater of my father's. Not even a framed degree or cigarette lighter, or whatever. Had he smoked? I had no idea. No passport. No birth certificate. If I didn't have a dim memory of him, the smell of wool and soap, riding his knee as he chanted, "This is the way the lady rides, clippety-clippety-clip," I'd think she'd invented him. She told me he was from England, and that he was in the Skidmore Geology department. Peran. I loved that name. It means "little dark one" in Cornish. When Mom used to read to me, I'd lie in the crook of her arm and spin her wedding band on her finger. It was heavy and radiated a warmth that I thought was a message from him to me.

In a box of her clothing, I hit pay dirt. Wrapped in a silk scarf was a blue ceramic horse the size of my palm. It wasn't realistic, more of an interpretation of a horse, with windswept lines, as if a sea storm had formed it. It had a pleasing weight in my palm. Like my mother's wedding ring, it seemed to warm my hand. I knew it was his.

"Julie?" my mother called from the landing.

I jumped, and my heart shot me with a guilt gun. I shoved the horse in my pocket and checked my watch. It was only 3 p.m.

"What are you doing up there?" she called up the stairs.

"Nothing," I said as I folded the box flaps shut, grabbed some papers, and met her halfway down the stairs so she wouldn't see that I had been in the box labeled hers. "Just looking for old report cards. I have to write an autobiography for English. You're home early."

Her classical oval face was tilted up at me, her fine eyebrows arched in slight irritation. For a woman of 51, she was really good-looking. Her hair was still naturally auburn and she had great bone structure, like those 1940s movie stars with high cheekbones. Way more beautiful than I'd ever be.

"I'll get them for you," she said, "I don't want you making a mess up there. I have it all in order."

My heart stabbed me again, this time with irritation.

"That's okay, I found them," I said with fake breeziness, waving papers a little too close to her face as I headed down the stairs toward her. She backed out into the hall. I tried to drape the papers naturally in front of my pocket to conceal my pocket's contents.

She stood there twisting her wedding band, her silence long and accusatory.

"What's up?" I said.

"Have you," she paused, "been in my room?"

Heat rushed to my face. I hoped it wasn't turning red. Should I deny it or make up a story?

"Oh, yeah. I'm sorry. I lost a pair of socks, and I was wondering if you had snagged them by mistake."

"Okay," she said slowly. "But other things were moved."

"Jesus, you're such a neat freak."

"Are you lying to me?" she said softly, her pitch floating upward disbelievingly.

Shit. I couldn't get anything past her. "Okay," I said, switching tactics. Offense makes the best defense, after all. "True confession. I was looking for pictures of Dad for that autobiography. Why don't you have even one?"

She stiffened and reddened slightly. "We all deal with grief in different ways."

"But I don't even know what he looks like!" I said.

"All you have to do is look in the mirror," she said, gesturing toward the round, wood-framed mirror that hung in the hallway. I glanced at my hazel eyes which annoyed me so much, because the lids always hung at half-mast, making me look tired, and my eyes couldn't decide which color they wanted to be. Light brown? Muddy green? They changed daily.

"But which part?"

"All of it–your dimples–the way your two front teeth are a little bit longer than the rest..."

Annoying, I thought, they made my canines look like fangs, for god's sake.

"...Your pointy chin," she babbled on, "your widow's peak..."

Good if you wanted to look like a vampire, I thought.

"You're adorable."

"Gross," I said.

"Even your build is like his. It's how the whole thing works together," she said.

"Mom, that's not good enough."

"That's all I have. I'm sorry. I know it's hard. But it doesn't give you the right to invade my privacy. My room is my inner sanctum. My retreat from the world. You know the deal."

Answering coldness sank into me like dust on those boxes above.

"Got it. I'm sorry." I turned my back on her swiftly and walked away, relishing this silent expression of anger.

I made excuses about homework and ate in my room that night. Yeah, okay. I can be passive-aggressive. I'm not proud of it. But it felt good.

In the privacy of my own room, the horse vibrated in my pocket like an incoming text. I pulled it out and wrapped both hands around it. There it was again. A warmth. An energy wave. My dad, talking to me. That little horse woke up a longing I couldn't put back to sleep: a flash of laughter and an answering light, like gold coins showering me from above as he dandled me on his knee. Who would I have been if my father had lived?

I was exhilarated, but also scared. I had worked hard not to feel things like that. I was Totally Normal Julie Sykes, after all.

So, yeah, it was a bunch of things that triggered stuff. However, the straw that broke the camel's back was when I became reacquainted with Damian Quinn at the SUNY Adirondack extension center a week later. It was like I was walking through a dull threshold into a bright place. I couldn't turn back. Around Damian, I had to stop pretending to be a normie, and that's when my world more or less exploded.

2

THE CRACKLE

EARLY SPRING, 1999

He was jogging through the North Woods on the Skidmore campus one day, when the crackle in his sternum became too strong to ignore. Four years ago, he'd crossed the Atlantic to take the position in the Geology department, drawn inexplicably to the area. It had to do with the dreams he'd had as a child, of a white-haired man, a bugler on the back of a horse-drawn carriage, a tomb. Peran had always been a restless soul, looking for his true home, and the dreams somehow pointed the way.

The trails through dense woods traversed a fault line that created steep hills and dips that made it a challenging workout. Trees, vines, and moss grew wild. The trail curved up a steep hill past a round stone structure that appeared to be an old well or silo some fifteen feet across, its upper walls knocked down to a few feet above the ground, its interior below ground level, the whole thing fenced in. The crackle of spirit energy mildly prickled his sternum throughout the Skidmore campus all the time. But, like sea air sizzling on power lines on humid days, the crackle was stronger in the woods, and strongest when he passed that well. Snow dampened the crackle, so perhaps that's why he hadn't noticed it until it intensified the third spring after his daughter was born, when emerald moss carpeted the stones on the forest floor.

His mentor had thought moving to the Queen of Spas was a good idea. Saratoga Springs was rich in spirit activity because of the fault that bisected it, allowing the evanescent healing springs for which the city was known to rise to the surface. Lord Cavendish had thought Peran could conduct spirit investigations from there. But ever since Peran had married Audrey, he'd renounced the Order of the Anima Arcanum.

When he met Audrey, thoughts of needing to find home vanished. Audrey became his home. He loved her intellect, her noble-minded ethics, and most of all, her no-nonsense, hardworking groundedness, so unlike his mercurial nature. The fact that she was beautiful only sweetened the package. He'd been on the longest run of emotional stability of his life. He hadn't had a single manic-depressive episode since he'd met her. He'd gotten so used to ignoring the crackle in his sternum that he'd ceased to feel it. Instead, he'd felt joy whenever he held their newborn child, Julie. He loved to wrap his palm around the back of his infant daughter's head, amazed at how soft and fragile this tiny skull was, and inhale the musky scent of puppy dogs and baby shampoo. He'd never expected to be a father. It had not occurred to him that making a family was the best way to find home. For an intelligent man, he mused, he could be surprisingly dense at times. A hint of laughter snagged his even breathing pattern, as he jogged uphill.

However, when Julie passed her third birthday, the crackle in his sternum had returned, as did the dreams, which crouched on his chest like a glowering beast the mornings after. He'd never told Audrey any of this. She was such a practical, earthy person that he knew she would scoff at his past profession. And why tell her now that he'd given it up?

As he jogged the winding trail toward the well this spring morning, his sternum crackled like he was being buzzed by an electrical current. His vision sharpened and fixated. A white-haired man in a top hat and frock coat stood with his back turned, halfway up the slope, adjacent to the well. As Peran came into the open, the man turned toward him and doffed his hat, silver-headed cane in the other hand.

Recognition splashed like ice water through his body at the handlebar mustache, the heavy jowls, the long sideburns. It was the man in his dreams. A bitter taste filled Peran's mouth, and the scent of almonds filled his nostrils. As he jogged around a curve in the path, the trees obscured the gentleman. When the bend curved back around, the man was gone.

That old longing for home, a true home, tugged at his chest like a shark on a line, and excitement thrilled through his arms and legs. This man was powerful. Perhaps he was connected to Peran's past, a past about which he knew little, as his mother didn't know his father's name. He and his twin sister, Athena, were the result of a one-night stand. They had grown up in a rat-infested flat in the east end of London, where children clustered in the stairwell hanging off banisters and played kickball next to trash bins in the alley. Sometimes, when his mother was particularly exhausted and in her cups, she'd say that his father was a wealthy man, an aristocrat of distinguished lineage. If she had known his name, everything would have been different.

Peran paused to catch his breath above the well, hands on knees. The man's spirit was still here. The crackle in his chest was unmistakable proof. Bollocks. He simply *had* to investigate. He would do it carefully, a few forays into the library. He would take no risks like he had that last time when he'd landed himself in hospital. He wouldn't get Anima Arcanum involved. No attempts to contact the spirit directly. It was just a lark. A harmless hobby. Audrey wouldn't have to know.

3
MEETING DAMIAN

SEPTEMBER 7 TO OCTOBER 10, 2016

You might be wondering why a woman who was already a junior in college was still living with her mother. I wondered that all the time. Rents were super high in the very white, very privileged city of Saratoga Springs. Even though my mom was a full professor at Skidmore, the only way she could afford to buy a house in Saratoga was to pick a multifamily house and rent out three-quarters of it. She didn't want me to spend my time working to afford an apartment. She wanted to make sure that I took full advantage of the free tuition at Skidmore, which was one of the perks of her job. That was the reason we gave, anyway, but also, my mom and I might have had a trauma bond over my Dad's death.

Samantha and her boyfriend, Jonathan, attended the local community college, SUNY Adirondack. They were both first-generation college-educated, and their families didn't or couldn't support them as they went to college. So, they were both working their way through, Jonathan at the Stewart's convenience store and Samantha at the Target Warehouse. Of the two of them, Samantha was definitely stronger. In any case, that put them behind me in credits. I didn't fit in at Skidmore, where most of the students were super-wealthy and wore designer clothes, the names of which I didn't bother to learn. Since Skidmore, like most private colleges, allowed students wide latitude in course choice, and SUNY ADK, like most public colleges, had a strict regimen and order, I arranged to take biology at the SUNY Adirondack extension center in Wilton, so I could hang with Samantha and Jonathan as they filled their sophomore year requirements.

Samantha and I were hanging out on the first day of class in the cafe-style lounge next to the snack machines at the Wilton campus. It was a bright September day, with no humidity and hot sun streaming through the wall of glass. Jonathan had stayed in his rusty old car to smoke a joint before class, and he was roaming the hallways, hands stuffed deep into his pockets, face impassive. Before you leap to conclusions, he claimed he had to smoke to slow his brain enough to concentrate, and the proof was in the pudding. He always aced his tests while high.

Samantha was describing her latest Wiccan spell while I teased her about it because I kinda thought it was all bullshit. Neither of us partook in any kind of drugs, she because members in both her family and Jonathan's struggled with heroin addiction, me because of my need to keep my "disability" under control. If I ever told Samantha about my disability, she would have been super supportive, but telling her would make it real, so I didn't.

I noticed Damian walking down the hall toward us. I hadn't seen him since my senior year in high school over two years ago. He was tallish and slender, maybe a little too slender, if you ask me, with a thin face, and light brown skin. His hair was closely cut as if it was growing out from a complete shave.

"Hey," Samantha said. "Don't look now. Damian Quinn is walking toward us."

Of course, I looked, and he saw me looking. I glanced away quickly, forgetting instantly how to act normal because I had always noticed him a little too much in high school. He was one of the few new kids our senior year. He lived at Jefferson Terrace, a housing project Saratoga was in total denial of, a place of broken homes and broken dreams, or so it was said, but I made it a policy never to judge people by their income level. Everyone thought he was a total geek when he first showed up. *There he goes down the hall*, we all thought as he passed us, seemingly content to walk alone in the crowd. I thought his shaved head with black stubble was pretty unsightly, myself. At first, I thought there was nothing remarkable about him except the strong, clean line of his jaw. What grabbed my attention later on, though, was this one time in the cafeteria.

"Hey, Jefferson Terrace!" Trent, a football jock, who had slapped my ass freshman year, yelled across two tables at him. "Why doesn't Jefferson Terrace celebrate Father's Day?" The answer to the joke, everyone knew, was because no one who lived at Jefferson Terrace had a father, or so the stereotype went.

Damian glanced up from his sandwich, paused with a faint smile, and said, "Because it's a holiday invented by Hallmark Cards?" That confused Trent and his friends, and they changed the subject like cats who missed a jump. Within a few months, people stopped making fun of him. He was self-assured in an indifferent way. It's not the kind of thing you can fake. I watched him from afar for the rest of the year, but I never got up the nerve to talk to him. I wasn't sure he even noticed me. There was a studied quietness to his movements, a dignity that set him apart from anyone else in the school. It was the first thing that drew me to him.

"Julie Sykes," he said, now, planting himself directly in front of me. "Damian."

"Yes," I said awkwardly, "I know. Damian Quinn."

"So, we need no introduction," he said.

"Apparently not," I said, trying to cover my nerves.

He smiled and that's when I noticed with surprise that his eyes, which appeared black from a distance, turned out to be a very dark blue. When I looked into them, I was double-surprised by how easily they let me in. I teetered inwardly, like I was going to fall into them. They were a whole world unto themselves of such depth, mystery, and knowing. And then his mouth. Don't get me started with his mouth. It was full at the center and thin and complex at the corners, a little wide.

Samantha nudged me, and I spluttered, "So, you're taking classes here?" Stupid, stupid question.

"No, I'm sightseeing," he said, keeping his face straight with a hint of a smile. I couldn't decide if that was a super-slick response or just cool.

Samantha guffawed. "I'm Samantha Barrett."

"Pleased to meet you," he said, shaking her hand.

"What are you taking?" I managed to ask.

"Biology 101."

"Dude! So are we!" Samantha said.

And that's how our friendship began. We both had an affinity for science, and over the next few weeks, we talked about all kinds of things, like how sunflowers, pinecones, and nautiluses spiraled to the same numerical tune (the Fibonacci sequence). As we talked, something very old and very new eddied inside me, slow and fast. I felt like I had always known him, and he seemed to know me almost better than I knew myself. Yet, at the same time, he was a mystery to me. He was evasive when I asked him about his family. I told him all I knew about mine, except for my childhood visions and the fact that they were coming back.

Professor Fish, the biology teacher, turned out to be a sarcastic but entertaining S.O.B. who wore a heavy gold chain and shirts that showed way more chest hair than anyone wanted to see, as if he hadn't quite realized that the 1970s ended over 40 years ago. But his class quickly became my favorite, outranking all my Skidmore courses. It was an easy class to pass because the tests were an exact replica of the complex notes that he painstakingly wrote by hand on the board before class every day. Other teachers would have just projected PowerPoint slides, but seeing all that data in his neat, spiky handwriting made it all particularly memorable. Even the spatial arrangement of his notes embedded themselves in memory. He clearly loved his subject. I also loved watching Damian take notes. I loved his handwriting, slanted squashed ovals— careful, consistent, and all his own. In contrast, my handwriting was irregular and mostly illegible, shifting with my moods. Damian's hands were unusually elegant. He had no business having such long fingers, smooth knuckles, and small veins.

One day in early October that *thing* I thought was part of my imagination started to happen again.

Dr. Fish was explaining cell structures that day. I was totally awed as I copied the notes off the board. I sneaked a peek at my fingertips imagining all that was going on under my skin. The very idea of mitochondria amazed me, those little oval energy factories that the body creates when under stress, and then eats when the body is inactive for too long. Maybe that's why I was always so tired on vacation– because my mitochondria were getting sucked into some kind of black hole. Help! My mitochondria are vanishing!

While Professor Fish was answering someone's question, I had time to scribble in the margin of Damian's notes, *"I'd change my name if I looked like that,"* referring to the broad flanges of the Fish's nose, his pale eyes, and his wide mouth. Even his shoulder-length 70s haircut made his head vaguely fish-shaped. Was he shaped by his name?

But really, I was trying to distract myself from the nauseating mixture of excitement and dread his lecture ignited. As I peered at my fingertips, I wondered, how did the different cell parts know how to form themselves and what to do? What bound them all together? And what lay between them? How could this wild universe be whizzing under the surface of my oh-so-ordinary skin? So much activity so far beyond sight. Maybe my visions *weren't* just my imagination. My emotions splashed through me light and dark, like when you drive under trees. Then I could see it. My fingertip seethed with particles, expanding, contracting, drifting.

Damian caught me gazing at my fingertips and nudged me with his elbow while he gestured with a quick pout at the board with his amazing lips to remind me to take notes. He smiled in that enigmatic way of his, either admiring me, or laughing at me, or both, all kinds of unsaid messages spiraling into one corner of his mouth. I flashed him a quick smile, relieved to return to the safety of *now*, but also a bit overstimulated by his mouth, and glanced at his notes to see how much I had missed. I fell back to transcribing notes off the board. As the clock hand reached the top of the hour, the room filled with the sound of rustling paper and backpacks being zipped, as students stowed their notebooks, much to the Fish's annoyance.

"What was going on there?" Damian asked as we headed out of the classroom.

One of the many ways that Damian made me nervous was that he didn't miss much. While it was a relief to finally have a friend whose sensory perception appeared to surpass the usual five, it also made me feel vulnerable.

"Wouldn't you like to know?" I parried. I didn't know if he was asking about my fingertips or my overstimulation.

"Indeed," he said. "Catch you later?"

"Totes," I said.

In a few short weeks, we'd developed our ritual meeting places, either in the North Woods or at Uncommon Grounds.

I couldn't tell if he was interested in being more than friends, or even if he was straight or gay. On the one hand, he had such elegant hand gestures that sometimes I was sure he was gay. I know that's a ridiculous stereotype. On the other hand, he touched me quite often and made startlingly direct eye contact. My heart tortured me with all kinds of jumps and squeezes when I was around him, but I was still a virgin.

"You should jump his bones," Samantha said as we headed out to the parking lot. "With that cute little ass? How can you resist?"

"Shut up!" I said as I swung the car door open too fast and it bounced at the apex of its arc.

"Candy-ass," she said affectionately as she tumbled into Jonathan's car.

Easy for her to say. Samantha and Jonathan had been having sex since eighth grade. They had been together so long that they barely needed to speak when they made plans. If Samantha said she was hungry, Jonathan would feel his pocket for his car keys, and wordlessly, they'd head out.

But I had always shied away from the whole thing. I don't know why. The idea of mixing all that energy with someone else's energy left me feeling jittery and slightly nauseated, and up until Damian, no one had ever been a serious contender.

4
THE ENERGY THING

OCTOBER 10, 2016

The next day, that energy thing got worse. I was waiting in line to buy hazelnut coffee at Uncommon Grounds. During the morning rush, the line winds all the way to the back of the room, but it moves fast. I took a deep breath, and my lung capacity mysteriously doubled, filling and filling with enormous skeins of oxygen. It felt good, but I wasn't totally conscious of it. When I stepped to the counter, I was sort of zoning, with my eyes in soft focus. The body of the nose-ringed woman who took my order seethed with tiny silver granules that rose like bubbles in a champagne glass. I blinked and focused, my lungs compressed, and there she was as solid as ever, clicking away at the keys of the cash register, a four-leaf clover tattooed to the back of her right hand.

Okay, I said to myself, *you're tired. You're seeing stars. Need that coffee more than you realized.* I have extremely low blood pressure, so it's common for me to see stars when I stand too quickly or haven't had enough to eat. It's amazing what you can ignore when you're determined not to see it.

That afternoon, I returned to Uncommon with Damian to see if I'd left my English book on the counter. It was one of those perfect autumn days, cool air, warm sun. The high dome of sky was so densely blue you could chew it, and sun-struck leaves shone like shards of red and yellow glass as we ducked into the roasty coffee shop. The morning rush was well over, so there was no line.

"I think I might have left a book here this morning," I said to the blue-haired woman behind the counter. "Did you find it, by any chance?"

"Haven't come across it," she said, glancing under the counter. "We usually put lost things right here. Who was waiting on you?"

"I'm not sure. She had a nose ring and a four-leaf clover tattoo on her hand."

"Oh." Short silence. "She had to go to the hospital." More silence.

"What happened?" I asked, my spine jingling like a string of silver coins.

"She just fainted. She was okay by the time the ambulance got here, but they thought she should go to the hospital to get tested."

"I'm sorry," I stuttered. Had I somehow caused it?

I did my best to cover my deep unease as we walked up Broadway toward the Skidmore campus. Broadway was the center of town, full of red, brown, and green Victorian storefronts and colonnaded hotels, but North Broadway, which was truly broad, was lush with every stripe of mansion you could imagine, Queen Anne, Second Empire, Edwardian, Tudor, you name it, the whole nine, with gatehouses, greenhouses, and fountains.

"What's wrong?" Damian asked.

"Nothing," I hedged.

"Did you know that girl?"

"No, no. It's just that— she looked fine this morning."

He studied me in silence, clearly deciding to hold space for me.

My favorite part of the Skidmore campus was the North Woods, where the walking trails spiraled up and down a fault line cleaved by a creek that periodically surfaced from and dove into rock. We walked through the cherry-chocolate scent of rotting maple leaves and the lemon-pine scent of hemlocks, sometimes in comfortable silence and other times deep in conversation, and we ended up sitting on a rocky ledge discussing the school newspaper club we had joined at SUNY ADK. The club consisted of Jonathan, who was the best writer of the group, Samantha, Damian, me, a few others who rarely showed up, and this kid, Payton, who had failed out of Skidmore and was planning to earn his way back in with what he thought would be super easy courses at the community college. Gradually our conversation turned to the news, another interest we had in common.

"It's getting harder and harder for me to listen to the news," I said. "It's so depressing and confusing. I don't know who to believe."

"Fair," Damian said, clearing a fallen leaf from the emerald moss we sat upon.

"I want to be one of the good guys," I said.

"You are," he said.

"How do you know? Climate change freaks me right out, and I'm not doing anything to stop it," I said, grabbing a few twigs and breaking them into y-shaped pieces. I placed them in the moss and set another stick across them.

"You bring your own lunches in reusable containers," he said.

"Yeah, but that's not enough." I paused and took in the beauty of the trees. Clouds of yellow leaves stippled the dark trunks, high and low, here and there, and burning bushes splashed the forest with sprays of fuchsia. "I feel like the country is collectively losing its mind. How could there even be a contest between Hillary Clinton and Donald Trump?"

"Politicians are all the same," he said.

"How can you *say* that?" I liked Damian so much that it would be a disaster if he turned out to be a jerk, politically.

"Whoa," he said. "Easy there." He set two more y-shaped sticks into the moss at right angles to mine and connected all four with crossbeam sticks.

"Trump's going around saying Mexican immigrants are drug dealers and rapists," I said. I couldn't keep the whine of exasperated incredulity out of my voice. "Until now, our racism has been latent. How is he still a viable candidate?"

"No, you're right. He's a dick. He's referring to people like me," Damian said, looking at the ground.

"Wait, you're Mexican?"

"No, but my mother's Puerto Rican, and her first language was Spanish."

"That's so cool," I said. It was the first time he had divulged any facts about his family.

"But Clinton voted to invade Iraq," he continued, "even though we all knew there were no weapons of mass destruction."

"She did? Well, no one is perfect. She knows her shit, though. And Trump is an orange baboon."

"Now you're insulting baboons," he said.

I laughed at his dopey cliche. "Fair. And the color orange."

I breathed in the amber light diffused through yellow leaves. The darkness of the trunks punctuated space in a way that made me see how three-dimensional life was. When you're stuck in your head too much, your surroundings become flat, mere abstractions.

I placed two longer sticks at the center of our four-square to create a gabled roof, and I began adding twig rafters. We worked in silence, sneaking back into childhood.

"People are getting *so crazy* these days. Maybe nature's plan to correct climate change is to infect us all with the stupid-virus so that we kill each other off," I mused.

"That virus is called capitalism," said Damian.

"Ah, so you're a communist," I said.

"More like a socialist."

"I'm not sure what I am, but taking care of other people makes sense to me. Communists, on the other hand, seem always to be advocating violent revolution, and I can't get on board with that."

"Capitalism is violent. Sometimes violence is necessary," he said with a shrug.

I searched his face. A piece of me turned cold inside. I really didn't know much about him. Perhaps my instant trust was misplaced. "You don't strike me as the violent type," I ventured hopefully.

He laughed. "I'm not, but there have been times . . ." His face darkened as his voice trailed to silence. I waited, hoping he'd complete his sentence. Instead, he laid twig rafters and began covering the gaps with bark to create a roof.

"I think that kid Payton is a Trumper," I mused. "I overheard him complaining about taxes and boasting about how he drank so much at a party last weekend that he barfed all over his best friend's car. He thought that was hilarious."

A look came over Damian's face like he wanted to puke himself. Then it cleared like water. " I don't touch the stuff myself," he said, "but I don't judge those who do."

"I don't drink much either, but you *never* drink?" Excessively rigid people worried me.

"Nope."

"Why not?"

He shrugged. "I don't like the feeling of losing control. But I don't mind if others drink. It's not a moral issue for me."

"Yeah . . . I don't experiment with alcohol or drugs, because— well, I have a pretty strange mind. It's already sorta on drugs." I thought uneasily of that girl at Uncommon. Had that fizzy static I'd seen been an illness? Was I psychic? Or had I hurt her? Images of *Carrie* jogged unevenly through my mind.

"What do you mean?" Damian tilted his head.

I found a flat rock to make a little table, and I set some acorn tops on it like bowls. "I don't know. I'm distracted by the weirdest things. I don't understand time. I'm always late for everything. It takes me forever to read. I can't tell if I'm super smart or just dumb."

"Oh, I can. You're super smart."

"You think so?" I said, my face flaming as hot as a burning bush with pleasure.

"Of course. You think fast."

"Really? But I read so *slowly*! I've always felt a little dumb that way."

"That's because you're making so many connections."

"How do you know?"

"By the questions you ask in class. You're always a few steps ahead of everyone."

"Wow," I took a moment to absorb this. "No one has ever told me that."

Damian smiled like he possessed secret knowledge as he added smaller rocks around the table for chairs topped with bits of moss cushioning. "You underestimate yourself," he said, now tucking blue-green lichen around the edges of the roof to create a gingerbread house effect. He was so artistic. Self-consciousness overcame me. I glanced at him again, but he seemed absorbed in the task. He had a slight bump in the middle of his long, narrow nose that gave it a noble line. Now he was stacking different types of bark into neat bundles, like provisions in a courtyard. We admired the different textures and colors of the bark.

"Those smooth gray strips are from beech trees," I said, and then named the crinkly white wisps from birch and the corky blocks of hickory bark.

"Where did you learn the names of the trees?" he asked.

"I spent a *lot* of time alone, growing up, reading and exploring. What about you?"

He worked in silence for a moment. A breeze stirred the trees, laden with earthy scents. "When you have two little brothers, you do a lot of babysitting."

I digested this. My peers at Skidmore mostly lived in dormitories. They had no family responsibilities, and most didn't need to work. Hanging out with Sam, Jonathan, and Damian reminded me not to take my privileges for granted.

"What are we making here?" Damian asked.

I shrugged, "A fairy house? A safe place from the big, nasty world?"

"Our house," he said and held my gaze a moment too long. Autumn-tinted light filled me up.

I blushed and tore my eyes away. On the one hand, I wanted him to crush me to him and kiss me, like one of those idiotic romance novels. On the other hand, I wasn't ready, and I didn't know how to say it. What if I lost him by never bringing it up? What if I brought it up and he didn't feel the same way? Misery and excitement twisted into a snarl in my stomach.

Damian could read me like a billboard, and that prospect felt like the twin sides of autumn, vivid yet deadly. You'd think the popularity of essential oils, meditation, and self-help books would have permitted me to reveal my energy thing. Especially with Samantha going all Wicca. But I didn't know Damian that well, and I didn't know myself. I thought my sanity depended on not seeing what I saw and not letting others see me as I was.

If I knew then what I know now, maybe I could have prevented what happened to Damian.

5
GEOGRAPHY OF NOWHERE

OCTOBER 19, 2016

Sometimes, a very small act like turning a page or stepping off a curb can set into motion a chain of events that leads to disaster. And when you look back, you think, if only I hadn't turned the page, if only I hadn't taken that last step, none of this would have happened.

In this case, the page was from a newspaper. October had turned cold and rainy, threatening to rot all the bright-colored leaves and pull them down too early. Damian and I sat together at Uncommon Grounds reading the *Saratogian* and looking for stories for *The Adirondacker*, as our newspaper was called. An article caught my eye: "*Decor and More* Coming to Wilton." Wilton was the next town over and really didn't have a town center. The picture showed a Victorian house of weathered clapboard and one of those squarish rooflines that lean in toward the top before flattening, you know what I mean? The front porch was falling away from the house, and the central square tower loomed over it all with little spear-pointed railings around the top.

"Hey, check this out," I said, hyper-conscious of the warmth that radiated from Damian where our elbows touched.

Damian glanced up from his section of the paper and leaned over my shoulder to scan the article, setting my heart into a tizzy. "Just what we need, another big-box store," he said.

"They won't stop until the whole place is a parking lot," I said, that line from the Joni Mitchell song echoing in my head.

Whereas Saratoga was a celebrated "city in the country" with a functional downtown consisting of broad sidewalks and lots of stores and restaurants for window shopping, Wilton was a sprawl of big-box stores with huge parking lots and no sidewalks, clearly designed for access by car. Route 50, which led out to Wilton, bisected Broadway at the north end, and because it was a four-lane highway, it was a big, nasty intersection.

I'm not sure why there was such a difference in how things went down in Saratoga vs. Wilton. Maybe it had to do with wealth. The affluent had more time and money to fight waste plants and big-box stores than the lower and middle classes.

"Isn't that the old house behind All-Mart?" I said as I reached over and snagged one of his pickles. He automatically pushed them toward me without missing a beat.

"You mean the *haunted house*?" he said in a mock creepy voice.

"The very one." I scanned the rest of the article, but I already knew the background material.

Behind All-Mart slouched a clapboard Victorian with a broken roof spine. Next to it, a lone oak groped the sky as if searching for its lost siblings. I had noticed it on the rare occasions when I had to go to All-Mart to get things you couldn't get anywhere else— like hangers. The vast, treeless parking lot and big-box store dwarfed the house in what used to be its own front yard, like a monstrously overgrown infant still trying to sit on its mother's lap, crushing her in the process. But the house wouldn't go down, people said. Something in it seemed to be pushing up, pushing back. And pulling at me.

The article explained that the town of Wilton had acquired the land and condemned the house when the owner died, like years ago. Local legend had it that whenever public works revved up their machines to knock it over, strange things happened. Rumors spread, and people stayed away from the house. Even the high school partiers didn't vandalize it. Or at least, I'd never heard about it. Development plans had been stalled for years, until recently. The article said a new plan was being submitted that very week before the Wilton town council, and it seemed likely to pass.

"Wouldn't it be cool if that house was really haunted?" I said. The mystery of it billowed and snapped inside me like sheets on a clothesline. The gray day seeping through the front windows of the coffee shop made the idea all the more delicious.

Damian smiled, and when he turned his eyes on me, I could feel their gaze, like halogen lights. There was that surprisingly vast midnight sky of his interior world, and there I was feeling slight vertigo.

"Yes?" he said, nudging me out of my suspended animation.

"Part of me has always wanted to see a ghost. I don't know why."

"Because of your father," he said. Even though I'd related the tiff I'd had with my mother over searching the attic for my autobiography, I was surprised he thought of it before I did.

"I suppose." My core began to vibrate. A faint sensation of swinging wildly in someone's arms surfaced and evaporated as soon as I tried to grasp it. "What about *your* father?" I deflected.

"My father?" Damian paused. "He's not in the picture, anymore," he said with a finality that discouraged follow-up questions.

In the starry night of his interior, I sensed a patch of denser stuff where no stars shone. Whenever I approached it, my mind fogged and I forgot the question I wanted to ask.

"What were you thinking a second ago?" he asked.

"Nothing."

"That was some kind of nothing," he said, smiling.

"I just sense, sometimes, that there's some part of you that you don't share."

"I tell you everything I know about myself," he said.

"Maybe there are parts of you that *you* don't even know," I said.

"Well, I hope so," he said, smiling again. "I want something to discover."

"Let's go discover that house," I said, flashing him one of my famous smiles. I wasn't sure about my looks, but everyone said I had a beautiful smile.

"So, when do you want to go?" he asked.

"Tonight?"

"Can't. Got a parent-teacher conference regarding my younger brother," he said, wadding up what was left of his lunch and untangling himself from his chair. Damian was long-limbed, and his clothes hung on him in straight lines that I found kinda sexy.

"So, who made it a brother-teacher conference?"

Damian shrugged his shoulders and smiled, eluding my questions as he always did. You'd think I'd be the kind of person to confront him, but if there was one thing I'd learned by hanging out in the woods, it was that if you want a wild animal to come near you, you have to stand very still—and leave him an escape route. "How about checking it out this weekend?" I said.

"Okay, it's a date."

I must have made a funny face or breathed differently. He was aware of it before I was.

"You know what I mean," he said, bumping me with his shoulder as we left the coffee shop. Was that a platonic best-buddy bump? Or was that a flirty bump? No idea.

We arranged for our usual late-night phone date to do our homework and we headed in opposite directions, I uptown and he downtown.

6

THE MAN WITH WHITE HAIR

SUMMER, 1999

Peran's visions continued through the summer, and they always occurred in the North Woods. One day, a horse-drawn carriage rattled by on a trail below. It jogged a memory. That carriage was in his dream last night. A bugler in a red frock coat and a tri-cornered hat stood on the back step and sounded the notes of the tally-ho used for fox hunts, three staccato low notes and one long, high note. It was a ridiculous conceit even for the Gilded Age. Three gold H's adorned the side of the carriage, polished to a high shine. A party of Victorian gentlemen and ladies laughed and chatted as they rattled along and vanished around a bend. Another day, he heard laughter and classical music ahead on the path, only to find a lone person in modern-day dress walking their dog.

He visited the Saratoga Room at the library and found out that the grounds had belonged to Henry H. Hilton, not related to the hotel chain. Hilton was a bit dodgy, a lawyer from a hardscrabble Scottish family who'd come into his fortune by befriending the fourth richest man in America, right after the Vanderbilts and the Astors, by the name of A.T. Stewart. Much to everyone's shock and speculation after Stewart died, Stewart had left his entire fortune to Hilton. Hilton moved up to Saratoga Springs from New York City in the 1880s, bought land, and built six lavish mansions on the property that now belonged to Skidmore. Where were the mansions? Were any left?

Not long after he learned of Hilton, Peran dreamt he was standing in a great room with thick, Persian rugs and silk-paneled walls. The room was large enough to have three separate sitting areas with carved camel-backed settees upholstered in rose velvet. Velvet curtains swept in loops from the top of twelve-foot arched windows to the floor. A man with white hair and long white sideburns in gentleman's clothes stood at the center. He opened his arms to Peran and said, "Welcome back, my son." Relief and joy flooded Peran even in the dream, and the feeling stayed with him for days. It strengthened his suspicion that he was related to Hilton. He had always assumed his mother, sozzled on gin, was thinking wishfully when she spoke of his father.

Of course, he told his wife none of this.

The dreams came back regularly, and the old man took him on winding tours through the mansions. They were specific and detailed dreams, room after room. There were twenty-six apartments for all their friends to come and stay, each outfitted in a different color scheme, gold, pink, royal blue, and red. In the main house, a royal blue Persian rug with a border of roses adorned the dining room floor. Carved mahogany chairs with rose velvet upholstery surrounded the matching table. A screen embroidered with birds of paradise stood in the corner. Wine-colored silk quilted the wall. The estate included a horse racing track and miles of trails where opulent carriages rode at night under flickering gas lamps. Women in silk and brocade gowns attended balls in the Lodge which also housed a gym and a pool room. By night Peran dreamt, and by day, his research confirmed all that he dreamt. He'd found the notes of the last caretaker, who'd written down the furnishings in exact and loving detail.

In the dreams, the old man gave Peran a heavy ring of keys that clanked everywhere they went. He insisted that Peran take over the handling of his estate and his business, but sometimes the picture would change to the houses in a derelict state, piled with debris, holes in their roofs, graffiti on the walls, young trees growing through rooms, and the feces of animals and humans in corners. When he awoke from the dream ruins, he felt heavy and waterlogged, as if mold and mildew grew through his veins. He walked into his classes groggy and disoriented. One night, he dreamt he sat at the mahogany table laden with roasts, puddings, and sweets. Hilton was pressuring him to fortify his empire. Peran's festering anxiety exploded and he cried, "You're mad. I can't do it. It's too late."

Hilton roared and slammed a crystal goblet of wine on the table so hard it shattered, and Peran woke with a cut on his brow. He assumed he had been sleepwalking, as he used to in his adolescence, but he knew there was a possibility that Hilton was making inroads.

7
SAMANTHA'S PROBLEM

OCTOBER 20, 2016

The weird energy thing happened to me again when Samantha came over to my house the next day. A car door slammed in the driveway below my window, and when I looked out, her back was turned to me as she pulled her enormous shoulder bag from the car. She was wearing her usual long black sweater, but it appeared to seethe with bits of white fluff. Then I realized I was seeing through her skin into her lungs, which appeared to be snowing. But these snowflakes were whirling, sticking to each other, and dropping into her stomach, which filled with gray putty.

"What's up?" I asked as I met her at the door. The vision was gone, but it didn't take psychic ability to read the expression on her face.

"Jonathan's English teacher accused him of *plagiarism!*"

"Oh, my God," I said.

Jonathan was hard to read. He usually didn't say much. We knew what he thought mostly from his quiet remarks to Samantha and from his English papers. Whoa—the guy was brilliant, but you'd never get that directly from him. He didn't have a deceptive bone in his seemingly boneless body.

"You *know* it's because he looks so grunge. They assume any guy with long hair does drugs—which he does—but that's not the point! They just can't believe he could be smart *and* do drugs."

I hesitated. "Didn't you say he'd been missing a lot of classes lately? That might be part of it, don't you think?"

"All she has to do is look at his papers from last year!"

"Does he have them?"

"No—he threw them all away. I'm so pissed off!"

"What happened?"

"Well—our class, we have to share our papers in small groups, and the teacher *insists* that they bring copies to class. They were working on this poem by some chick about a fish."

"Oh, I love that poem. Elizabeth Bishop." Oil is floating across the water at the bottom of the boat, and she has caught this enormous old fish with a bunch of broken hooks hanging out of its jaw.

"Yeah, that's the one. Anyway, Jonathan made this fucking brilliant connection between the rosettes on the side of the fish, which I guess is, like, a military thing. Then this shithead in his group handed in his paper, like, a month later, and, even though he had changed the wording of every single line, it still followed Jonathan's ideas exactly, in the same exact order. He must have put more time into the revision than if he'd written the damn thing himself. It was the rosette reference that caught the teacher's attention."

"So what happens now?"

"I don't know. I guess he has to prove that it was his paper first or he will fail the class, and that will mean he'll have to return his financial aid money, which he already spent."

"You want to walk it off?" I asked.

"Walk!" she said with disdain. "It's freezing out here!" She hugged her black sweater more tightly around herself and glared at the trees.

"Come on, it's like sixty degrees!" I said.

"I hate the outdoors."

She made me laugh. "How can you be a Wiccan and hate nature?"

"I do my spells indoors." We both giggled.

I talked her into walking downtown. The North Woods was way too much nature for her.

We headed down Broadway.

"So what *has* Jonathan been up to?"

She grabbed my arm and leaned in as we walked. "Cocaine."

"Jesus," I said. Jonathan was mostly into Cannabis. Cocaine was too addictive and expensive for me to even consider.

"I *know*. He said he only tried it once, and he didn't even like it, but what's next? Heroin?"

"No, he's not that stupid. He saw what it did to his cousin." For second, an amber patch glowed in Samantha's stomach, like a mass of writhing roots. Samantha made no secret of the fact that both her parents had been addicted to heroin when she was very young. Her father was one of the lucky ones who kicked the addiction and cleaned himself up and was now a firm believer in Narcotics Anonymous. Her mother had strayed farther and farther from home in search of a fix, until, eventually, Samantha's father had told her not to return until she was sober. NA called it tough love. They said sheltering and feeding her would be "enabling" her. I had my doubts.

Samantha burped loudly, and the amber glow in her stomach vanished.

"Excuse *me*!" she shouted and then laughed, embarrassed, fanning herself. Underneath her sarcastic, vehement exterior, she was a Southern belle who could easily belong in the Riggi mansion we were passing, a new stone castle, home to forty Chihuahuas, built in 2012 with an enormous water fountain out front. "He promised me he was all done with it. I'm scared to death. I won't be able to *handle* it if he gets hooked on heroin." She pounced on certain words like a cat on a fly.

"He hasn't tried heroin, has he?"

"I don't think so—yet anyway. I did a protection spell with a piece of obsidian. It's really a spell for protection from demons because I couldn't find one for drugs. Heroin is definitely a kind of demon, don't you think?"

"Sure," I said, keeping my raging skepticism to myself.

"He promised to keep it in his pocket."

"You really think that's gonna help?" So much for good intentions and restraint.

"Quit being such a skeptic, Jules," she said, giving me a playful arm whack.

"I'm sorry, you know I totally love and respect you. But all the work your father has done to get your mother back didn't work. Do you really think a spell alone could protect Jonathan?"

"Every little bit helps. Thing is, Jonathan's problem is that he's too smart. It can be like a disability. Makes you different from everyone else. You see things others don't see. His mind goes, like a million miles an hour, and it's so tedious waiting for the rest of us to keep up. That's why he smokes pot. To dumb himself down."

"That's probably why he won't get hooked on cocaine. It will just speed his brain up."

"Hence my fear of heroin," she said miserably.

I gave her arm a squeeze.

You'd think with my particular disability, that I'd be into things like Wicca. But that stuff seemed like such a total crock. Maybe even dangerous. It's a little grandiose, don't you think, the idea that you can make a bunch of money fall in your lap by wearing green or some such thing? Like, who has that kind of control over life? And there was Samantha trying to ward off evil for Jonathan, when she herself was haunted by her mother's abandonment. It seemed like projection and avoidance to me. And at a time like this, when people were denying climate change, it was obvious you could get lost in "magical thinking" and go seriously astray. Samantha was avoiding her own problems by trying to heal Jonathan. But then again, who was I kidding? Maybe I was doing the same thing with Samantha.

8

THE ADIRONDACKER

OCTOBER 21, 2016

Shortly after that, *the energy thing* happened again at school, and this time Damian confronted me. We were working on the *Adirondacker* together with Jonathan and Payton Wilkinson. Sometimes we ate lunch in the dining area, finishing last-minute edits. I think I already mentioned that Payton was a Skidmore dropout, and like most of the Skiddies, he drove a BMW. His father was a major developer in town. If he didn't raise his grades at SUNY ADK and re-apply to Skidmore, his parents threatened to take away his Beamer, a threat that made us all quiver with fear, lol.

I had been feeling a little spongy that day, kind of waterlogged. Payton leaned over my shoulder to look at the edits Damian and I were making, while Samantha and Jonathan sat across from us, Samantha on the arm of the couch draped over Jonathan, who edited a different story.

I had gone to the Wilton historical society to research the haunted house and I'd pitched a story about suburban sprawl for the *Adirondacker.*

"I found all these cool pictures of what Wilton used to look like," I said, "all these farms and taverns, sort of spread out. And there was even a trolley that went between Saratoga Springs and Wilton every hour."

"My grandfather used to have a farm out that way," Jonathan said, looking up from his pages.

"Oh really?" I asked. He so rarely spoke, I was all ears.

"Yeah. They couldn't keep it up. Got into a lot of debt."

"I'm sorry," Damian said.

"That's so sad," I said.

"It was a long time ago," Jonathan said and went back to his editing.

Today, Wilton is basically a four-lane highway with national food chains and shopping plazas. Housing developments are tucked into the woods with curvy roads that swoop in and out of each other like a maze, where the houses are all beige, and no one has sidewalks.

"What's so sad?" Payton interjected.

"I've always assumed Wilton began as an ugly development, but the town historian wrote a plaintive message at the end of every Wilton calendar urging the town council to preserve the hotels, taverns, and granges. One by one, they burned down, fell down, or were sold," I said.

"Yeah, well who wants to book a room in a moldy old hotel, anyway," Payton said. "Give me a Comfort Inn, any day."

"Oh, like you'd ever stay at a Comfort Inn," Samantha scoffed.

"Well, I wouldn't, but I wouldn't mind owning one or two…if the taxes weren't so high."

"Another BMW sob story," Samantha said, rolling her eyes.

"What I don't get is why no one tried to lay out a new town map and develop the area into a walkable city, like Saratoga Springs," I said. With only one access route to Wilton and no public transportation, we get traffic jams all the time, and we don't even have that high a population.

"It's not profitable. Besides, Wilton residents hardly pay any taxes."

"They also don't have any libraries, public bathrooms, or any of the other things taxes usually buy."

"Big deal," Payton said. "You libtards are always over-regulating everything, creating a nanny state, letting Mexicans over the border to get on the dole. That's why the economy is so bad." He spouted off about how great Donald Trump would be for the country because he was honest, and Hillary made speeches on Wall Street. I just about choked on my smoked turkey sandwich.

"I thought you were into Wall Street and making money," I said. "And the guy can't string together one grammatical sentence." My heart hammered with anger, but Damian leaned into me, silently warning me not to take Payton's bait.

I took a deep breath, and that's when Payton's face went all cubist on me. All the different planes of his face shifted around as he nattered on about Trump making America great again and all that crap. The edges of his face jutted in and out like drawers, and one eye floated to his chin and the other out to his ear, as if he were trying to piece himself together, or trying to stop anyone from looking in by presenting a surface to each potentially prying eye.

"We're done here," I said pointedly to Damian and stood up. Damian gathered the proofs and shoved them into his backpack.

"Okay, Payton," Damian said, cutting into his diatribe. "Thanks for your help."

"Oh, sure, no problem," Payton said, not getting the irony.

I shouldered my backpack and headed for the exit, but Payton followed yammering the whole time, oblivious to my oh-so-subtle conversation-ending cue. I dug my nails into my thigh and Payton's broad cheekbones and sandy hair returned.

We finally scraped Payton off like gum on the bottom of our shoes when we left the building. He wandered off to impress someone else with his brilliance.

Damian and I headed for my Mom's car in the parking lot. Since we lived within walking distance of her workplace, I was allowed to borrow her car to drive out to the SUNY ADK extension in sprawl-city Wilton. Damian didn't own a car, but he rode his bike everywhere. That's what kept him so lean.

"You okay?" Damian said.

"Yeah. No. I'm fine." I pulled the keys out and hit the unlock button.

"What's up, Sykes?"

"Nothing. Really," I weakly evaded. "Payton's such a narcissist, not to mention a racist. What does he have against Mexicans?"

"Seems like he really got to you. You were in suspended animation for a moment there."

"Nah. I'm just tired."

Damian tilted his head and eyed me skeptically. "Okay. You don't have to tell me—*yet*," he said casually, straightening the lapel of my wrinkled linen shirt. "But I'm gonna catch you later." Need I mention my heart palpitations? "Also, don't forget we have that exam Monday."

"Oh, shit. I *did* forget," I said as I unlocked the car door. He'd parked his bike next to my car and leaned over to unlock it.

"Want to study over the phone tonight? I have a double shift at Hamlet and Ghost this weekend."

"Sure, but I have an evening class at Skidmore that doesn't end until 7:30. I won't be able to start until eight. Is that okay?"

"Perfect," he said.

He swung his long leg over his bike and pushed off in one coordinated move, and glided away.

Images of Payton's jutting head returned. *You didn't see that*, I told myself. *You just have a graphically vivid imagination.* Everyone imagines things once in a while. It's just synesthesia, that's all. Some people see color when they hear music, or perceive scents when they look at numbers. The animated cubist painting was just a really good metaphor for Payton's ego-defense system. *You're normal. Totally Normal Julie Sykes.*

9
CONFESSION

OCTOBER 21, 2016

That night, we studied until two a.m. Well, the actual studying had probably stopped an hour before that. I was sitting in the middle of my room on the floor wrapped in a blanket, hunched over my textbook, with my notes splayed all around me. I was determined to keep going until we'd reviewed all the material, no matter how tired I was. But by one o'clock, waves of sleepiness had brought all thought to a standstill. By two, I clung to consciousness by the skin of my eyelids, but each successive wave of sleepiness weakened my anchorage. I finally closed my book and lay back on the floor.

"I need to sleep, but I don't want to hang up," I said.

"I'll stay on until you fall asleep," Damian said

"Okay." I smiled into the phone, hoping he could hear my smile. I don't know how long we had been drifting through silence when Damian whispered, "Julie Sykes," as if from the inside of my brain, like a pale puff of air barely rippling my slack sail.

"Hmm?" I was lying on the floor, cradling my cell phone in the crook of my neck. I pulled my father's blue clay horse out of the cigar box and snuggled it under the blanket with me.

"What do you see?" Damian asked.

"I see a blue horse, his body shaped by wind." I rolled onto my side, curled up, and pulled a blanket over me.

"And what else do you see?"

"I see walls the color of bark and stone," I murmured as another wave of sleep pressed my eyes closed.

"What else?"

"I see my favorite books on a shelf." I didn't need to open my eyes to see *A Wrinkle in Time* and *The Golden Compass*.

"And?"

I slanted a dim glance through the top right square of my window. "I see the moon, and the moon sees me, God bless the moon and God bless me." The warmth of my body was reaching a pleasant roasting point that made all my muscles drop off my bones. "What do *you* see?" I asked, trying to imagine him on the other side of town in his own room. No image came.

"A worn rug, a crack in the wall," he said quickly, without emotion as if to get it out of the way. "Tell me more of what you see."

"I see slanted walls."

"Is that all you see?"

I surveyed the room blearily. "I see a black and white photograph of a woman dancing. She is wearing a trench coat over a filmy skirt that flares as she spins." My mind hovered inside the lip of sleep, where thoughts begin to slip and slide, turning upside down, and shooting sideways in what seems like the most normal way, but isn't. "She's the weaver of dreams."

"What *else* do you see?"

"You want me to describe my whole room?" I whined. All the muscles in my body seemed to have puddled like warm milk underneath me. "I'm too tired."

"Go to sleep, then. I'll stay here with you."

"Okay," I said, pulling the blanket a little tighter. We drifted silently again without time. The phone slipped farther from my ear.

"Now tell me what you *really* see."

"I see atoms, I see truth, I see the silver stars of people inside out." I succumbed to whatever my slidey mind suggested.

"What else?"

"I see people's waterfall thoughts and black-hole wounds."

"Yes."

"I see shadow-wishes and ghost-fears," my words tumbled pleasantly free. "I see," I pinched my fingers together, smiling at my silliness, "the tiny, shredded moss of what we've forgotten we are." I was totally babbling, unaware of what I was saying, loopy-stoned, drunk with sleep, not even sure I was speaking into the phone.

"Tell me about the people we know—about today with Payton."

Sleep evaporated. My eyelids flew open. I sat up, eyes clear and fresh, pumped awake by my beating heart. He was really listening.

"I was just rambling," I said, trying to cover my tracks as I gripped the phone.

"But it's true, isn't it?"

A paranoid wave discolored my thoughts. Had he lulled me on purpose? Had he sort of hypnotized me?

"I don't even know what I said."

"You said you saw silver stars and waterfalls and moss. Inside people."

"No, I didn't," I said. My wrist, neck, and temples bulged with pounding blood.

He was silent.

"I was being metaphorical," I hedged.

"You can trust me, Julie."

My insides shook slightly. I got off the floor and climbed into bed.

"Can I?"

"I swear."

I burrowed under my blankets and hugged my favorite pillow,

the one that was made of silky, heavy down. "I don't know what I see."

"Yes, you do," he asserted quietly, but firmly, more on my side than I was, as it turned out.

"I don't. I think I just have an overactive imagination."

"It's more than that," he said.

"How do you know?"

"I know." He brooked no argument.

"I don't actually see anything—extraordinary—I mean," I ventured. I was too tired to resist. "I feel it."

"Feel what?"

"No, I see it, too. Earlier today with Payton. His face got all cubist on me. Sometimes I think I see sickness inside people, or worry."

"What was it with Payton?"

"I'm not sure. Maybe I see how people are inside."

"Tell me exactly what you see."

"I'm not allowed to see it," I said, turning into a five-year-old pleading with her mother.

"Why not?"

"I don't know, I knew at an early age—it was engraved in my mind, 'Thou shalt not see.'"

"Who was the engraver?"

"Life, I guess." I lay in silence for a while, and he waited, too. "Actually, the first time I remember getting that message was when I was very small, maybe six or seven." A memory I had never clearly recalled flooded back to me surprisingly intact. "It was after my father died, I'm pretty sure because he wasn't there."

"What happened?"

"My Aunt Peggy, my mom's sister, came to visit with her husband—what was his name? I can't remember."

"Go on."

I could almost see his face, his wide, moist eyes, but that was all. "Why can't I think of his name?"

"It doesn't matter. Go on."

I stopped for a minute, searching the memory.

"It was the first time I'd met either of them. My mom and my Aunt Peggy weren't on the best terms, and she lived somewhere far away, like Seattle. I liked her immediately when she came through the door. She had this—" I paused to edit myself, but then said what I really saw, "this bright, dappled energy, like sunlight shining through a thousand leaves. I should tell you what her face looked like, but I can't."

"No, I want to see what you see," he said.

Surprise caused a prickle in my nose and eyes, which was as close as I got to tears in those days. No one had ever wanted to see this part of me, including myself.

"She had a flowered dress," I said, and when I dredged up that detail, more details came with it, like snails on seaweed. "She had a smooth, pink face and full, gray hair. Elisha, my cousin, was hugging her leg. She was about my age, maybe six or seven. Elisha had this—I don't know how to describe it—this dense, rubbery matter all around her."

"She was overweight?"

"No, quite thin, actually. It was her—energy, I guess. See, that's just it—I don't know what I was seeing. But at that time I didn't know it was any different from what other people saw."

"That wasn't the first time, then," he said.

"No, I don't think so, but it was the first time I became conscious of it, I guess."

"So then what happened?"

I described how Aunt Peggy said Elisha and I should go off and play together and "become best friends," but Elisha was as dull as a dirty sock. I couldn't reach through that rubbery stuff to get anything out of her.

Then Uncle What's-his-Name came through the door, looked at me, and smiled. That's when this—thing—exploded inside of me. A rock materialized inside my stomach and whammo-ed into a boulder. His face was off-kilter, his eyes too widely placed. As he stooped to grab me, he said in a patronizingly high voice, "Hey, girlie! Who've we got here?" I screamed, pushed him away, and ran out of the room.

My mom came running after me into the next room, "What's the matter with you? That's no way to behave when guests arrive."

But I was crying so earnestly that she must have realized this wasn't a simple case of bad manners. She took me onto her lap, and I clamped my arms and legs around her while she tried to calm me.

"I told her he had worms," I now related to Damian. "She had no idea what I was talking about."

"But you saw something," Damian interjected. "What did you see?"

It was strange to stop my self-editing reflex and say instead what I usually omitted:

"This big hole in him," I said, "a ragged, oval hole, that started where his nose should have been and went all the way down to his crotch, and the edge of that hole was seething like a million worms." I stopped speaking as the memory expanded. I had never been able to describe it to my mother when I was a child, but now, as I matched the words to my felt-sense correctly, they reverberated and expanded, like a church bell ringing a clear note that carries for miles.

"My mom later told me I wouldn't talk to him or touch him for the entire visit. She was really mad at me. My Aunt Peggy stiffened and her eyes grew dark whenever she looked at me. Much later I found out he was molesting my cousin Elisha, and that my Aunt Peggy had her suspicions, but she didn't do anything to stop it."

"Wow. The hair on my arms just stood up. What happened to her?"

"Well, Aunt Peg divorced him, eventually. We only saw Elisha and Aunt Peg once more after that, at another cousin's wedding. Elisha had the same kind of hole as her dad, but smaller, and right above her crotch, and then that rubbery gray matter seemed to block it from spreading to her heart."

"That's pretty intense. But it also sounds kinda," he hesitated, testing the waters, "cool."

"It wasn't. Especially when everyone was denying it."

"So that was when you learned to hide," he said.

"No. There were other times. I got a lot of little messages." The picture of the dancer on my wall drew my attention. The incongruity of her coat and tutu and the wildness of her gesture validated the split inside me. "I got another message to zip it from my mother—maybe around the same time."

"Tell me."

"I said to my mom one morning while we were driving somewhere, 'Why are all those lines wiggling around your head?' She didn't even look at me. She just kept on driving, and said, 'Nothing is wiggling around my head.'"

That was all she said, but the iron doors came slamming down all around her. The message was clear: *You don't see that. It's not there. I don't want to hear about it.*

"So that's why you shut it down," Damian said.

"I guess. It wasn't really a conscious decision at that stage." I shook inside as I confessed all this to him.

"How did you do it? Shut it down, I mean."

"I don't know. When I was a kid, I could kind of control it. I could shut my eyes or my chest to it, and it would turn off. Or I could open my eyes to it and it would turn on. I think I shut it off so often that after a while, it wouldn't open anymore. And I was fine with that. But in the last few weeks, it has been *happening* again."

"I *knew* something was going on. I could see it."

"What have you been seeing?"

"You get this certain look on your face, like you are listening for the words of a song from a different world. Then you yank yourself out of it. But now you don't have to hide it anymore, around me anyway."

"It makes me feel like I'm crazy."

"Julie. You're one of the sanest people I know. You really see people. You see yourself. You ask questions. You think. You're truly alive."

"You have to promise not to tell anyone any of this, Damian. Truly."

"Not even Samantha?

"No. I've never told her."

"Maybe you should. She's clearly open to alternative views."

"Maybe."

"I promise. I never tell anyone what we talk about, anyway, Jules. No one knows we are going to visit that house, right?"

"Right. I know."

"I'd never betray you, Julie Sykes."

His energy surrounded me like a warm breath.

After we hung up, my body still shook at the core. I had never told anyone, even myself, what I told Damian that night. Talking made it real. It felt good and bad at the same time. Good, like a raspy cell phone connection that finally clears. Bad, like one of those nightmares, where you go to school and realize you're not wearing pants.

Curled under my heavy blankets, I cast my mind like a fishing net over the storm-tossed ocean of my past. Squares of moonlight slanted across my quilt like white sails, pure, clean, and free. My past was enveloped in murk, but as I lay there, it cleared.

Then it hit me. That gray mist that had engulfed us after my father died belonged to my mother, not to me. She wasn't always enshrouded, but whenever she was, her grayness exhausted me. Because of this "disability," I got confused and couldn't tell the difference between what was inside me and what was inside her.

Now I remembered what my mother said once about going to a doctor and taking Wellbutrin. She was adamant that her depression was all physical and hereditary. There were things my mother was refusing to see and trying to stop me from seeing, and I wasn't okay with that anymore.

10

FALLING THROUGH

SUMMER, 1999

One warm day in late summer, after a particularly vivid dream, Peran jogged through the North Woods, hoping the run would force oxygen into his blood and work the ache from his head and sinuses. He and Audrey were having difficulties. He had decreased his medication dose because it blunted his visions, and the depressive episodes had returned. He was finding it hard to get out of bed some days, but he always did. The demands of classes and work were sufficient motivation, but he was forgetting things in class and falling behind in his grading.

Audrey couldn't help but notice his depressive episodes, and she asked if he had cold feet about being a family man. He was shocked at the implication. He had confessed to her that he was on medication, but he made it sound like he suffered from mild anxiety, and she had accepted that story. Now he thought he read regret and fear in her eyes.

How could he tell her that he'd always had these depressive episodes? That he'd been hospitalized at certain points in his life for what others called hallucinations? That this hospitalization was how he'd met Lord Cavendish, who was a psychiatrist, but also the head of Anima Arcanum, a society that most in the academic world would spurn and snidely refer to as ghost hunters? He had to admit that the "lark" had grown into an obsession. But he resisted calling his sister Athena in to make it an official spirit investigation, and he rationalized that this was proof of his devotion to his wife. For, if he called Athena in, he'd be returning to the old life before he'd come to America.

Still, there was no way out but through. So there he was jogging, when, as if on auto-pilot, he left the path and bushwhacked down to the round stone structure. From maps he'd found in the Skidmore library of Henry Hilton's estate, he hadn't been able to ascertain whether it had been a well, a silo, or part of a tower from one of the Hilton's houses in the complex. He scaled the fence and jumped into the pit, four feet below ground level. The gray rock walls had been spray-painted by college students.

His dream from the previous night billowed inside him like smoke as he touched the walls. He was sitting at the mahogany table with Hilton at its head. Seated halfway down the table was a middle-aged man with a face that was bloated and red, as if he'd spent a lifetime drinking. He wore a soiled wool overcoat, and his greasy fedora sat on the table next to the fine china. The era of this guest's clothing appeared to be late 1930s or early 1940s. His eyes were glued ravenously to the sumptuous spread of fruits and cheeses before them, arranged like a Caravaggio painting. Hilton poured the vagrant a glass of deep red wine. The vagrant gulped so fast it dribbled out the sides of his mouth and stained his shirt front. Then they were outside. He wasn't himself anymore, but one of Hilton's sons. Hilton was accusing him of destroying the family fortune and reputation by carousing with women of ill repute. Shirt fronts were grabbed, throats were hoarse from shouting, spittle flew, and faces were tumescent with fury.

Now, as Peran bent over to examine the gray stones closely, pain coursed through his sinuses, and the ground gave way. He tumbled among rocks and debris ten feet into a hole.

"Bloody hell." He lay on his back looking up at the light streaming through the ragged hole above, shielding his eyes as dirt and gravel continued to sprinkle around him. Gingerly, he moved his arms and legs to see what was hurt. All seemed to be in working order. As he twisted to a sitting position, though, his coccyx bone and spine blasted him. Fortunately, the pain subsided to a low ebb in a matter of minutes.

He stood and examined his surroundings, breathing in the cool, earthy air with a hint of mold. He pulled out his flip phone, using the illumination to see where he was. It appeared to be a basement, and at the far end, a rectangular threshold loomed into darkness. His years of training kicked in, and he performed the grounding ritual to protect himself from any unwanted spirit activity, a quick matter of deep breathing, visualization, and rubbing dirt to his pulse points. But the unknown beckoned. The weak daisy of light from his phone swam over debris beyond the door, piles of rubble, a bed roll, a few empty bottles, shoes, and rags.

He stepped into the darkness where the temperature was a few degrees lower, and as he neared the pile of rags, a shot of adrenaline spritzed his body. The pile of rags was a human skeleton. There were six of them, stacked together. The spirit energy was strong here, but not from the bodies. Cautiously, he probed. They were oddly preserved, having dried out rather than putrefied, and there was no discernible smell. They looked more like mummies, with their skin wrinkled, tight, and dry. Some wore clothes that appeared to be from the 50s, but underneath was one that must have been from the 1930s, the same as the man at the table in his dream with a fedora still on his head. At the perimeter of the room were wood shelves that had fallen away from the wall with a few broken wine bottles on the floor. Evidently, this had been a wine cellar once. There was another door at the back slightly ajar, but when he picked his way through the debris and tried to push on it, it was clear the room beyond had collapsed.

His heart pounded with excitement rather than fear. This discovery. This mystery. He couldn't walk away from it. He was tied to it by an umbilical cord, figuratively if not literally. But guilt and dread swung back like a heavy pendulum when he thought of Audrey and the baby. Engaging with spirits opened anyone near him to danger. If he acted fast, he could call the police and that would settle it. They would cordon off the area and prevent him from investigating. They would match the bodies to missing persons' files. Then again, he'd have to explain what he was doing there, and dead bodies found on a college campus would headline nationally if it got out.

Nothing in his research explained the presence of these bodies. Over the last year, he'd learned more about how Hilton had attained his fortune. He had been hired by A.T. Stewart as his lawyer when he was only twenty-five. Stewart was known as the "Merchant Prince" and was the inventor of the first department store. He had amassed a fortune of 70 million by 1850, which was the equivalent of billions today. The Stewarts had lost two children and were too heartbroken to try for more. So when Hilton quickly moved to a key position in Stewart's business, people noticed. Soon access to Stewart was constricted. They had to talk to Hilton instead. Was Hilton a practitioner of mesmerism, a fad that fascinated high society in those days? When Stewart died in 1876, Hilton ended up with his entire fortune and control of all his businesses.

He moved to Saratoga Springs, bringing Mrs. Stewart with him, and he bought the Woodlawn Estate, where Skidmore now was. He amassed 1,500 acres of land and began building lavish mansions all over it. He hired Olmstead (famed for the design of Central Park in New York City) to design Woodlawn Park. They filled in marshes, leveled hills, and dammed creeks to create a small lake stocked with fish and swans. He had a stable built for 60 horses, not to mention a 22-acre chicken house and other farmland. There was a horse racing track on his property for summer entertainment and people skated on the lake in winter. Though he was disapproved of, as were most of the nouveau-riche, everyone accepted invitations to his events, and hundreds came from miles around to ride the carriage roads through his park in flickering gaslight.

It wasn't long before he created a national scandal with a million-dollar renovation of the Grand Union Hotel on Broadway by forbidding Jewish patrons from entering. Saratoga was frequented by New York City's Jewish millionaires.

Why had this lavish estate been abandoned? Why had the houses been allowed to rot? What were these corpses doing here? They had died or been killed at different points in time. Peran's mind raced. There was no turning back. The headache was gone. Out of the grog and mildew rose a phoenix of ambition. He would solve this mystery and, with it, the mystery of his own heritage.

He decided to call Athena and to re-activate his connections with Anima Arcanum. With her skills in energy weaving and her degree in forensics, she could help him fill in the blanks. Lord Cavendish would approve of the mission, he was sure.

He would have to come clean with Audrey. This was his destiny. He had to obey the calling, and she would have to accept it.

He would have to remove the bodies as soon as possible, even though it would destroy some clues, because it wouldn't be long before the hole was discovered. For now, he climbed out and did his best to cover it with branches.

11

HAUNTED HOUSE

OCTOBER 24, 2016

After days of jewel-like autumn weather, Saturday dawned as gray and padded as an asylum cell. I woke up feeling characteristically shy about what I had uncharacteristically told Damian. But I flung myself through the North Woods at a rapid pace, trying to shake the shyness off as I jogged. The fog saturated the tree trunks to nearly black, and burning bushes stippled the woods with clouds of fuchsia.

As I jogged, I wrestled with a million conflicting emotions. On the one hand, I was bursting with excitement, like a child on Christmas morning. The possibility of finding a ghost infused life with richer colors, like fog draws out the deeper colors of tree trunks. The mystery of it sharpened the edges of life. On the other hand, I felt as dopey as a Scooby-Doo cartoon. I didn't believe in ghosts and all that New Age crap. On the third hand (when did I grow a third hand?), I wanted my visions to be real and outside of me—patterns that others could see, a sign of wisdom rather than psychosis. On the fourth hand, this unmoored me. How was I supposed to act with Damian now that I'd confessed my deepest secrets?

I decided to pretend nothing had changed when we met late that afternoon with our bicycles. We had agreed that checking out the house at night would require lights and would draw attention. Daylight would be our best cover. Still, my heart valves pinched off my blood flow for a nanosecond that actually hurt when I caught sight of his lean figure next to his black bike waiting for me at the corner of Van Dam and Broadway. I forgot to mention that when Damian let his hair grow back in, he turned out to be handsome—a little too handsome for comfort. His body looked so relaxed and comfortable in its own skin that it made me want to jump out of mine.

"How'd that parent-teacher conference on Carl go?" I asked, striking a jocular note.

"Oh, he's up to the usual trouble," Damian said, rubbing his neck.

"What kind of trouble?"

"Failing math, smoking in the bathroom, stupid, death-defying skateboard stunts in the school parking lot. That kid has no fear."

"I wish I had no fear," I said with a smile.

"Fear is useful," he said, looking stern. "One of these days he's going to break his back." He rubbed his neck again.

"Okay, Grampa," I teased.

Damian's face darkened for a second.

"I'm sorry. I didn't mean to offend you," I said speedily.

"Not at all," he said as his face cleared. "I plan on becoming an old man someday. And that's because I know when to be afraid, which is more than I can say for Carl."

We came to Route 50 and walked our bikes as far from the white line as possible because it was a trucking route and people drove fast and didn't look out for bikes or pedestrians. But it was also the most direct route, and the shoulder widened further out where we'd be able to ride.

"Huh. My fear just inhibits me," I said.

"You don't strike me as a person who fears much, Julie Sykes."

The pleasure of hearing myself characterized in such a positive way splashed hotly through my body.

"You, too," I managed to choke out.

"So what do you think we are going to find at this house?" Damian asked.

I was thankful for the change of subject. "I don't know," I said. "Probably just dusty windows. As much as I'd like to believe in ghosts, I don't."

"No? What about your visions?"

"Those aren't ghosts—those are—I don't know what they are—energy things. I think I might have synesthesia– you know, that disorder where your senses are all mixed up and you smell color or see sound?" As I acknowledged our conversation last night, my face burned. "What about you?"

"Me?"

"Do you believe in ghosts?"

"Yes. I think I do," he said, thoughtfully.

When he spoke, his whole body was cool water, filled with light. Or else I was smelling a hint of rain in the air.

"Why? Have you ever seen one?"

"No, but it seems possible. I feel it here," he said pointing to his chest.

"Ah, the all-knowing solar plexus, ancillary to the brain. Is it here?" I jabbed him playfully in the ribs, "Or here?" He tweaked my hip, pressing his thumb inside the curve of my hip bone, a hugely sensitive tickle-spot on me. I laughed. "Hey, watch the Vulcan death grip!" I said, pushing him off.

"Do you know what solar plexus means in Latin?" Damian asked as I fell back in place beside him.

A car with a broken muffler rumbled by and I waited for the sound to die down.

"No. What?"

"The gathering place of the sun."

"That's pretty cool. I wonder how it got that name."

"Some scientists . . . because the nerves that come together radiate like the sun."

Have I mentioned that knowledge like that is a turn-on for me? The fact that he was in touch with his intuition. The fact that he cared enough about a word to look up its origin. Yum.

The traffic was so loud at this point that we had to stop talking and decided to ride our bikes. The shoulder narrowed so that we had to ride single file to stay well clear of the cars and trucks. The intersection of the Northway and Route 50 had no crosswalks or lights at the entrance and exit ramps. It was a classic example of how suburban sprawl is designed only for cars and actively discourages human interaction. Fortunately, there was a light at Old Gick Rd. that created a temporary lull, so we dashed across the four lanes, and then cut through All-Mart's vast parking lot, always full of cars.

The Victorian house with a square central tower hunched beyond the dumpsters and drainage ditches next to a single oak tree, now bare and black against the sky. A ten-foot, chain-link fence hemmed them both in, posted with no-trespassing signs. The roof gave the house a graceful character, with four sloping sides that curved gently inward to a flat top trimmed with wrought-iron railings that had rusty spear points. The four-sided tower roof echoed the main roof which I later learned was called a mansard roof. Time had stripped the paint from the cracked clapboard siding, and shutters leaned. The windows and doors all arched with keystone centerpieces.

Sadness settled around my shoulders when I noticed how the front porch sagged away from the house, and one of its six brown pillars jutted off to the side, spoiling the house's former symmetry. The builders of this house had been proud, probably owners of the hundreds of acres of farmland that used to surround it. Now tin cans, garbage, and a single rubber boot littered what had once been the front lawn. We found a depression in the ground under the fence and dug it out with some tuna cans lying around in the grass. Then, with a quick look over our shoulders, we belly-crawled under.

The front porch looked like it was about to cave in, so we circled to the back. When I first approached the back door, a sprinkle of icy droplets pricked my body all over, like fine silvery pins. I glanced at the overcast sky. "I think it's starting to rain," I said.

"I don't feel anything," Damian said, looking skyward also.

The glass in the door clattered in its frame as I pushed it open into a broad hall floored with wide planks that had once been glossy with varnish but were now worn gray. At the other end, a broad staircase rose from the front door to the second floor. Judging from the high ceilings and detailed wood and plaster trim, the owners had once been wealthy. The smell of earth mixed with a stale hint of coffee and licorice wafted out at us. Brown floral wallpaper peeled off in patches revealing crumbling plaster and lath. "Stay Out," had been spray-painted in neon turquoise on the wall. Near the door, a dusty jacket hung on a peg over a pair of cracked rubber boots still caked with dried mud. Clearly, the money had run out before the life of its inhabitants.

"Wow," I whispered. "No one ever cleaned this place out." The romantic notion of a ghost collapsed, flattened by human failure.

Damian checked the label of the jacket. "K-Mart. Our first ghost," he said, referring to the fact that K-Mart was drummed out of business in the area by All-Mart.

It was a navy blue down parka, with duct tape covering a few tears here and there. The arms of the coat bent at the elbows holding a shape memory of a body. "I'm not sure this was such a good idea," I said, even though the idea was mine. That weight on my shoulders was sinking in, making my lungs feel woody. "What if no one took the body away?"

Damian squeezed my shoulder and said in a voice velvety with repressed laughter, "They took the body away."

In the living room, a maroon couch and chair slumped, still holding impressions of the people who had once sat there. The velveteen had been worn bare on the overstuffed chair that faced one of those 1950s TVs, encased in a wooden cabinet.

"Maybe someone is squatting here," I said. Our city's answer to homelessness was to arrest the homeless for vagrancy or put them on buses out of town.

"We'd see marks in the dust," Damian said, stepping ahead of me. When we turned to leave the living room, another message sprawled over the doorway in navy blue paint: "I pulled back the curtain and saw God with the devil."

"Creepy," I said. "Guess we were wrong about people staying away from the house, unless the owner was getting poetic at the end of his life."

I walked on the outsides of my feet, slowly rolling my weight inward to make as little noise as possible. The floor creaked anyway, the noise crackling across the deep-bowl silence of the house.

In the kitchen, close to the floor, someone had spray-painted, "Kill Me" in black. The heavy cast-iron sink was propped on two-by-fours, a makeshift curtain tacked to the edge. A red-painted hand pump stood on the drainboard. Two coffee mugs rested upside down on a coffee-stained paper towel next to a kettle on the stove, as if the owner were returning for a late afternoon cup. The stove had a compartment for a wood fire. Damian peeked inside at the ash.

"He shopped in the twentieth century but cooked in the nineteenth."

"Did the guy like it this way?" I asked, looking at a cheap plastic clock that contrasted sharply with the cast iron stove. "Or did he not have enough money to change it?"

Though coated with dust, everything looked neat and rooted to the spot, and the house's energy curled around my ankles like a cat.

"Maybe we should go," I said abruptly.

"Let's look upstairs first."

With an effort, I unstuck myself and followed Damian back out into the hall. But as we mounted the stairs, lead seemed to fill my legs. Damian no longer seemed to be humoring me but was driven by his own curiosity.

We found four bedrooms upstairs, three of which were filled with boxes, broken lamps, and chairs.

One bedroom was neat and spare with a four-poster bed still made up and a bulky wooden wardrobe. Damian slapped the mattress and a cloud of dust rose.

A boulder of tension expanded in my stomach. I didn't like how Damian was touching everything, but I didn't know why it bothered me, so I kept quiet.

The scuffed wardrobe tilted on three legs. The door hung open, and Damian pulled it wide. Inside, clothes hung on pegs around the edge. The heaviness that filled me turned to fatigue. "Why are his clothes still here? Didn't he have any relatives to clear the house out? It's so odd," I said.

Damian shrugged his shoulders. When he fingered a shirt, it felt like he'd plucked my stomach lining.

"Don't!" I grabbed his arm.

"What?"

"I don't know. His clothes still have his—well, his body oils on them. I mean, isn't that creepy to you?"

"Body oils?"

"I just—let's go. It's not romantic anymore. It's super depressing."

"But this would be such a cool hangout. It could be our—"

Something heavy thudded against the wall in the hallway followed by a rubbing sound, as if someone were sliding along it. A spray of acid stung my stomach, crackled up my arms, and finished off with a frizzle at the top of my head.

"Did you hear that?" I said.

Damian nodded, focusing.

"Let's get out of here." My scalp tingled.

"Wait," he grabbed my shoulders. "Let me check first."

He poked his head out into the hallway. Empty, of course. He creaked slowly down the stairs, pressing against the wall, making the same sound we'd just heard. I stood at the top, fighting B-movie visions of psychos jumping out to slash him or demonic forces snatching him through the wall into nowhere. At the bottom, he peered into the kitchen then around the banister to the door we'd come in by.

"No one's here." His voice cut a measure of normalcy through my fear. "Come on," he beckoned with his hand. "It was probably a squirrel inside the walls. We get them at our house."

"It sounded a lot heavier than a squirrel."

"A raccoon, then."

As we descended, the crown of my head itched so acutely that I thought I might have picked up fleas.

"Gross," I said and scratched my head hard. But the itching only increased.

Damian was ahead of me in the kitchen. A shaft of thin, watery sunlight emerged from the clouds and shone through the dirty window. Something opened in my chest, steady, permeable, perceptive. When I crossed the kitchen threshold, a dark shape flickered across the light in front of Damian, and the smell of burnt coffee pricked my nostrils.

Time caught and stuttered for a fraction of a second, fluttering like pressure changes in my ear, and inside that fraction, I saw the outline of a masculine hand, brown skin contrasting with the white mug, soundlessly slamming it on the table and sending up a spray of coffee. My eye was transfixed by each of the individual droplets as they arced through the air and spattered the wall and curtain.

Then I blinked. The moment collapsed. And the image was gone, as if I hadn't seen it at all. I shook my head.

"Did you see . . . ?"

Damian turned around, but the look on his face cut my words short. A few beads of sweat stood out on his pale upper lip.

"You okay?"

"I dunno. I feel like I'm gonna puke." That rock re-materialized in my stomach.

"Let's *go*." I grabbed his arm and pulled him down the hall and out the door.

As soon as we were outside the fence, we both felt better. The clouds had thickened and lowered, with not even a speck of the sun that I'd seen seconds earlier in the kitchen. Night was beginning to stain the sky a deeper gray. As Damian breathed in the cool air, the color returned to his face.

"You saw it, too?" I asked.

"What?"

"That guy," I said.

"What are you talking about?"

"In the kitchen. I saw a Black guy—or a guy's hand—slamming down a coffee mug—right in front of you."

Damian studied my face. "What do you mean, exactly?"

"I don't know. It looked like someone was standing in front of you, and all I saw was his arm coming down to the left of you."

"But how could you have seen something in front of me when you were behind me?"

"Right. I don't know," I said, doubting myself.

"Was it one of your visions?"

"All I've ever seen is splotches attached to living people. Never the shape of a person. And never by itself." I replayed the scene in my mind. He was right. Damian's body should have obscured my sight.

"Maybe you can see ghosts and never had the opportunity before. Tell me again what you experienced. Every detail. Even things that seem irrelevant."

"I don't know if I saw something physical and real, or if it was an image in my head. But it was so distinct and so particular it seemed real. I think I even remember where the coffee splashed."

"That's very cool," he said, looking at me speculatively.

"But I thought you saw it—I thought that was why you got sick."

"What?" He sounded almost irritated. "No. I don't know what *that* was . . . a stomach thing. It's gone now."

I brushed a fragment of wallpaper from Damian's shoulder. The motion made me realize how light and energetic I felt in contrast to the heaviness inside the house. "I've got to go back in," I said

"Why?"

"Just for a second."

"You're not afraid anymore."

"Yeah, it's gone. I've got to check something out."

"I'm coming with you," Damian said, "but let's make it quick. It's getting dark."

Inside, we knelt beside the kitchen table and examined the wall. There, exactly where I had seen them fall, were brown drip marks of coffee. And they were still wet.

12

JUMBLED IMPRESSIONS

OCTOBER 24, 2016

As we walked our bikes back toward Saratoga Springs, we picked through our jumbled impressions. It began to sprinkle. The fact that we both felt the coffee drops on the wall made it hard to dismiss the whole thing as a figment of my imagination. What had I seen? A ghost? Remnants of leftover thought? In TV shows, mediums touch physical objects to get a read on a missing person, as if those objects retain human energy like a glass holds a fingerprint. Maybe the medium gets a read off of the oils of the fingerprints themselves. We knew from a special forensics unit in biology that even a trace of dirt on someone's shoe has characteristics so unique that you can identify where that person had been. And DNA can be gleaned from a few skin cells. Maybe psychic ability wasn't supernatural, but acutely natural, like, they worked off microscopic physical clues. I told Damian about the concept of rapid cognition, which I learned from *Blink*, by Malcolm Gladwell. What looks like an intuitive guess is really the mind making a rapid series of accurate calculations. Maybe I had picked up a few microscopic clues and pieced together an event that had occurred in the house earlier. Someone had thrown a temper tantrum in that room and slammed down a cup of coffee.

"Why are you trying to talk yourself out of what you saw?" Damian asked.

"I'm not. I'm just trying to explain it rationally."

"I thought you *wanted* to see a ghost?"

"I did. I do. But I kinda don't."

"Remember Fish's unit on quantum mechanics? He said that all solid objects were really seething atoms," Damian said.

"Sure, and the sensation of solidity is the electrons of one thing repelling the electrons of another."

"If that's how fluid physical reality is, ghosts don't seem so very far-fetched," Damian said.

I thought about it. The nucleus is like a little sun, and the electrons orbit the nucleus like planets. These atoms have invisible rings or wider orbits around them, and when the electrons get excited by light or heat, they jump to these outer orbits. When they relax, they return to their inner orbit. "The thing that blows my mind," I said, "is that the space between those particles is much greater than their mass. We are made of more space than mass!"

"Right," said Damian, "so what if death means the container for the smaller orbit is gone, but there's a wider invisible orbit where an entity can stay organized?"

"It's plausible," I said with mixed emotions.

"Whatever it was," said Damian, "it has a connection to the physical world. We both felt the moisture of those coffee drops. And," as a car zoomed by and he grabbed my elbow and pulled me further from the road, "*we'd* better stay connected to the physical world, too."

We decided that we should investigate the history of the house to see what the story was.

"Do you remember anything in that article on how the owner died?" I asked.

He didn't.

"I don't have a clue where to start looking for answers," I said.

"My mother's friend is a secretary at the Wilton town hall. She'll help us out."

We decided to go after school on Monday.

Cars whooshed by as we mounted our bikes and rode the rest of the highway extension toward home, the sounds of their tires amplified by the wet pavement.

We stopped a few blocks away from my house.

"I'll leave you here," he said. He brushed a strand of hair away from my face, which set my nerves jangling like wind chimes in a hurricane. There it was again: that surprisingly dark blue of his eyes, that easy entrance, that smile I couldn't quite interpret. His mouth was capable of holding more than one expression at a time. A billion tiny gas burners flared under my skin. I was about to fall into his lips when an iron hand from within seized my stomach and pulled me away from him.

"Well," I said, "see you Monday." So lame.

"Right," he said, tucking his hands in his pockets without missing a beat.

Shame crashed and tumbled inside me.

"See you Monday," he said, hopping on his bike like a dancer, one leg on the pedal, the push-off leg extending into an arabesque as he swung it over his seat to the other side. He didn't look back as he sailed away. Was he mad at me?

I marched my bike toward my house at a brisk pace to thrash away the painful mix of disappointment, fear, and excitement. Only when he was out of sight did I attempt to mount it. I wasn't as graceful as Damian, and it would be just like me to fall flat on my face. I wanted to kiss him so badly that the inside of my cheeks itched. But I Just Couldn't.

I was furiously berating myself when a flash of gray flickered in my peripheral vision. The hairs stood up on the back of my neck. I turned my head, but no one was there, just a car parked in our neighbor's driveway, a gnarly young maple next to it. I searched the area. Had I seen it? I closed my eyes and breathed in and out. Yes, it was a woman. With long, white hair and a flowing, gray dress. What the heck was going on?

A yellow glow from our neighbor's windows filled me with wordless longing. It was easy to imagine a peaceful family inside with a mother and father sitting at the table, smiling at their only child. No such scene awaited me at home. I quickened my pace and leapt onto the porch.

13

MOTHER-DAUGHTER DANCE

OCTOBER 24, 2016

The second I opened the door I knew how angry my mother was by the set of her back, the curve of her neck, and the way she rinsed a plate and almost threw it onto the drying rack, but slowed her hand expertly before touchdown so that it slid soundlessly into place. The lack of greeting was a dead giveaway, too. No extra sensory perception needed to figure that out.

Guilt swamped me as I remembered the fight we'd had earlier that week over how messy I was, and we negotiated Saturday afternoon as our weekly date to clean up. The wild, windy mystery of my afternoon with Damian and the ghost lady flatlined.

"I'm sorry, Mom," I said quietly, hoping to forestall a fight.

"Sorry doesn't clean the house."

"I'll do it now. I just forgot."

"Forgot? How could you possibly forget?" She turned around and leaned a soapy hand on the counter, her finely carved features drawn into a scowl.

"I don't know. I just did."

"This is the time we both decided on. We discussed this *ad infinitum* three days ago." She wasn't yelling, but each word twanged with tension.

"Could we just stop arguing?" I said.

"No, we need to work this out. I can't live in a pigsty, I—"

"I know, I *know*." Tangled darkness welled up inside me and threatened to overflow. Instead, I said, "Why can't you even say 'hello, how are you'?"

The crease between my mother's brows smoothed out to a lesser crease of worry. She silently dried her hands on a kitchen towel and took a deep breath.

"I'm sorry. You're right. How are you?"

"Never mind!" I ran out of the room and threw myself on my bed, steeped in betrayal. I had come home from this mind-blowing experience, and she flattened it with total banality. I mean, I know on the scale of things that matter, cleaning the house counts, but is it worth destroying a relationship over? The worst of it was, she didn't have a clue what she was missing. I was a vast universe, and all she saw was an irresponsible college student.

Later at dinner, spearing a cube of marinated, baked tofu with a fork, my mother asked, "How's Damian?"

"Fine," I said, pins of annoyance needling my stomach. Why did she have to be so invasive?

She threw her hands up. "I thought you wanted me to ask how you are."

"Not because I told you to." It was one of those divided moments when the rational part of you knows you're being unfair, but the other part of you does it anyway.

My mom fell silent. The auburn wave of hair that rose and fell over her forehead and framed her classically symmetrical face made a part of me rush toward her. I wished she approved of me. I wished we connected. I wished I resembled her. She was so beautiful. After a few silent crunches of stir-fried veggies, I said, "Mom? Do you believe in ghosts?"

She examined my face for a long moment. Then a door closed in her eyes. Like, I literally saw them go dull. I read her way too well. Not a muscle had changed on her face, yet I knew exactly where her emotions were going: to some private place she never let me into.

"Why do you ask?"

"No reason. I just—you know when you see something move out of the corner of your eye, and then you turn to see what it is, and nothing is there?"

"Sure, it happens all the time. But there can be so many causes for a thing like that, a bird flying by, someone's shadow, fatigue, even a little phlegm in your eye."

"Gross, Mom."

"What, you never have phlegm?" She brightened.

"Well, it's not exactly dinner conversation."

"And this is?"

"Yeah. It's philosophy. Isn't that what you academic types do at the dinner table, talk about deep stuff like the meaning of life?"

"On the rare occasions that we *actually* have time to *have* dinner with each other."

"Seriously though, what do you think happens when we die?" I pressed.

In a blink, my mother aged ten years. "I think we . . . end," she said flatly. "Our energy disperses. That's it."

"I have a hard time believing that," I retorted.

"Of course you do, you're only 19."

"Well, I'm old enough to see that you're not telling me something."

My mother's eyes snapped up from her plate.

"Something important," I said, surging ahead, knowing I was flinging myself off an emotional cliff, "something I have a right to know."

"What are you talking about?"

"You know exactly what I'm talking about!" My sudden anger surprised me as much as it did her.

"No. I don't," she said like she was chewing wood.

"I'm talking about my father," I said. She sucked in her breath, and a pang of fear plucked my insides. I'd gone too far.

She dropped her eyes to her plate and sighed. After the longest minute of my life, she said, "What do you want to know?" She said it quietly, like a war prisoner, resigned to her fate.

"Why don't you ever talk about him?"

"It's painful."

"But you've kept him from me all these years!"

She met my eyes for another long moment. "I never thought of it that way."

"Do you have *any* pictures of him?"

"Somewhere," she waved her hand and lowered her eyes to her plate.

"Where?"

"In the attic, I suppose." She averted her eyes.

"Can you show me where they are?"

"I don't want to go up there. It's a mess. Finding them would take days."

"But I *need* to see them."

"I know you do, and you have a right to. But I'm not ready to dig all that up again. I'm sorry. We'll do it another time. Just not now." She stood. "It's your turn to do the dishes."

Later that night, I called Samantha.

"Ugh. I'm so mad at my mom," I said.

"At least you have one," Samantha returned.

"Sometimes I wish I didn't."

"Don't *say* that."

"No, you're right. And I don't mean it, either. I'd just like to trade her in for a different model."

Samantha laughed. "Hey, I've got good news about Jonathan!"

"What?"

"His professor believes that it was the other kid who plagiarized! When she examined his notes and other writings, she saw that he had characteristically long and complex sentence structure. The other kid's sentences were all short and choppy."

"Whew. That's a relief. What happened to the other guy?"

"She withdrew him from the course."

"Harsh."

"Oh, he totally deserves it. When we confronted him, he lied straight to our faces. Didn't blink, blush or even shift his eyes. I never knew people could lie like that. I mean, with my mom, it was always crystal clear when she was using, but she was on drugs."

I didn't know what to say.

Samantha's grief over how her mother put heroin ahead of her family welled up chronically throughout her life, playing out in all kinds of ways including nightly binging and punishing diets. But that was also why her relationship with Jonathan was as solid as a rock jetty, carving a safe harbor within a dangerous ocean. And here I was withholding information from her about my vision thing and the haunted house, which I knew she'd totally love. Was the sin of omission the same as lying?

"Anyway, how are things going with you and Mr. Hottie?" she said.

"Shut up!" I said.

14
ANIMA ARCANUM

FALL, 1999

"Hello, sis," he said, giving Athena a tight hug at the Newark airport. They were fraternal twins, but their likeness was striking. Both had prominent noses that formed a distinguished hook, large eyes, with unusually thick eyelashes, and high cheekbones. Both were lean and muscular, but Athena had gone prematurely white at the age of 35, whereas Peran's hair was still brown.

"Lord C. sends his regards," she said, hugging him back just as tightly.

Lord Cavendish had been the only other person to understand that Peran's "hallucinations" were visions and that they were the most acute when he was the most unbalanced. In the hospital, Cavendish had been able to help Peran find a balance of medications that allowed him a measure of emotional stability but that didn't quash the visions. When Athena came to visit Peran in the hospital and touched his arm, Lord Cavendish noted how her touch changed his energy measurably. Peran's blood pressure normalized and his oxygen level reached 100%. Cavendish quickly ascertained that she, too, had psychic powers, though they were different from Peran's. Outside the hospital, once he'd gained their trust, he introduced them to the Societas Anima Arcanum, the Society of Soul Mysteries, dedicated less to the proving of the mystery of ghosts, than to achieving balance in situations where restless spirits plagued the living. Independently wealthy, Cavendish fully funded the endeavor. They only solved cases when there was a pressing need, which in most cases meant among the super-wealthy and politically powerful.

"How is the bloody bastard?" Peran said, lapsing back into British slang.

"Charming as ever. He has procured a villa on North Broadway for me, not far from campus. I can set up my labs there."

"That's grand."

"I can't wait to meet your family," Athena said.

"Uh, about that. I'm not sure we should let Audrey know."

"What? That's bonkers! Not to mention disappointing. I thought you came clean with her!"

"I did. And she threw a wobbly," he said using the word they'd always used when their mostly mild-mannered mother lost her temper and screamed at them after she'd gotten into the liquor.

He would never forget the look on his wife's face when he confessed that until he'd met her, teaching geology was only a side gig for him and that his real purpose in life lay with the work of Anima Arcanum. She had looked at him that night like she seriously doubted his sanity and was even a little afraid of him. When he tried to explain, she grew angry.

"Why am I only hearing this now?" she'd fairly hissed, trying to keep her voice low so as not to wake Julie, now two years old. "This is a serious breach of trust!" Her nose drew down tight to her face when she was angry, and instead of reddening, she paled, which made her features all the sharper.

"Because I knew you'd reject it. Reject me. This is part of who I am," he told her.

"It's not. It's not!" she said as if denying it could change it. "It's a mental illness."

"She is adamantly closed-minded," Peran told his sister in the airport, as they waited at the baggage claim carousel.

"But why?" asked Athena.

"I gather she's from a long line of academics and atheists, and she believes only in things for which there is verifiable evidence. Anything else is dangerous hogwash that leads to mass murder, according to her—like David Koresh, or Hilter."

Sadness waterlogged him. "The only way I could get her to trust me was to agree to abandon my pursuit and to never bring it up again."

"That's a bad idea," Athena said. "Suppressed things only gain power. And if she sees you hanging around with another woman, she'll think you're having an affair. She'll find out, and then she'll never trust you again."

"Give it a few months," Peran said. His wife's outright rejection of the things he held dear wounded him deeply. He did his best not to show it, but he could feel himself pulling away from her.

"Well, I'm knackered. Let's get home, and then tomorrow, I want to get to work on those bodies."

15
WILTON TOWN HALL

OCTOBER 28, 2016

Since Wilton had no town center, it made a certain backward sense that the town hall was in the middle of nowhere, but it wasn't that far from SUNY ADK, so I drove us there to do some research on the haunted house.

Damian's mother was good friends with Maureen, who was a town clerk. She sat at a monolithic metal desk and presided over all she surveyed with large, cat-like blue eyes.

"Hey, kids," Maureen called out as we entered. Her voice was sharp and strong, as if she'd been around the block a few times and found the block difficult but still good. "Damian! How's it going?"

"Not bad. How are you?"

"I'm great. At least, that's what I hear." She laughed at her own joke, an easy, loud laugh that filled the room. "Who's your friend?"

Damian introduced us.

"How's your lovely mother?" Maureen turned back to Damian.

"Good, I guess." He shrugged.

"Sid still having his *little problem*?" She whispered the two last words. Sid was Damian's youngest brother.

"No," Damian said, smiling faintly. "He's better." I could have whacked him for the revelation of yet another unshared bit of his life, but I restrained myself. The way she said it made it seem like it was something embarrassing, like bed-wetting. I knew from a child development class last year that bed-wetting was a sign of family stress.

"You're such a godsend for your mother, Damian. I don't know what she'd do without you. But you didn't come here to talk *family*. What can I *do you for*?" she said, ironically as she rested her chin on her hands, eyes wide and expectant.

"Well, we're doing a project for the school paper, and I was wondering if you could help us out," Damian said.

"I'll do my best. What do you need?"

"You know that old house out behind All-Mart?"

"Oh." She made her mouth a perfect O. "*That* house." She widened her eyes theatrically.

"What do you know about it?" Damian asked.

"Well," she paused, "what do you *want* to know about it, dearie?" She cat-winked at us with both eyes. They say cats blink like that to tell you they're not going to eat you. I wasn't so sure about Maureen.

"Like, who lived there, how he died, whatever you can tell us," Damian said, keeping his voice casual as if he was a little bored by the project.

She scanned the office to see if anyone might overhear. "Come back here with me. I have to do some—filing." She picked up a stack of papers and we followed her toward the back of the office into a room filled with putty-colored file cabinets.

"It's quite a story," she said, once we were inside. "Grab a stool." We sat, and Maureen drew the door of the room almost closed. "The man who used to own that house was named Jacob Johnson. He had lived there forever. It was built by his great-grandfather in the 1880s. He was descended from an elite Black family who thrived in the

1890s. See, his great-grandfather, Blanche E. Johnson, was born a slave, but rose to prominence as an investor, farmer and eventually a senator. His family at one time owned hundreds of acres. Farming was how most people in these parts made a living. But his business went the way of most farms, undersold by corporate agri-businesses out west. Only I'm sure his family had a target on their back."

"Wow," I said, stupidly, "I didn't know there were rich Black people back then."

"Oh, yeah," Maureen said. "There was a pretty well-to-do black community right here in Saratoga Springs."

"No kidding," I said. "How come we don't know this?"

"Duh," Maureen said, rolling her eyes. "Urban renewal. They build parks and shopping malls over black communities to drive them out. Anyway, by 2008, Johnson's holdings had dwindled to that falling-down monstrosity out there on Gick Road and about six acres. The farm was long gone and Jacob Johnson was the last of his line.

"All-Mart approached the town council to buy some land out there, so the council developed this whole 'economic stimulus' plan, and they decided they would bring a few more stores in—make it pretty much what you see there now—except," she paused, "without the house, and," another ironic pause, "more stores.

"But Jacob Johnson refused to sell. The area had been zoned rural residential. That didn't stop the town council. They turned right around and re-zoned the area to commercial."

"Wait. You lost me," I cut in. "What's all this zone stuff?"

"The town is divided into areas where houses can be built or stores. Some areas, like downtown Saratoga Springs, are mixed."

"Wait. So all of a sudden, he wasn't allowed to live there?"

"No, when they change a zone, everything there gets grandfathered in. But no new houses can be built. Most people don't want to live right next to the mall, so they sell."

"What did Jacob do?" Damian asked.

"He still refused to sell. He would come to all the town council meetings and yell his head off about how he was born here, his father was born here, how white people were always building dams, parks, and shopping malls on black land, yadda, yadda, yadda. The Johnsons had to sell off parcels of their land bit by bit, and the area got developed until there was just this six-acre plot right in the middle of the town council's new commercial zone. So contractors for All-Mart started bull-dozing a plot of land that was practically on top of Johnson's house, thinking he'd sell, and *of course*, this made Johnson wild—almost got into a fistfight with Michael Wright."

Damian whistled and said to me, "You know who Wright is, don't you?"

"I don't."

"But you grew up here."

"Sorry," I said.

"He's our local real estate magnate," Maureen said. "Owns a *lot* of property in downtown Saratoga Springs not to mention the Wilton Mall. And he was also on the planning board—a slight conflict of interest, if you ask me, but no one does," she paused abruptly, "ask me— that is," she rolled her eyes and grinned.

"No kidding," said Damian.

"Why?" I asked.

"Don't they ask me?" Maureen quipped.

"No, I mean," I trailed off.

"Just teasing, doll," she said. "See, if town council members buy and sell property regularly, they have the power to change the zoning laws to suit their pocketbook. And that's not right," Maureen said. "At least, I don't think it is."

"Me, neither," I said.

"Finally, the town lawyer cooks up this plan. Ever heard of 'eminent domain'?"

We both shook our heads.

"Well—it's a law that allows the government to take over private property—to buy the owners out—if there is a public need for the land—like a highway or a railroad. Something like that. But in the

1950s the Supreme Court ruled that you could declare 'eminent domain' to build privately owned stores."

"But how can they do that?" I cried. "You mean All-Mart can come along and force you out of your own home?"

"Well, they can't take it. They have to buy it, but, yeah. They can kick you out of your home if the city or the state or the federal government thinks it serves a public need."

"To shop?" I said.

"To shop and provide a tax base, improve the economy, yadda, yadda, yadda."

"Wow, I can't believe that," I said. Damian shook his head like he was world-weary.

Maureen nodded. "So the city declared eminent domain, wrote a check out for 'fair market value,' and condemned his house. That's when Johnson," she paused a beat, "shot himself."

"Oh, my god." A shiver crawled down my spine like a column of ants. "How come no one knows this?"

"Every town has secrets. And there's more. You won't find this in the news, either. Every time they try to knock that house down, something happens: equipment fails, people get hurt."

"That part of the story gets around," Damian said.

"Yeah, but what you don't know is that Bill Ferguson, our director of public works, got bitten by a timber rattler, when no one has even *seen* a rattlesnake in this area for fifty years."

"Wow," we said in unison.

"And that's not all. The fire department sometimes uses condemned buildings for training new firefighters, but they couldn't burn that house. I was there. They would pour gasoline and light it, and it would burn off without catching the building. They even heaped rags together in a big pile and soaked it in gasoline. When they lit it, it burst into flame, then smoldered and went out."

"So the rumor is true," I said.

Maureen laughed her big laugh. "*The truth will out.* But I *know* you don't know this," she leaned in closer. "The whole project got canned when Michael Wright had a stroke soon after Jacob died. Lots of people think the ghost of Jacob Johnson did that. Lots of people being me," she winked.

"Did he die?" Damian asked.

"He's still alive, but he's a babbling idiot, if you pardon my language. Irreparable brain damage, the doctors say. He's been in a nursing home the past seven years. I mean, nobody said anything, but words like 'cursed' started to float around. So the town council and development company quietly dropped the whole thing."

"Wow," I said lamely.

"We read they're talking about knocking it down again," said Damian.

"Yeah. Décor and More wants that spot."

"Are they going to do it?"

"I don't know. Probably. You can't let a little thing like a curse stand between you and millions of dollars." Her laughter ricocheted like a bullet off the walls and file cabinets. "Well, that's all I know. Don't tell anybody I told you," she said. "And don't get any ideas about going into that house." She shook her finger at us and pierced us with her blue cat eyes. "It's not safe. Floorboards could break—or the ghost of Jacob Johnson might get you." She laughed.

16

EMINENT DOMAIN

OCTOBER 28, 2016

Back in Saratoga, I chose the parking lot a few blocks from Uncommon Grounds so I could avoid the nerve-wracking prospect of parallel parking in front of Damian on Broadway. As we walked down the street, the gray sky settled heavily into my chest, and my legs felt like they were raining inside.

"I can't believe how slimy the town council was to Jacob Johnson," I said.

"I can," Damian said. "That's why Jefferson Terrace exists. Zoning boards don't want the riffraff living next door ruining their property values," he added speaking of the place where he lived.

"Indeed," I said. "But there's a difference between exclusive zoning practices and deliberate plotting for individual gain."

"Not much difference in the outcome," Damian said.

"True."

I wanted to believe that Jacob's spirit was still there, seeking some kind of justice. But I didn't know if I really did. As much as I loved Samantha, I didn't want to be as flakey as I thought she was with all her stones and spells.

Uncommon Grounds is in one of those flat, short, 1970s buildings sandwiched between tall Victorian brownstones, built when Saratoga Springs' economy was struggling.

"How many other secrets are these buildings hiding?" I wondered aloud as we pushed through the front door. "What other lives have been bulldozed along with woods and rolling pastures?"

"Oh, lots. Starting with the indigenous people," Damian said.

"You can say that again. We are so out of touch."

"We pay a price for all this convenience," Damian said as he searched for a table to snag.

"Some pay more than others," I said.

"We all pay. We just don't know it."

The rust and ocher interior of Uncommon was hung with the paintings of local artists. It had been the first coffee shop of its kind in Saratoga, but it wasn't long before Starbucks moved in across the street. We were indignant. Didn't they have enough stores? Weren't they making enough money? Couldn't they let local coffee stores have a little piece of the local pie?

To the town's credit, the place was jamming, as usual, every table filled, cups clinking, college students typing on laptops, and conversations swirling high in the air with the smell of slightly burnt coffee. Damian ducked out to lay his jacket over one of the outside tables to reserve it and joined me in a line that curved all the way back to the coffee roaster, which resembled a giant's head with one protruding lower jaw.

"After Maureen's story, I'm wondering if I really *did* see a ghost, " I said. "It explains why his spirit might still be hanging around—I mean, *if* it is."

"Because of the suicide?" Damian asked. It was so loud in there that we didn't have to worry about being overheard.

"No, I was thinking because he might be trying to protect the house. But what's the suicide factor?"

"I was raised Catholic."

"Really," I said. "What other juicy tidbits of your past have you been hiding from me?"

Damian shot me an uncertain look but smiled in answer to my smile. "You can't go to heaven if you kill yourself."

"Oooh," I said dramatically. "So, you go to hell?"

"Purgatory."

"If there's one thing I definitely *don't* believe in, it's hell," I said. "I don't picture God as a torturer on high. I can't picture God at all, as a matter of fact, except as the sum total of the universe."

"He's *supposed* to be beyond imagination. Beyond description. Besides, according to the catechism, God doesn't do the torturing. Satan sets that up. But the point I was trying to make before you started dissing my family's faith," he said, nudging me.

"I'm sorry!" I interjected, my face flaring, and sweat prickling my back.

"I'm kidding! I stopped believing in organized religion a long time ago."

I was relieved.

"But the *point* I was trying to make is that earth might be purgatory for Jacob."

"You don't believe in God, but you believe in ghosts?"

"I said *organized religion*."

"So what *do* you believe?"

He told me about a book he'd read called *The Gaia Hypothesis* that posited the idea that the Earth and the universe are conscious. All the different parts work together to make up a conscious entity. Excitement raised invisible hairs on my arms, and my heart beat faster at how close this was to how I saw it.

"That's exactly it," I said, resonating at my core. "Life is so mind-blowing whether you're looking out at the stars or into a skin cell."

"That's one of the many reasons I like you, Julie Sykes. You are fully alive."

I blushed. "Takes one to know one," I choked out as we reached the front of the line.

"Has someone taken your order?" asked a guy with dreadlocks and an eyebrow ring. I ordered my usual: steamed milk with a squirt of hazelnut decaf. Damian ordered an espresso (yuck) and a plain white bagel (forbidden fruit in my house) with cream cheese.

"So why would Jacob go to purgatory for committing suicide?" I asked after we sat outside.

"Because, supposedly, we are God's property, and it's the ultimate sin to destroy God's gift. And because you die without receiving your last rites."

"Is it also a sin to cut down God's trees?" I said.

"No."

"A little hypocritical, don't you think?"

"So what else is new?" Damian said, grinning. "I think suicide is wrong, though."

"I don't know. If your life is truly *yours*, you should have the right to end it," I said, eying his bagel.

"It's selfish. If you bring a child into this world, you should stick around and raise them no matter what kind of pain you're in." Anger darkened his voice.

"Oh my gosh, did someone in your family commit suicide?"

"What?" Damian's eyes widened. "No, no. Nothing like that."

I searched his face and thought I saw winter thaw churning over rocks and tumbling around bends. "Then what? You seem angry."

"Me?" His intensity smoothed out instantly.

"No," I said. "I was talking to the guy behind you."

A smile tucked the corner of his mouth. "I'm not angry." He pushed half of his bagel at me.

"Thank you," I said.

"I never get angry," Damian said.

I couldn't really argue with that. I'd never seen him act out angrily, whereas I was easily irritated and outspoken about it.

"Anyway. Poor guy," I said, turning back to the subject of Jacob. "I wonder if he had any family left."

"We should look up his obituary in the library," Damian said. "It should be in the papers."

"Good idea. Maybe we could get in touch with one of his relatives. I want to help his—spirit." It seemed like I was beginning to believe.

"Uh-oh," said Damian.

"Uh-oh?"

"Well," he shrugged. "You never know what you're getting into."

He was right. It's not a good idea to mess around with—well—the supernatural—even if you don't believe in it. It was a problem waiting to happen, and I should have known that the instant I touched those wet drops of coffee on the wall of Jacob's house.

17
A PLAN BEGINS TO FORM

OCTOBER 29, 2016

The next day, in biology, The Fish was lecturing on experiments with subatomic particles in these things called "particle accelerators," which are underground tunnels miles long. Scientists can't actually see the particles, but they know they are there because when they smash particles into each other at high speeds, they leave light trails. He stood at the lectern of the blue-carpeted amphitheater that was our classroom, and we sat at semi-round desks on risers around him as he explained that the old TV sets used tubes that were small particle accelerators. Unbelievable. Truly the stuff of science fiction, only fact. They have found that when some particles are split, the two parts continue to act in concert with each other no matter how much distance is between them, as if they are still connected.

My heart sped and my mind whizzed. I nudged Damian and wrote "Ghosts?" in the margin of his notes. He wrote a question mark next to it. I wrote, "Couldn't energy particles be split away from the body particles and still act like they were alive in some form?"

He wrote, "But if one particle was acting dead, that would imply the others would act dead, too." My heart sank.

"You two want to share your fascinating exchange with the rest of the class?" Dr. Fish said sharply.

"Sorry," I said.

Jonathan had been called into Stewarts to pick up a shift, and that left Samantha without a ride, so she missed class that day, but they had arranged to meet us after class to work on the next issue of *The Adirondacker*.

Damian and I headed to the writing center computers, a wide-open room with windows on the hall. We found Jacob Johnson's obituary with ease. He died on October 11, 2008. It didn't mention the manner of his death—only that he was "found" alone in his house. It said the house had been built by his great-great-great grandfather and that he was the last in the line.

We headed back to town to Congress Park to have a late lunch. October couldn't decide if it was winter or summer. Today it was summer, warm and sunny. We sat on a bench facing the duck pond with the octagon stone war memorial off-center in it.

I unwound the full-size Price Chopper bag that contained my lunch (my mom and I were both obsessed with reusing and recycling and *never* bought baggies). "How can we help Jacob's spirit rest—I mean—"

"If there *is* such a thing," Damian finished my sentence ironically.

"Yeah."

"We could call the people who do ghost tours around town and see if they know of an exorcist," Damian mused.

"I'm sure we'd have to pay them, don't you think? Besides, this is *our* project."

A sparrow landed at the end of the park bench we sat on. It chirped and cocked its head in the direction of my sandwich. Damian threw it a crumb. "Then I guess it depends on why his spirit is hanging around. You mentioned that you thought he might be trying to protect the place. Hence the *curse*. In which case, maybe we should let him continue to protect the land," he mused.

"Maybe he can't let go of it. Maybe he's in pain. Maybe because all his ancestors lived in that house and because they built it, all their energy is trapped in the house, and it's holding him there," I said.

"Or maybe he's afraid to leave because that's all he ever knew," Damian said.

"I've heard of that—that some spirits get confused, don't know they're dead, and just need to be told."

"Go toward the light!" Damian said.

"What spirit? What light?" Samantha swooped down on us with Jonathan behind. The sparrow flew away. Damian and I locked eyes. We weren't sure we wanted to tell anyone about the house. It was sort of our thing.

"We were talking about our research for the sprawl series," Damian said. He was a little too smooth at covering up.

"Bullshit," Samantha said. "Who died?"

Jonathan looked at us with his doleful brown eyes and a faint smile. His ponytail had snuck over his shoulder and curled against his neck like an exhausted kitten.

"Nobody we know," I said, looking at Damian for help. He shrugged his shoulders slightly.

"Come on," she said, hitting me on the arm and plopping onto my lap. "Spill it, or I'll never speak to you again." She pinched my cheeks.

"Ow! Okay, okay!" I said, laughing. I glanced at Damian and he nodded. "Damian and I have been checking out that house behind All-Mart and—"

"You went *without* me?" she yelled.

"Sorry. We just—"

"That's okay," she winked, and her voice rose and fell suggestively. "I understand."

"Behave," I said, shaking my index finger at her.

"So, tell me. It really *is* haunted, isn't it?"

"Maybe," Damian said.

We told her how I'd seen the coffee cup slamming down, the coffee drops, and that we'd learned Jacob Johnson committed suicide. We didn't tell them how we learned that, and Samantha didn't seem to want to know.

"Way cool," she said, jumping up and clapping her hands. "I can't believe you didn't include me in this. You *know* I'm a Wiccan. This is my thing!" This surprised me. I didn't think Wiccans were into ghosts. "We have to have a séance! Let's talk to him and find out what's bothering him so we can help him pass over."

"Wiccans do séances?" I asked, trying unsuccessfully to keep incredulity out of my voice.

"No, I mean, sure. Whatever."

"There's only one problem," I said.

"What?" she said.

"Who here is a medium?"

"I am! I read all about it in this book. You close your eyes, join hands and say," she interrupted herself and waved her hand. "You'll see. I can totally do it. You want to do it?" she said with a little hop. "Let's do it!"

I was split. One part of me said, *Try it, why not?* The other part was saying, *Who are we to mess with spirits,* real or not? It was easy for Samantha to be cavalier about it because she'd never actually experienced anything supernatural.

"We'll burn sage to cleanse it!" Samantha said as if reading my concern. It sort of irritated me that she was now ad-libbing a mixture of Indigenous American spiritualism and Wicca.

However, some essential fibers of my being must have gotten snagged in the branches of that lone oak outside Jacob's home. The idea of a ghost bloomed darkly inside me, a rich and promising darkness, like the scent of new-ground coffee and dark chocolate.

"I suppose we could try it someday," I said.

"No!" Samantha practically screamed. "It *has* to be night."

"Why?" I asked.

"That's when you *have* séances," she said, rolling her black-lined eyes with disdain.

"But if a spirit is there, it's going to be there whether it is night or day. We were there during the day."

"Night is better. More spirit activity. Better communication. More fun."

I didn't think so. It's hard to see at night, easier to get confused and scared, but I went along with it anyway. Don't you hate it when you do that?

"And let's do it on Halloween!" she said.

"Oh come on!" I said with disgust. "That's *such* a cliché!"

"No, no, that's when the skin between the two worlds is the thinnest! Besides, we can't go trick-or-treating anymore. Come *on!* We *have* to!"

"I have to take my little brother trick-or-treating," said Damian.

"Aw," Samantha cooed. "That's sweet."

Damian shrugged. "That's family."

"Okay, let's go after you finish!" Samantha said. "We can pick you up, right?" she said, looking at Jonathan.

"Your wish is my command," Jonathan said.

I conferred with Damian and he nodded. "Deal."

I won't pretend I wasn't excited.

18
SÉANCE

OCTOBER 31, 2016

Halloween night, darkness slid open like a cat's eye. A warm wind swooped from what felt like thousands of miles away, nuzzling Damian and me along the street to our pick-up point on Nelson Avenue.

My mother was going to spend the night on a friend's front porch on Caroline Street which was locally known as the best place to go trick-or-treating. The whole street outdid itself in purple lights, cobwebs, and skeletons, but her friends were informally known to have the best display in the neighborhood with their front yard full of zombies, witches, and skeletons popping out of coffins. She and her friends loved sipping on a glass of wine, working the fog machine, watching kid reactions, and handing out candy. Trick-or-treaters swamped the area in costumes that ran the gamut from All-Mart Spiderman costumes to original papier-mâché dragon heads and alien masks. I told my mom I was getting together with friends to celebrate Halloween, which was true, sort of. I just didn't give her the details, and she knew I wasn't the type to get into drugs or excessive alcohol.

Jonathan's beater car rumbled unevenly to a stop along the curb under the yellow streetlight. "Yoo-hoo," Samantha called, waving a scarf out the front window at us. Damian and I tumbled into the back seat and were enveloped by the smell of leaking gas, cannabis, and Sam's perfume. Samantha was the only one who'd donned a Halloween costume as a Romani fortune teller. "I thought I'd dress the part, JK," she said, showing off her long spangly skirt, head scarf, and a black birthmark.

Jonathan offered Damian a toke of his joint, but Damian declined, giving Jonathan a squeeze on the shoulder. I declined, too. Damian draped his arm across the back of the seat, and when he gestured as he talked, his hand accidentally brushed against my hair, which set my whole body tingling.

"You smoke too much," Samantha complained, batting with her scarf at the smoke from Jonathan's joint.

"You want me to drive so you can take it easy?" asked Damian.

"If anything," Jonathan said coolly, "cannabis makes me a better driver. More focused. I do my homework stoned." We all knew he could pull straight A's when he wanted to. Apparently, it made him a better talker, too, because he had strung together more words in that sentence than I'd heard him say all year.

"It's true," said Samantha begrudgingly. "He acts like he's on speed without it."

"There's no accounting for the difference in brain chemistry," said Damian. "All it does for me is make me paranoid."

"Hmmm," I said, mockingly. "Very interesting."

Damian's hand capped my head, his long fingers easily encompassing my crown.

"Quit talking about drugs," Samantha interjected. "Let's talk about ghosts!" The green dashboard lights illuminated her pale skin. "I brought candles and the black cloth for the windows." The plan was to send someone in ahead to cover the windows so that no one would see the lights from the road. The candles were another thing that "had to be" according to Samantha.

Jonathan elected to take us on a slow tour through the neighborhood where my mom was hanging, the well-heeled east side of Broadway, up and down Phila and Spring streets, as well as Caroline. Tri-colored, turreted, gingerbread houses unfolded their balconies under broad maple trees that still hung onto their orange and yellow leaves for the most part. Fake cobwebs stretched over bushes and banisters, along with orange and purple string lights and piles of jack-o-lanterns cut into loony grins and creepy witch faces. Most of the young kids had already gone off to bed, which left a few teenage stragglers, and adults on front porches. Tines of unnamable longing raked my insides, uncovering, to my surprise, a pit of emotion where I couldn't distinguish sadness from joy. It had something to do with the contrasts of the seasons, intense color heralding imminent death, or the fantasy happy childhood of a two-parent family contrasted with what I had. All of us, except Jonathan, were from single-parent families.

"So who knows a real ghost story?" Samantha asked.

"I heard that house used to have an aviary—" Jonathan said, pointing at the yellow brick mansion we were passing. Four two-story pillars fronted the house, and a wrought-iron fence surrounded it, its ornate curlicues painted glossily black.

"Speak English, Jonathan," Samantha cut in. "The natives are restless."

"A big birdhouse, then," he corrected placidly. "When the workmen started gutting it, I'm told, windows and shutters banged open and slammed shut all over the house. Then a flock of red birds flew out of nowhere and out the window."

We all oohed and aahed.

"I woke up one night," Samantha said, twisting in her seat to face us, "and I swear an old man was sitting at the foot of my bed. I couldn't move for, like, ten minutes. I was frozen, like this huge weight was pressing me to the bed. When I opened my eyes, he was gone."

"You just said you opened your eyes," I said. "That suggests they were closed when you saw him."

Samantha seemed confused for a second. "No, I mean I opened them wider."

"See, I think there's an explanation for most of that stuff," I said, not knowing why I was being such a party pooper. "When we sleep, our bodies are paralyzed so that we don't walk. But for some people, the wires get crossed."

"Don't you remember those pictures on the Psychical Research Society's website?" Samantha said. We had spent a fair amount of time in sixth and seventh grade playing with Ouija boards and attempting levitation.

"Those photos are so easy to fake," I said. "Like the one with little white orbs supposedly in a graveyard. All it takes is a speck of dust close to the camera lens."

"Yeah. And the ghost lore is pretty contradictory. Why do some of those pictures look like people, some like smoke, and some like white dots?" Jonathan asked.

We all stared at him.

"How come some can talk and some can't?" he continued.

"This is no time to play devil's avocado or whatever," Samantha said.

"Devil's advocate," Jonathan corrected her without a trace of laughter.

I stifled a grin as I tried to imagine what the devil's avocado looked like.

"What does advocate mean, anyway?!" she said, hitting him.

"It's like a lawyer," explained Damian.

"Can't the devil represent himself?" I joked.

"Shh! Don't talk about him!" Samantha said, plugging her ears.

"Anyway. I'm with Jonathan," I said, annoying even myself. "Don't you think there'd be hard evidence by now if ghosts really existed? I mean, we all see this car, that tree, and that house. We can all agree on the shape, size, and color. Why isn't it the same with ghosts?"

"You're the one who saw that thing in the house in the first place," Samantha quipped, flapping her scarf at me.

"But it could have been a hallucination," I said to our warped reflections in the black windows.

"Or a premonition," Samantha shot back.

"I'm not even sure I saw it," I said. I felt exposed and wanted to drop the whole thing like a hot rock.

"What do you *mean*? How can you *say* that?" Samantha said.

"I don't know," I said falteringly, "I just—it could have been inside my head. It wasn't, like, *real*."

"Reality is pretty subjective," Damian said.

Jonathan smiled in the rearview mirror at Damian and nodded like he was rocking to a song inside his head. "Yeah, brother, preach it."

"And the drops of coffee!" Samantha practically yelled. "You both felt it."

"Reality is established by mutual agreement," Jonathan said, quoting somebody-or-other.

"Okay professor," I quipped. "But—maybe it was just a leak. Have you ever thought of that?" I lay my head back against the seat. This car was so old it didn't have headrests. Damian, whose hand rested along the rear dash, tapped the center of my forehead with his thumb.

"You're refusing to see," he whispered. "Exactly as your mother demanded." The warmth of his breath tingled all the way down to my you-know-what.

Jonathan stepped on the gas as we turned onto the four-lane arterial going toward the shopping strip. Within minutes we were pulling into All-Mart's enormous blacktop bib, a serving tray for all the people it consumed, like that *Twilight Zone* episode, "How to Serve Man." People thought All-Mart was serving them when, really, they were serving it.

"Let's park here," I said, "and walk the rest of the way, so we don't call attention to ourselves."

"Walk?!" said Samantha, "You mean outside?" Jonathan looked at her blankly in the silence of the just-cut engine, exited the car, came around to her side, opened her door, and ceremoniously offered her his arm.

The doors of All-Mart opened and closed, swallowing up and spitting out a surprisingly steady stream of people for nine o'clock on Halloween. As we climbed out of the car, a dry wind blew my hair in my eyes and made the trees roar.

Damian held his fingers up as a crucifix in the direction of All-Mart. "Talk about evil spirits," he said. "When you walk the aisles, you can practically hear the cries of children in India tied to looms."

We turned the corner and stepped into darkness. As we stumbled silently through the weeds, the house came into view, its curved mansard roof graceful at night over the arched trim that gently glowed from distant streetlights. It felt good to be part of a team, as if we were superheroes off to accomplish a mission.

As we neared, I thought I saw someone standing by the fence that surrounded it, a woman in gray with a flowing dress and long white hair. The headlights of an oncoming car momentarily silhouetted her for an instant. Then, as soon as the car passed, she was gone. I waited for someone else to comment, but no one said anything.

Damian and Jonathan walked ahead, and Samantha squeezed my arm. "This is so crazy!"

The fence jingled gently when we pulled the bottom edge up for each other and scooted underneath.

"You didn't tell me we had to climb under a fence!" Samantha said through gritted teeth before she knelt on the ground.

"You're going to have to shimmy on your stomach," Jonathan said.

"Easy for you to say, ya skinny lizard," Samantha said. She grunted as she flattened out and pulled herself through, muttering, "Honestly. The things I do for my friends."

When we were all inside the fence, we paused a moment in silence looking at the old house, absorbing its isolation, its former Victorian grace. The windows winked like blind eyes, and the clapboard glowed as bones in the light of the distant highway. The central tower with its square mansard roof loomed. I was afraid of what I might see if I looked too hard at the tower windows.

"I'll go first and cover the kitchen windows," Damian said quietly.

"So gallant," I said. "But I could do it if you don't want to."

"I need you to watch my back," he said, turning up the collar of my coat and snugging it around my neck. Then he was off, the suede resonance of his voice, textured with suppressed laughter and *je ne sais quoi*, tickled my ear, warmer than the October wind.

"I'm *not* going in until you've lit the candles," Samantha chimed in adamantly. She doled out one candle to each of us. "And also, put this in your pocket," she said, thrusting little black pebbles at each of us.

"What is it?" I whispered.

"Onyx, to protect us from being possessed by evil spirits."

Seemed dubious to me, but we all did as she said. She was the boss all of a sudden.

"Just curious," I said, "why aren't we using our phone flashlights?"

"It could cause interference," she said. "Everyone knows ghosts can travel via electric lines."

"Hm," I said, but I obeyed.

As I approached the back door, icy droplets pricked me all over again.

"Did you feel that?" I asked Damian.

"What?"

"I felt it the last time. Like cold water or static electricity pricking me all over."

"Maybe it's spirit energy," Damian said.

We stepped carefully onto the back porch feeling for loose boards. Damian opened the door first with me right behind. That coffee-licorice smell rushed to meet me. The hall was pitch black, but once my eyes adjusted, the faintly pinkish night sky caused by city lights reflecting illuminating cloud cover seeped through the windows. I took a deep breath and held it. Damian moved ahead of me into the darkness, but within a few steps, I couldn't see him anymore. Samantha and Jonathan waited on the front porch for the okay to enter.

When I edged my way along the wall, it got darker. I assumed it was because Damian had succeeded in covering the windows in the kitchen. I was surprised, then, when Damian's hand roughly groped for mine. My fingers closed around blunt, sausage-like fingers that I instantly knew were not his. Shock seared me like an electric current. I let go. At that very instant, Damian's voice sounded from the kitchen: "Here we go." He struck a match and illuminated the kitchen doorway where he stood, a full ten feet away from me. The skin on my hand burned with the sensation of those rough fingers. My heart beat so hard it pushed a wave through me. I swayed and caught myself.

I looked around hoping to find that Jonathan had somehow gotten ahead of me, but they were still a yard behind me, poking their heads through the door. The blue parka swung slightly on its hook in front of me. That must have been what I felt, I insisted to myself. I swallowed several times to quell the puking sensation. I decided not to say anything to the others. I didn't want to send everyone into a total panic. Imagination plays tricks, after all.

Once Damian lit a few candles, Samantha and Jonathan came in, looking in awed silence at the patchy wallpaper with "Stay Out" spray-painted on the plaster and the banister curving up from the lathe-turned newel post.

"Wow," said Samantha. "This place is seriously haunted."

As I watched them poke their heads in and then out of the living room and move down the hall, I was still jittery, but my heart calmed somewhat.

"Let's peek upstairs," Samantha said. "But stick together."

Damian led the way with me bringing up the rear.

"Keep an eye out for broken boards," Damian warned. The candles we each held made it harder for me to see, lighting things above but increasing the darkness below as we creaked slowly up the stairs. I reviewed the sensations in my hand—the roughness and hardness could have been the sleeve of the coat hanging by the door, crusted with dirt and cracked with age, but hadn't it pulled out of my hand? Was I still moving when I felt it? I rubbed my fingers against my jeans, trying to erase the sensation. Another swallow kept the bile where it was supposed to be.

At the top of the stairs, Damian stood aside and let Sam and Jonathan look into the bedroom. She poked her head in, and Jonathan stayed behind her.

"Okay, I've seen enough," she said, filling with purpose and efficiency like an investigator. "Let's do this thing, smudge the place with sage, and get out." She turned toward us and brusquely took charge. "Where did you see the—what you saw?"

"In the kitchen," I said.

"Then we'll have the séance there. Come on. Move." She pointed down the stairs. We all turned around obediently and shuffled back down, our feet thudding hollowly all the way. As we entered the kitchen, we heard a very high, soft, screeching sound. The black window cloth billowed slightly.

"What was that!" Samantha jumped.

"Nothing," I said, "just the branch of that oak tree scratching against a window."

"Is the window open? Why did the cloth move?"

"I'm sure there are a lot of cracks in the windows," I said.

The sound grounded me. I debated telling them about the hand I'd grabbed but decided again not to. I'm not sure why. I guess I wanted to try the séance, as stupid as it seemed. If I told them, everyone might panic. Maybe also, seeing their expressions would make me feel my feelings. It was easier to carry on if I kept it to myself.

"Okay," said Sam, gesturing a pipe-down motion with both hands. She took a deep breath. "So where exactly were you standing?"

"Right here," I said, tapping my hand on the white, porcelain-top table. "Someone slammed a coffee mug down on this table. And the drops splashed right over there." I pointed to the window Damian had covered in cloth.

"Ectoplasm," said Samantha knowledgeably.

"Ecto-what?"

"When spirits break through the material plane, they emit a kind of slime," Samantha said. "Now, Julie, you hold onto this end of the saturated object—no wait—"

"Saturated object?" I squinted at her.

"The table—saturated with spirit. Now shut up. Remain standing, everyone. I'll hold onto this end of the table, then, Jonathan, you're next to me. Then Damian," and she arranged us so that we formed a chain that began and ended with the "saturated object" otherwise known as a table.

I closed my hand around Damian's long fingers, and he laced his pinky between my last two fingers. Yeah, I shivered. That was definitely not his hand in the hall. It was that stupid K-Mart jacket.

"It's okay to see," he whispered. I glanced at his eyes, but in the candlelight they were black. Still, his hand felt warm, strong, and infinitely calm. I squeezed his hand hard, not wanting to let go.

"Okay. Everyone take a deep breath," Samantha commanded.

Her full face was rosy with excitement and confidence. We did as we were told. It felt good to breathe in, and my lungs opened like a thirsty flower. "Okay, now breathe out. Close your eyes. Cleanse yourself. Breathe in good, clean light and breathe out the toxins." We breathed together again. Someone's breath was trembling. By the fourth or fifth breath, we were all in sync. I had to give it to Samantha, it worked to connect and ground us.

"Now. This won't work if everyone doesn't believe. Do you believe?" Samantha asked. We opened our eyes and stared at each other in the flickering candlelight that illuminated the bottoms of our faces and cast dark shadows above our eyes. Damian wore an expression I couldn't read, but he squeezed my hand gently. We all nodded, regardless of what we thought.

"Okay. Close your eyes again and breathe. Oh, Great Spirit," Samantha babbled, casting a protective circle and calling upon the spirit in the house to come forward and tell us what it wanted.

At first, I had a strong urge to laugh, but as I listened to my breathing, the smell of the house suffused me, and my mind puddled. I forgot where I was and was floating pleasantly on my breath, lavender veils swirling under my eyelids, when the air pressure changed in my ear, like when you're in a plane taking off.

My body snapped to attention. I opened my eyes, but everyone else still had their eyes shut, and Samantha was still talking, her voice muffled through my closed ear drums. Then my ears popped, relieving the pressure, and Samantha's voice became clear. "We call on you to safeguard . . ." But my scalp itched. I couldn't scratch it because my hands were held. I wiggled my shoulders around, hoping to alleviate the itch. It only itched worse. I closed my eyes, trying to concentrate or relax, or whatever I was supposed to be doing.

The air pressure fluctuated inside my ear once, twice, three times, at ever-increasing speed, until it was fluttering as disturbingly as when one back window has been left open in a moving car. Thick hands roughly groped my shoulders, neck, and face, and a spear of shock stabbed my gut. I yelled, "Cut it out!" thinking Jonathan or Damian was playing an asinine joke on me. But when I tried to let go of their hands to fend them off, I realized simultaneously that they were both still gripping mine, Jonathan on my left and Damian on my right. Then red exploded in my mind, Damian yanked me sideways, Samantha screamed, and we all crashed to the floor, arms, feet, and table legs flying in all directions.

When we recovered our senses, Samantha sat up and yelled, "What the fuck happened?" We sprawled around her.

"Shhh," Jonathan said, rising on all fours to grab the tumbled candlestick which had miraculously stayed alight and was about to set the place on fire. "The table broke, that's all."

"My bad," I said, shakily. "I lost my balance, and I must have knocked Damian over and he—" We all looked over at Damian and stopped. He sat up gingerly, one hand to his stomach, and—I kid you not—he was green—seriously green, even in that light. Then he leapt to his feet and started for the door but doubled over and vomited some liquid, which even in that light, we could see was deep yellow bile.

"Gross!" Samantha said.

"Damian, are you all right?" I stupidly asked, jumping up after him. I rubbed his back, but my heart felt as if it had swelled to twice its normal size and was painfully and unsuccessfully trying to squeeze blood through its swollen valves.

"Sorry," he said, still bent over. He patted his jeans looking for a tissue. I grabbed the paper towel from the stove that the coffee mugs had been resting on. He wiped his mouth and spat. "I guess I've got some kind of stomach thing going on."

But I knew with a slither in my belly that it had to do with Jacob's spirit.

"Let's get out of here," Samantha said. Her spark ignited us, and we all scrambled for the door. Our feet thudded on the back steps, swished through the weeds, and I scraped my back on the fence as we squeezed under it. We jogged a fair distance from the house before we stopped and looked back, our collective pants sawing the air unevenly. Jonathan jammed both hands in his pocket, raising his narrow shoulders to his ears, his doleful eyes large and round. Damian wiped his mouth again with the back of his sleeve, and the wind flew over us like a giant eagle, lifting the scent of the house off us.

"What happened? What-the-fuck just happened in there?" Samantha demanded.

"I don't know," I said. "Damian?"

"I think I've got a stomach bug or something."

"But you got sick the last time we went to the house," I said.

"No," Samantha cut in impatiently, "I mean the table. It exploded."

"It was me." I said, "I felt this weird—"

"Don't tell us now—I'm too freaked out," said Samantha, palms outspread. "*And* I'm *freezing*," which was odd because it wasn't cold at all.

Later, with the car idling and the heat on full blast, I told them what I had felt, leaving out the hand in the hallway—feeling embarrassed for keeping a secret that might have endangered them. With the dome light on, the car windows were opaque, and we were cocooned from the night.

"This time I can't deny it. Something touched me. It wasn't in my head. I felt it on my body, and it wasn't any of you, because we were all still holding hands."

"I didn't feel a thing, thank *God*," Samantha said as she rubbed her arms and shivered.

"Me neither," said Jonathan. "Except when you knocked us all flat, that is," he smiled.

"What about you, Damian?" I asked.

Damian paused, thinking. "Nothing, really. I was sort of distracted, 'cause I started to feel so sick."

"But is it weird that I'm also kinda jealous?" Samantha said.

Jonathan rolled a joint as I studied Damian's narrow face, the neat sharp corner of his jaw. His expression was blank. His secretiveness, his always-under-control-ness was beginning to seriously irritate me.

"How did the guy kill himself?" Jonathan asked.

"We don't know," said Damian.

"With a gun," I said. I related my vision of the red explosion. I had the creepy feeling that it might have been murder, too, but I kept that to myself.

"It's a poltergeist, for sure," said Samantha. "I'd like to help, but sorry—I'm *not* going in that house again. And if you do, you're on your own!"

"Some friend!" I said with an exaggerated grin, reaching over the seat to squeeze her shoulder. But I was relieved, to tell you the truth. I wasn't sure I wanted to go back, either. Ghosts are much more romantic in concept than in person. Irritation at Samantha rippled through me, for insisting we come on this fool's errand in the first place—and at night, when the unknown takes shape in the darkness. And I was worried. What if *I* was the source of the trouble? What if *I* was manifesting these disturbances? There was a theory that poltergeists were really teenage psychokinetic angst, a sort of extrasensory tantrum.

But even though I routinely saw some pretty freaky things, and even though my father died when I was young, and even though I was angry at my mother, I didn't feel like an angst-ridden teenager. And I'd only ever *seen* energy patterns before. Never felt human shapes.

The smoke from Jonathan's joint swathed us in gray felt. I slid back into the cracked vinyl seat, slack with fatigue.

We should have left it alone at that point. But deep down, under the layers of placation, worry, and fear, another very new emotion stirred: pride, a secret pride that I had been chosen, that I was special, that I had supernatural power. I wanted to know more, even though I wasn't sure what it would cost us, about my power, about Jacob, and about what was happening to me and to Damian.

I tipped my head back against the seat, bumping into Damian's hand. He pulled his hand away quickly, which wounded me more than it should have.

Far reaches of infinite black rushed the car, and gently rocked it as the wind dipped and took off for distant plains.

19
FORENSICS

END OF NOVEMBER, 1999

The first thing Athena did after the contractors set up her lab in the gatehouse at the back of the Broadway villa that Anima Arcanum acquired for her, was to lay out what was left of all six corpses on stainless steel tables. They were all male, and by measuring the radio-carbon levels in their tooth enamel and comparing it to environmental radio-carbon levels between 1900 and now, she was able to estimate when they died. As their clothing suggested, they had all died in different years between 1910 and 1948 at uneven intervals that didn't seem to correspond to anything obvious.

Peran walked with her to each body as she explained.

"There were no marks on their bodies that suggested violence; however, the preservation of their bodies struck me as odd and rang a bell. I did a little research, and sure enough, arsenic has a tendency to preserve the body. Only two of them still had remnants of stomach tissue. By boiling a section of them and subjecting the liquid to precipitate tests, I was able to find arsenic in both."

"Brilliant," Peran exclaimed, eyes gleaming.

"But two doesn't make a pattern, and it's possible that the arsenic poisoning may have occurred by accident."

"The city historian devoted an entire chapter in her *Saratoga History* to he-who-shall-hence-forward-be-referred-to-as-H," Peran said, observing the Anima Arcanum caution of not saying the name of the spirit in question to avoid accidentally raising it. "She blamed the destruction of the houses on vagrants looting and squatting, but other newspaper accounts mentioned grass fires."

"It was common to use arsenic to color clothing and wallpaper in the Victorian era," Athena mused, "so if these blokes were squatting there, it's possible they could have absorbed enough arsenic over time to kill them."

Peran pondered this. "But you wouldn't find it in their stomach lining unless they'd consumed it, yeah?"

"Good point," Athena said. "Now, these two blokes," she pointed to the ones from 1930 and 1940, "could have died of natural causes. If they broke in on a cold winter's night hoping for shelter, they could have frozen to death. Particularly if they were drunk. You said you found wine bottles?"

"It appeared to be a wine cellar or some sort."

"Can you go back and find a few? I could test their contents."

"I'll see what I can find," Peran said, excitement sparking in his eyes at the thought of returning to the site.

"What I don't understand is, why were the mansions abandoned and allowed to rot?" said Athena.

"For one thing," Peran said, "He squandered most of his money on excessive luxury. By the time he died, he'd spent down his seventy million to a million and a half. He damaged his fortune when he posted anti-Semitic signs in the Grand Hotel, which caused a sensation across America and started a boycott of his department stores. When his debts were settled, there was only $800 thousand left, not enough to maintain the estate."

"So, why not sell?"

"He left a maze of a will. I found it in the NY State records. It prevented his heirs from selling or transferring any part of the estate."

Athena whistled. "But why?"

"Pure conjecture on my part. My guess is that he wanted his legacy to stay intact, and he wanted his bloodline to be the sole inhabitants of Woodlawn. There was a lot of prejudice against new money, and if he could establish a legacy, that would change."

"So, they didn't have enough money to keep the estate, and they couldn't sell it. What a mess," Athena said.

"He stipulated that each of his children should get $50 thousand apiece after the estate's needs were met. But he gave his executors the right to hang onto the money and dispense it 'as needed,' whatever that meant."

"Sounds to me like he didn't trust his children not to squander the money," Athena said.

"Spot on. He left half that amount to the son who was named after him. Apparently, when they were flush, H Junior spent a million dollars on the wardrobe of some French woman he met on a transatlantic cruise."

"My word," Athena said.

"The children sued, of course, and the whole thing was tied up in court for 20 years."

"What a bloody mess."

"Finally, there was an estate sale where they sold off his artwork — he had amassed a lot, including a seven-foot-wide marble statue of Hiawatha by Augustus Saint-Gaudens, mentioned in the Longfellow poem. But get this, the statue disappeared. The people who paid for it never got it."

"Sounds like a bunch of ne'er-do-wells surrounding the estate."

"It's like it was cursed," Peran said. He swayed for a moment.

"You look a bit peaked," Athena said. "Have a seat."

"I'm fine. I skipped brekkie this morning."

"Fancy a cuppa? You need to keep up your strength," Athena paused and gave him a knowing look, "*and* your medication."

Peran waved that away. "Anyway, the curse. In 1916, seventeen years after H died, a congressman by the name of Loft was going to buy the estate and turn it into a hotel and golf course. A financier named Morse offered to go in on the deal. But I guess Loft didn't have enough money to go through with any renovation. Then he died rather suddenly. Morse brought in woodcutters and denuded the place. Three thousand trees were cut down, and then he abandoned it. He later landed in jail for defrauding his own bank."

"That's not a curse. That's capitalism," Athena quipped.

Peran said nothing.

"Meanwhile, someone or something poisoned these men," she added. "What are you sensing?"

"There's definitely a spirit there. I've seen H on the trail, and I feel it, here," he pointed to his sternum. "And then there are the dreams. Maybe what is keeping him here is that the estate was never settled."

"Is there an ongoing threat to life?" Athena asked. For Anima Arcanum to take action, the haunting had to meet a set of criteria, this being the first.

"I'm not sure. There haven't been any reported deaths in the woods, and I haven't traced his descendants, yet."

"And how is it all affecting you?"

"It has created problems with Audrey, and I've been a little more down, lately, but nothing to worry about."

"You're looking a bit thin, too. Have you been following the grounding protocols?"

"Of course," Peran said, irritated.

"What have you found works?"

"Don't patronize me," Peran said.

"Okay," Athena said, slowly. "But to be sure, maybe you shouldn't do any more exploration on the property on your own, yeah?"

"I work there, remember?"

"Right, but on second thought, wait for me to accompany you to find those wine bottles, and please don't go near the well again without me. We don't want another Cornwall," she said, referring to a case from their past where he'd been hospitalized.

"I'm not ready to suggest any kind of official Anima Arcanum action," Peran said. "But there's something here. Something that I think connects directly to us."

"What do you mean?"

"Remember what Mum used to say about the bloke who knocked her up?"

"A long-lost descendant of H, you think?"

"Exactly. I felt drawn to this place, and the dreams are similar to ones I had when I was a tyke."

"Without our father's name, we have no way of proving that," Athena said.

"Other than a summoning."

"You know how unreliable that can be. Dead spirit memory isn't any more accurate than living memory. Anyway, it doesn't follow the protocol."

"Always a proper rule follower," Peran said with a smile.

"Someone has to be." Athena smiled back.

"Well, he is buried in the Greenwood Cemetery in Brooklyn. We could get a DNA sample."

"How on earth are we going to get the body exhumed?" Athena asked.

"There are other ways."

"Go on. Need I remind you that grave robbery is also not in the protocol?"

"We'll see," said Peran.

"Have a cuppa before you leave, what say you?" She headed to the door and gestured for him to follow.

Peran checked his watch. "I guess I could fit that in. I only have one more stack of finals to grade today."

"Hey, with Christmas coming up, do you think I can finally meet the family? We could concoct a story about how I'm here on a research grant."

"I think that could work," Peran said slowly. "I'll run it by Audrey tonight."

20
WHY NO PICTURES

NOVEMBER 1, 2016

When I woke the following day, excitement battled with fear. Was I Julie the-psychokinetic-tantrum-thrower? Or was I Julie, *the powerful*? Had we gotten in touch with something from the other side? The idea was both comforting and terrifying. What would happen if I stopped fighting my visions and leaned into them? Could I contact my father? Longing tugged at me. At the same time, I remembered Damian pulling his hand away from me in the car. I wandered downstairs in search of my mother.

"Hey, gorgeous," she said, looking up from the stack of papers she was correcting in the dining room. Sunlight glanced off the French doors, illuminating her delicate, pink skin. Age was starting to crumple it ever so slightly.

"How are your students this semester?" I asked, looking at her stack.

"Pretty good. I've got a talkative bunch. They're coming up with great ideas."

A salmon-colored sea anemone waved delicately at her core. I didn't shut my vision down this time, enjoying the sense of power it gave me.

"Did you have fun at Felicity's porch party last night?" I asked.

"Oh, yes. The weather was great. First time in a long time that it was warm enough for all the trick-or-treaters to show off their costumes. Felicity had made these huge butterfly wings out of pantihose and wire, but they kept sweeping wine glasses onto the floor, so she had to abandon them. I was hoping you'd stop by."

"We drove by and waved."

"Oh? You were with Sam and Jonathan?"

"And Damian."

"Ooo," she said suggestively. "Is it getting serious?"

"I like him. A lot," I said. "He's smart and responsible."

"When do I get to meet him?"

"He works a lot."

"Maybe you can bring him over sometime to study. I'll just pop in for a quick hello and then make myself scarce, I promise."

"Deal," I said. She was cute when she wanted to be. "Maybe tonight. Speaking of which, can we clean the house early today?" I asked.

"Sure," she said, looking surprised and happy. "I like the impact this Damian is having on you. Which rooms do you want to take?"

I don't know why annoyance suddenly pricked me all over.

"The attic," I said, perversely.

Her internal anemone clamped shut. "We've been over this."

I shook my head to clear my vision, sad that I'd shut her down, but also unable to stop the ball I'd set in motion from rolling. "But Dad's pictures are up there."

"No, they're not." She put down her pen, took a deep breath, and massaged the spot between her brows.

"But you said—"

"I know what I said—I'm sorry. I should have told you the truth."

My chest closed, heaviness descended, and the sunlight through the windows seemed cold. "You *lied to me?*"

"I didn't lie."

"You said—"

"Okay. Okay. Technically I did. I'm sorry. But," she sat up straighter and squared her shoulders. "The truth is, there are no pictures."

"What?" My voice careened upwards.

"I'm sorry."

"You're telling me you don't have a single picture of Dad?" I shifted over to one hip.

"Right." Her face was a stone wall.

"Why not?"

"Look," she spread her palms outward as if to contain my welling anger, "he didn't have that many pictures, to begin with. He didn't have many possessions at all."

"Not even wedding pictures or baby pictures?"

"Neither of us was handy with a camera, so we didn't take a lot of pictures. It wasn't like now when everyone has a cell phone."

"But you must have had some."

"I got rid of them."

"*Why?*" The height of my anger surprised us both.

"You want to know? You *really* want to know?" she said angrily. "I burned them."

"You *burned* them?"

"I was distraught. After he died, I went into a rage and took everything that reminded me of him and burned it—to—to," she searched for the word, "to cauterize the wound."

"Didn't you think to save even one picture or letter for me?"

"I wasn't thinking. I could barely function. It was all I could do to look after you."

"But I don't even know what he looks like," I shouted. "Or sounds like. It's all a huge blank. Like I'm the daughter of a ghost."

She paled when I said that, jumped out of her chair, and tried to hug me, but I fended her off.

"Please Julie, I've really bungled this. I can see that now. I thought by not sharing my pain I was protecting you. But now I see how selfish I've been. Please, sit down." She took my arm and pulled me toward the living room, "I'll tell you whatever you want to know."

I let her pull me to our couch, and we sank into it. "I know you said he looked like me, but I want to hear how *you* saw him. Was he handsome?"

She closed her eyes for a long moment. Then, like a person resolving to jump into a cold pool, she spilled it all at once. "He had eyes like a lake in August, greenish-brown. He had a sort of sad, serious face that lit up startlingly with a beautiful, bright smile. He was taller than you and lanky." She patted my arm. "Your body is more like mine, but your face," she cupped my chin, "is all his."

"Is that why you are angry at me all the time?"

"Oh honey, I'm not angry at you all the time."

"Why are you so angry at him?"

She sighed. "I'm angry that he's gone. I want him back."

"You loved him?"

"Like trees love the sun."

"What did you love about him?"

She paused, looking inward. "He had this electric energy, this passion, this charm. And, of course, I've always been a fool for a British accent."

"Am I . . . like him?" I glanced quickly away.

She mused in silence, pinching the fabric on her knee.

"He used to laugh a lot. He was very physical. He ran in the North Woods all the time."

"The North Woods? That's my favorite place."

"Really," she said, speculatively. "How come I didn't know that?"

"I don't know. Tell me about the day he died."

She sucked in her breath.

"You said you'd tell me anything I wanted to know."

She nodded vigorously, took another deep breath, and exhaled forcefully through her lips. Then she slouched back into the couch and sighed. "There's nothing to tell, really. He kissed me goodbye, walked out the door, and collapsed on the way to work. He died instantly. No forewarning, nothing. He was here and full of life one minute, then completely gone the next."

"But how did you find out? Tell me the *story*."

"There isn't a story. It's an anti-story."

The familiar anger rushed in like a dark tide. My stomach clenched.

"I deserve to know."

"You do, you do. But I'm just so tired all of a sudden."

A gray fog seemed to envelop me, making me feel logy. "Please. Don't shut me out."

She gazed at me for a long moment.

"Like I said," she said standing up and walking away from me, "it's not much of a story. He kissed me goodbye like he did every morning, and a few hours later, I got the call that he had collapsed outside his office. It was an aneurysm. Anyone can get them. There's rarely a forewarning. It was a fluke."

"See? Why was that so hard to tell me?"

"I had yelled at your father that morning. I guess I always wondered," she sank back down onto the couch, "if I had handled him differently . . ." she trailed off as she put her hand to her neck.

I hugged her. "It's not your fault, Mom."

"No, I know," she said quietly. "I'll see if I can dig up a picture online, somewhere, okay?"

"Okay."

Later, after we finished cleaning, I retreated to my room. I whipped open my laptop. I don't know why I'd never thought of it before. His obituary. I typed in the word after his name, and there it was, Peran Sykes. But the picture didn't load. I pressed the refresh button, and the little wheel of death spun around and around. I cursed and slammed my fist on the table. That did nothing, of course. "Why won't anyone let me see my father?" I said.

The picture loaded. But it couldn't have been right. It was a black and white photograph, blurred around the edges in the style of old photographic portraits, of a Victorian gentleman with white hair, a handlebar mustache, and long white sideburns. Then my computer had some kind of hissy fit and shut down. When I got it to restart and returned to the page, the picture wouldn't load again.

21
SOMETHING'S OFF

NOVEMBER 1, 2016

Barely able to contain myself about my mother's revelations and the bizarre experience with the picture in my father's obituary, I called Damian to ask if he wanted to meet at the coffee shop.

"Yeah, okay." He sounded irritated. It was already 11:30, so I knew I hadn't woken him. He was so controlled that I'd never seen him express irritation toward anyone else, much less me. I realized, uneasily, that I had become dependent on his steady, endless approval. I didn't want to be dependent. His mood infected me the same way black ink dropped into water coils and spreads.

As I got dressed, the onyx pebble Sam had given each of us caught my eye, sitting on my dresser where I'd emptied my pockets after the seánce. I pocketed it. What the hell. It couldn't hurt.

Damian was already sitting when I got to Uncommon Grounds. He was crouched over his bagel sandwich, eating it with great concentration. A streak of yellow light seemed to split his forehead. It stopped me short. But when my stomach clenched, the streak vanished. I glanced back at the front windows, to see if the sun was creating an optical illusion.

"Hungry?" I injected my voice with humor because usually he waited for me, and we ordered together. He startled like he was surprised to see me. "What's your problem?"

That hit me in my gut. The flood of new information on my father that I had been so ready to spill clogged my throat. This was a side of Damian I had never seen. I didn't know how to respond, so I got in line at the granite counter, stalling for time. A woman with a nose ring and olive parachute pants took my order, and a man with a blond 'Fro slid my bagel and coffee across the counter in no time.

"Are you feeling okay?" I asked as I sat. He jerked his lunch back toward himself as if he was afraid I was going to take it.

"I'm fine."

"I mean, that stomach thing you had last night at the house . . . is it gone?"

"Like I said."

My stomach balled up tighter.

"So, how would we go about investigating a murder?" I said, trying to push past it.

"Murder?" He looked up quickly from his bagel, becoming very still.

"Yeah, I've been thinking about it. In every ghost story I've ever read, the spirit sticks around to resolve some unfinished business. What if Jacob was murdered?"

"Who would want to murder the guy?"

"I don't know, anyone who wanted him out of that house," I mumbled.

"But they didn't need to kill him to get him out; they played the 'eminent domain' card, remember?"

"That's true. I just wondered about that image—that red explosion. It seemed like blood to me."

"Or your imagination."

That hurt. And also, it totally contradicted everything he'd said so far about my perception. Red flags waved all around him. I briefly contemplated the idea that I should use my vision to see what was wrong with him, but all the unknowns filled me with dread.

"Anyway," I said. "I still think we should look into how Jacob died. How could we do that?"

"Police reports." He went back to concentrating on his bagel. He was taking small, meticulous bites, and examining the bagel after each bite, which was odd because Damian generally didn't think much about food. It always appeared to be an afterthought.

"But are we allowed to see them?"

"Probably not," he said.

"Maybe Maureen could find something out for us."

"Maureen?" His eyes zeroed in on my mouth, concentrating. "Maureen," he said again, drawing the syllables out like a sigh and smiling, finally.

"Maybe you could call her."

"I'll do that," he said, looking happy.

I reached over to grab his pickle, more as a gesture of affection, really, but he pushed my hand away roughly.

"Mind your manners," he said, glaring. His eyes were gray like hematite marbles, repelling entry.

"What is up with you today, Damian?"

He stared at me in silence, as if considering. Regret flickered over his face, instantly replaced by indifference.

In the next instant, I was too disgusted to wait for an answer. Everyone I had ever trusted was turning out to be untrustworthy. I jumped up from the table, leaving my food uneaten, and pulled the door so hard on my way out that it bounced back and hit me. The sight that met my eyes outside the door slammed me even harder: an older woman with long white hair, dark eyes, and a flowing gray dress was sitting at one of the sidewalk tables, looking at me intently over her coffee cup.

I stopped breathing for a minute as images shuffled like a deck of cards through my mind: the flicker of gray near my house, then again near the haunted house, and now. She set her coffee cup on the table, stood, and walked away.

"Hey," I said faintly as she began crossing the street. She kept walking. "Hey!" I said louder. Conviction and anger welded into action, and I sprang after her. "Are you following me?" She was halfway across the street, her strides long and graceful, her dress and hair flowing behind her. I leapt off the curb and a car screeched to a halt just in time. The driver laid on her horn and gestured angrily at me. The light had turned, a stream of traffic cut me off, and the woman in gray reached the alley a block beyond and stepped out of sight. When I got there, she was gone. What the hell was going on? I shoved my hands in my pockets and found that onyx pebble again. Some protection.

22

WORLDS COLLIDE

NOVEMBER 2-3, 2016

I slept badly that night, waking often, stewing over my mother, the haunted house, the lady in gray, Damian's weird behavior, and that yellow streak cleaving his forehead. What if we had opened Pandora's box? Could Damian be possessed? He certainly wasn't behaving like himself—or what I knew of him so far. But then again, we'd only really gotten to know each other in the past two months. And was that woman flesh or spirit, stalker or imagination?

When I did sleep, I dreamt I was awake. Sunday morning finally released me from the battle, and I rose with the uneasy feeling that I had a foot in two different worlds, one the ordinary, day-lit present over which my mother stood staunch guard, and where everything was drab, superficial, but safe; the other world of haunted houses and visions, where everything tilted off balance and the air swirled with charcoal shadows, full of possibility and danger. The two worlds pulled at me, each repelling the other. Also, guilt suffused the whole thing because I had led Damian from the first world into the second, and now I didn't know if I could get him back.

I waited all day for him to call, but he never did—another sign that something was wrong. We usually talked daily. I called Samantha. Jonathan was with her, so every time I delivered a detail of the story, I had to wait for her to tell Jonathan.

"Maybe he's got PMS," she said.

I laughed in spite of myself.

"No, really," she pressed, "I read somewhere that guys have hormonal cycles, too."

"If you say so," I said. I could hear Jonathan's muffled voice in the background, so I waited.

"Jonathan thinks you're blowing it out of proportion." She paused listening to Jonathan. "All he did was refuse to share his food."

"But it was more than that. It was completely out of character—and the whole way he was eating. All his gestures were wrong." I didn't tell her about his eyes and the yellow streak, or the bad feeling I had inside.

"What if," I paused, "What if the house—"

"Oh, my God. He's possessed," Sam gushed with sudden energy. "I *knew* we shouldn't have gone into that house."

"But you were the one who—"

"We should *not* mess with that stuff. We're going to have to perform an exorcism."

"Okay," I said hesitantly. "I mean, it couldn't hurt, right? Do you know how to do one?"

"Yes, I mean, *no,* but there's a whole chapter on it in one of Starhawk's books. I'll study up on it. And meanwhile, don't go *near* that place."

Before my bio class on Monday at SUNY ADK, I walked around feeling skinless and tender, worried that I'd run into Damian and worried that I wouldn't. I wasn't sure I was buying the whole possession thing, but my boundaries had definitely been crossed. I'd let Damian into my world more deeply than I'd let anyone, even my mother. And now, it turns out, he couldn't be trusted.

My lungs opened and closed like sea sponges, riddled with giant holes that absorbed the particles of other people, bits of hair and skin, thoughts, and feelings. My molecules seethed like snow on a TV screen, black and white chaotic bits grinding together at my sternum with each intake of breath. Every time I breathed in more particles from other people, the bits jittered and multiplied until I was frayed around the edges. I ran my hands over my arms to smooth and mend my boundaries, but the bits jittered all the harder, like a heart on too much caffeine.

He didn't show up for our biology class. He hadn't missed a single class so far. Later, as I attended my classes on the Skidmore campus, crowds of happy faces bobbed along the hallway, unconcerned and uncomplicated, free of shadow. Oh, how I wished to be returned to boring normalcy. Even though Damian didn't attend Skidmore, every time I turned a corner, my lungs closed, and my muscles tensed, preparing for the impact of Damian. What would I say? What would he be like? What if he had multiple personality disorder? I had read that those things could surface in your early twenties.

By the end of the day, I was exhausted by the constant opening and closing of my body. When I got home, I was so disgusted with my wimpiness, that I resolved to call him. I closed my bedroom door, sat on my bed, hugged a pillow to my stomach, and dialed, mentally armoring myself as the phone rang. "Julie Sykes," Damian answered immediately, warmly. My whole body relaxed, and my armor melted.

"What happened to you in class today?" I asked.

"Huh? Oh," he yawned, "I've been . . . out of it." He spoke slowly with sleepy pauses. "I must be sick or something. When I woke up this morning my legs felt like stone. I could barely move them. I was *so* tired."

"Maybe you should see a doctor."

"No, I'm better now. How are you?"

"I'm pretty shaken up."

"Why?"

"Because you were—so—weird Saturday."

"Was I? Wait. What did we do on Saturday?"

"At Uncommon Grounds."

He was silent.

"You were downright... mean."

"I'm sorry. It's all pretty fuzzy. I do remember feeling, sort of—" he paused as if searching for the right words, "angry, like my brain was pushing against my skull. What did I say?"

"I don't know, it was nothing, really—it was just—you were different—about things you normally don't care about—like, you told me to mind my manners when I tried to take a bite of your pickle."

"You're right," he laughed warmly, "that *is* certifiable. Mind your manners. Where'd that come from? I don't even like pickles."

"Now you're making fun of me."

"No, Jules, really. I'm sorry. I wasn't myself. How can I make it up to you?" His voice was rich and full. Have I mentioned how round the sound of it was, how when he spoke, his voice vibrated in my chest and seemed to order and soothe my very atoms?

"Never mind," I said, happy to push it all far away and never look back. "Don't forget to vote tomorrow."

"Whoa, right. That snuck up on me. Huh."

"Hilary is gonna win, right?" I asked, looking for assurance.

"I don't see how Trump could win," he said.

"I know, right? Oh, and did you call Maureen?"

"Maureen?"

"Remember? You said you'd call her."

"Oh... right, about the—murder theory. I remember now. Man, I was in a fog. But I'm on it. Julie Sykes, psychic detective," he said, like a voice-over on a series trailer.

"Damian, what if something in that house has infected you?"

Deep silence, a sudden vacuum. Did he hang up?

"Damian?"

"I'm here. You mean, like a curse?"

"Or something."

"Naah. Stop worrying. I caught a stomach bug. Honest."

23
OPENINGS WITHOUT CLOSE

NOVEMBER 4-9, 2016

I awoke Wednesday morning feeling that everything had changed. For one thing, Trump won the election. No one I knew saw that coming. It felt like I had been transported to some other country or a sci-fi movie. I wondered if liberals were going to be dragged out in the street and shot. They'd know us by our reusable shopping bags. I'm only half joking, or joking in the way you do when you're navigating a swamp of poisonous gases and trying to decide which hummock is safe to step on and which will suck you into the muck.

How could this racist, narcissistic criminal who had gone bankrupt multiple times and routinely didn't pay his bills, who lied plentifully and obviously, who grabbed women's crotches, and called people names like a second-grade bully, have gotten elected? How could so much of the country choose him? I mean, he couldn't even string a grammatical sentence together. We had become a nation where naked hostility and aggression were admirable.

For another thing, while Damian was normal, I was not. The

physical world kept melting at odd times with no discernable pattern. My lungs would open and my body would buzz like it was made of jittery bits, and then trees, walls, and tables would become murkily transparent. If I tried to ignore the visions and carry on, I'd get seasick. If I stared right at an undulating wall, I'd get hypnotized. It was like trailing your hand in the river and watching how it changes the shape of the stream. To turn off the vision, I had to do things like shake my head really hard. But over the next few days, even that wasn't working. At home, I could jump up and down to make it stop. But you can't do that in the middle of the hallway at school, so I'd have to slip into a bathroom stall to shake myself.

In biology, I always listened harder when Dr. Fish began with, "And you won't find this on any SAT exam . . . ." That's when he'd tell us some amazing fact. So, when he said it that morning, I managed to focus for a blessed second. He explained fractals, which are divisions found in nature where the same pattern of the overall thing is repeated in subsets of it, like the branch of a snowflake forms the same pattern as the snowflake itself, or the leaf of a fern is the same shape as the entire frond. And it turns out that our blood vessels and neurons do this, as well as coastlines and rivers. Then he showed us a psychedelic video of the Mandelbrot equation, which sets this pattern into infinite motion. It was a circle with three buds, and when you zoomed into the bud, that, too, was a circle with three buds, and when you zoomed into that, same thing, on and on, and the whole thing spiraled in this pattern much like my visions. It was both disturbing and cool, like maybe there was a deep-down order to all that chaos. If I could find the order, these bursts of vision wouldn't be so bad.

At our *Adirondacker* meeting, Payton gloated insufferably over the Trump win. It was all I could do to not strangle him. He was a smart guy, and that made it all the more sinister that he couldn't see the obvious. Seeing an obvious truth that everyone else denies is a special kind of pain. It's a sickening twist in your viscera, a tortured bend of mind and spirit, an anguish. Jonathan and Samantha, both slumped together in a loveseat, staring off into space in a deep funk. Damian was quiet, alert, and watchful.

After the meeting, as Damian and I walked down the hall, all at once, my cells bloated like a blowfish, my lungs went porous, and everyone streaming around us toward the doors melted and undulated. I tried to blink it away. Everything rippled. I stopped in my tracks and unconsciously grabbed Damian's arm.

"What's up?" he asked. I shook my head, trying to find a still point of focus. People ahead of us were disappearing through the glass doors into a blaze of light where cars rumbled to life in the parking lot.

I turned my head to look at him, but all I saw was a white starburst with dark blue edges. Right down the center of the starburst, like the eye of a lizard, was a dark, jagged line that blinked on and off, like a crack in space-time, like a flickering void: there, not there, there, not there.

"I can't turn it off," I said, and my words sent ripples of nausea through my body.

"Your vision thing?"

"Yes." I couldn't look at him. I tried to find the walls.

"What do you need?" he said. I held onto the solidity of his voice.

"I don't know—hit me or something."

Someone pushed past me, accidentally knocking me sideways with his backpack, and my regular vision snapped back. The ground solidified, my flesh gelled, and Damian became Damian with two eyes, a nose, and a mouth. I breathed a sigh of relief to the bottom of my lungs as I watched the last few normal people walk through the doors.

Damian steered me into an out-of-the-way sitting area. I sank into a brightly colored overstuffed chair, and Damian pulled up another chair and sat opposite, on the edge of his seat. "You okay?" he asked, leaning toward me.

"Yeah," I said. Now I was uncomfortable for a different reason. He was sitting so close his knees were on either side of mine, and I was having trouble looking at his face, those eyes letting me in so easily, that strong jawline, that sculpted, complicated mouth. I tried not to let on. "Lately, this vision thing has a mind of its own. I'm having a harder and harder time shutting it off. And where it used to be just a vision thing, it now seems to be a whole-body thing."

"Maybe you shouldn't fight it. Maybe instead of trying to turn it off, you should try to turn it on."

"Why?" I asked. His lapis gaze surrounded me, steadied me. I wondered how I ever could have doubted him.

"Maybe it's trying to tell you something important."

I closed my eyes a second and leaned my head back while conflicting emotions grappled inside, dark-flying dread, ruby excitement, numbing fatigue.

"Yeah, I could almost accept it, but it *majorly* gets in my way," I said. "And what if I'm doing this to other people? Like that girl at Uncommon Grounds—what if I made her sick? And what about you? You really *got* sick. What if *I* did that? I brought you to that house. Maybe I'm like Carrie."

Damian shook his head and rubbed his chin. "No. You're not doing anything to anybody. You're seeing what is really there, what no one else can see. In the hall just now, nothing happened to anyone else but you."

"But I saw something in you, too."

"Oh?" He pulled back a fraction of an inch. "What did you see?"

I described the starburst and the crack down the center.

"Maybe you're seeing the remnants of that flu I had. I'm mostly over it now. Julie, this is a gift. What would it mean to you if you let yourself be what you really are?"

"But who am I?"

"A person who sees what is beyond sight."

"A freak."

"In whose eyes?"

"In the eyes of normal people."

"But who is really 'normal'?" Damian tilted his head.

"I don't know. The ones who don't think too hard about life. The ones who haven't been scarred by death or abuse. The ones who can discuss shampoo seriously. I can't even make my hair stay out of my eyes."

"Your hair is beautiful."

I could feel my face flame. I avoided his eyes. "You, of all people, must know that everyone is truly bizarre—complicated deep down, whether they know it or not."

"Yeah, but *they* don't know it."

"You have to trust what you see," Damian said.

"But how do I know if what I'm seeing is real? What if it's a weird brain defect?"

"You know, in here," Damian tapped his chest with his long fingers.

"Right. The gathering place of the sun."

"It's like a resonance. What's in here matches what's out there, and you know it's true."

"Like the grand inquisitors," I teased.

"I can't speak for them." He smiled. "I can only speak for myself. I believe what you see."

Love and admiration for Damian burst my heart open. I mean, how did he get to be so wise? I wanted to hug him or kiss him. But I didn't.

"Okay," I said.

"The problem, as I see it," Damian said, "isn't what you see, it's *when* you see it. You have no control over it. If you listen to it, if you pay attention, maybe you can learn to turn it on and off at will."

"But how?"

"Think back to the hallway, to where it last happened. What were you doing right before?"

"Nothing. Spacing out."

"Okay. So maybe it happens when you are relaxed. Try spacing out."

"You can't *try* to space out. That's a contradiction in terms. If you're trying, you're not spacing."

"Okay, so relax." He was holding both my hands between his, and he inched a little closer, his knees brushing against my outer thighs. Heat rushed up my legs. I pressed my thighs together so tightly my knee bones ground into each other.

"I can't," I said.

Damian circled behind my chair, putting his hands on my shoulders. That was anything but relaxing. His hands were so warm and eloquent. Their heat was telling me things, long, complicated night-whispering things. I tried to appear relaxed.

"Lean back in the chair and try to let go. Stop holding yourself up."

I tried for a second. I closed my eyes and stretched out. But my mind was like a jungle with bird thoughts flitting from branch to branch.

"No, Damian," I paused, "this is too weird." I grabbed one of his hands. My body was too tight, and I knew it was pointless.

"Try."

"It's a good idea, just not here, not now."

"Okay, forget it," he said, clasping my face between his hands, tipping it up, and looking down at me with a rueful smile. He pushed my face from side to side between his palms. "You've got to learn to relax, Julie Sykes." His eyes opened over me like the night sky, and I wanted to float up into them, into him, and let go of me. Instead, I pulled back. I remembered that dark absence flickering inside him and the friability of my physical boundaries.

"I'm hopeless," I said, smiling and wiggling out of his hands. I took a deep breath and forced a fresh, confident tone. "Hey, did you call Maureen?"

"Yeah," he said, easily changing pace without so much as a flicker. "She said it would be hard to get the information, but she thought she could."

24

GRAVES' DISEASE

WINTER, 1999-2000

Over the winter months, Peran's health declined. He lost weight even though he was ravenously hungry and eating all the time. His skin took on a gray hue and a shock of white hair sprouted at the nape of his neck. He was irritable and moody during the day, and it was common for Audrey to find him walking in his sleep. Both Athena and Audrey worried, and since they had met, they now conferred with each other frequently. He spent more and more time in the North Woods and researching Henry Hilton.

One day, he arrived on Athena's doorstep overexcited, as he always was whenever he uncovered new information on Hilton. Against the pallor of his skin, his eyes glowed darkly.

"Get this! Two years after the H's benefactor died, someone broke into his mausoleum and stole his body," Peran said, referring to Hilton without saying his full name.

"What?" Athena said.

"Well, it was still fairly common at the time for people to steal bodies for scientific research."

"But not two years after they died," she said.

"I know. Several relatives had taken H to court to return some of Stewart's estate, and there was talk of foul play, and of exhuming the body. That's when his body was stolen."

"My word," Athena said.

"There were some ransom notes, but they were fraudulent, and anyway, H refused to pay, much to everyone's consternation. Some thought it was one of his sons who stole the body or maybe one of Stewart's relatives, angry that they'd been cut out of the estate, trying to force his hand. A few people pointed fingers at H himself, hiding evidence of murder.

"Arsenic does stay in the body for some time, but I'm not sure how many people knew that then," Athena said.

"Eventually, a bag of bones surfaced, but it was never confirmed to be S's bones. Perhaps H buried S's remains somewhere on this property, and that's what is keeping him here." Peran said.

Athena nodded. "Or maybe the spirit is S himself?"

"Don't think so. It's H who is haunting my dreams."

Over many weeks, with only the evidence of apparent intuition, Peran was able to lead Athena to all the sites on the Skidmore campus where the original buildings of Hilton's Woodlawn Estate once stood, despite the lack of any physical evidence. He was able to confirm it via maps he found in the Skidmore library's special collections. Vision and spirit incorporation was one of his strengths, but it was also his Achilles heel. Though he wasn't admitting it, it was clear to Athena that he was under the influence of a spirit.

Her expertise was energy sensing and weaving. She, too, felt how the spirit energy was strongest near the cavity under the well. It manifested as a fizz of energy like heartburn in the back that left her heart racing and her stomach churning. It was all hunger, this spirit. Not much mind energy left, if it had ever had any. Not all spirits tried to enter people, but this one seemed to have that as a primary aim, she concluded. The first contacts from any spirit were the weakest, but if one didn't take precautions, the spirit could change the body like a drug does and carve permanent passageways into it to make it more receptive and less autonomous. How one prevented this depended on the nature of the spirit. In this case, she guessed accurately that if she alkalized her body before going near the well by drinking a mixture of greens, and if she shored up her physical, limbic, and spirit energy boundaries with meditation, the spirit couldn't touch her. But Peran, being an incorporator, was much more susceptible to invasion.

Audrey convinced Peran to see a doctor about his weight loss and constant hunger. The doctor diagnosed him with Graves' disease or hyperthyroidism. But Athena knew it was the spirit. It had made inroads into Peran. She could feel the heat radiating from his sternum like an infection. Athena insisted Peran take the green drink daily, but his chemistry was quite different from hers, even though they were twins. Also, he seemed to crave the spirit connection.

Nevertheless, he allowed her to perform her energy weaves on him, rituals involving the balancing of the four elements. H's energy was high in fire, and each weave required more and more earth element. She couldn't tell if her weaves were helping.

She began working with hematite. It had grounding properties and strengthened the blood. It provided focus, and Peran seemed to be getting increasingly scattered. There had been student complaints about him losing their exams and missing classes without notice.

She sewed hematite beads into a vest that he agreed to wear when he was on campus, but the spirit continued to connect to him in ways she couldn't detect energetically. What she came to understand, finally, was that the spirit wasn't so much entering him as siphoning off his energy, pulling him out, one strand at a time. And the more energy it siphoned, the more the spirit developed mind energy, and the more that happened, the more entranced Peran became with it, as if he'd found his long-lost father.

"It's definitely Hilton," Peran said.

"Name!" Athena reminded him.

"Yeah. Sorry. I wasn't sure at first, but now it's clear."

"Then do you think guilt is keeping him here? Over the murder of S.?" Athena asked.

"I don't think so. In my dreams, he demands that I take care of his estate. He wants his children to come home. He doesn't realize it's all gone."

"Next order of business should be to make him realize that."

"I'm not ready to be rid of him," Peran said.

"But that's our job."

"We need a better grasp of the dynamic," Peran said.

Athena was dubious.

A few months later, Peran again arrived at Athena's doorstep, wool hat pulled low over his ears against the snowy day.

"You'll never believe it! I bumped into a descendant of Hilton."

Athena did her best to breathe a protective shield around them both as Peran had become cavalier about saying Hilton's name.

"He's a lawyer and owns a real estate company. His name is Michael Wright. I was perusing some of the listings in the window of his office, and we struck up a conversation. I don't even know how it came up. He said he was related on the maternal side, through one of H's daughters. And look what I've got here." He waved a glossy real-estate circular in a plastic bag.

"A brochure?"

"DNA! His hands have been all over this thing. Might even be a piece of hair."

"I'll see what I can do," Athena said, taking the bag.

When she told Peran that Michael Wright's DNA showed he was a distant relative of theirs, Peran was elated. "I *knew* it. That's why I was called here. Everything has been pointing to that. Now we know who we are," he gave her a huge hug. But his breath smelled of rot and stress hormones. Athena drew back in alarm.

"What? Aren't you happy?" he asked.

"Peran, we've always known who we are—at least since we met Cavendish. Having a paternal ancestor doesn't change anything."

"It changes everything. It means we never belonged to that rat-infested tenement in Bermondsey."

"No one belongs there. You say it like class matters."

"It does matter."

"What? This isn't you. It's that bloody spirit. From all I can tell H was a reckless narcissist obsessed with money. Possibly a murderer. Excuse me if I'm not elated to be related to *that*."

"Harsh."

"It's bloody realistic. And we have got to expel him before he twists you any further."

"You don't know what you're talking about," Peran said, backing away from her, his face rigid with disdain.

"As a matter of fact, I've contacted Lord Cavendish, and he shares my concern," Athena said.

"You've been talking about me behind my back?"

"Pretty easy to do with your head always turned," she retorted.

He slammed out of her house and didn't answer her calls for the rest of the week.

25
A QUESTION OF MURDER

NOVEMBER 10-14, 2016

The next week, Maureen called Damian to say she had news and she'd meet us at the coffee shop. I met Damian in front of the YMCA —or what used to be the Y; it was slated to be replaced by—let's see—what does Saratoga really need? Luxury condos. Real estate prices had gotten crazy, rents had gone up, and waitresses, janitors, and teachers now had to live elsewhere. My mom kept her rents well below the market rate out of decency.

It was getting nippy. The trees were bare. November is always a dismal month. Gray and cold without the benefits of snow. Damian's younger brother Carl arrived a block ahead of him cruising on a skateboard down the hill, straight at me. I was considering leaping into the bushes, but right before he reached me, he did what I later learned was an ollie. Then he "ground an edge" along the retaining wall of the bank. The clatter and scrape ended abruptly at the edge of the wall as he flew into the air, did a grab, and slammed back onto the sidewalk. He circled back around to meet me and graced me with a breathy "Hey," which was an honor, really, coming from him.

A figure from inside the bank rapped on the window angrily. Carl flipped them off as Damian caught up to us.

Carl didn't look anything like Damian with his white, freckled skin, light blue eyes, and reddish blonde hair. If I didn't know better, I wouldn't have pegged them as brothers.

"We've got troubles, now," I said, thumbing over my shoulder toward the bank window. "They're probably calling the cops as we speak."

"You could save them the trouble," Damian said, "and come with us to the police station."

"No fuckin' way," Carl said, rolling his eyes.

"Hey—language," Damian said with a smile, gesturing to me.

"Sorry," he said, both sheepish and proud. He reminded me of a German shepherd puppy, still small, but you could tell by the size of his paws and pungent body odor that he was going to be huge.

"Not a problem," I said.

"Friggin' Saratoga," Carl said, then squeezed his voice high and wagged a finger. "No bikes, no skateboards, no teenagers loitering." Now his husky voice returned: "Everyone else has free speech, but we can't even hang downtown. Fuck them. I'm gonna cruise right up their asses."

Damian slapped him lightly on the back of his head.

"Oh, sorry," he said again, laughing.

As we walked downtown, Carl rolled along slowly beside us, commandeering our attention. He talked loudly and continuously with sweeping hand gestures as he told me way more than I wanted to know about the latest skateboard star and all his best tricks, using a lot of terms I'd never heard before.

Both Damian and I spotted a cop on horseback two blocks ahead. Fortunately, he was leaning over talking to someone on the ground, so he hadn't spotted Carl yet.

Damian took note of the situation and looked down thoughtfully, still nodding his head as Carl ranted about the idiots who didn't know the difference between a rail stand and a primo slide.

"So," Damian cut in as Carl paused to breathe, "how loose do you keep your kingpins typically for that kind of maneuver?" Carl hopped off the board and flipped it into his hands without so much as a pause in his gait and launched into a salivating lecture on his trucks and other technical details I totally spaced out on, his voice cracking and changing all over the place.

By the time we passed the cop, Carl, still talking a blue streak, had his board tucked under his arm. The cop scrutinized us, and Damian gave him one of those universal man-code nods, short and barely perceptible. The cop tipped his chin back and turned away.

"I gotta get outta here," Carl said, noticing. "Pigs." He abruptly turned down the alley toward the library. "Don't let the stink rub off on you."

"I'll catch up with you at the Rec Center," Damian called after him. "Five o'clock."

"Yes, Mother," Carl called back. We could already hear his wheels rattling along the pavement, safely out of the cop's sight—and earshot, hopefully.

"That was pretty smooth," I said.

"What?" Damian put his hands in his pockets.

"How you maneuvered Carl off his board without him realizing it."

"Ah," he smiled, "years of experience. You can't tell him what to do. All you get is a fight."

"So, you just sorta—manage him?"

"It's an acquired skill."

"More like an art." I paused. "He doesn't look like you at all. Who does he take after?"

Damian looked away. "That's my father's side of the family. All Irish. Loud storytellers." A smile plucked itself out of a scowl.

"Your dad's a good storyteller?"

"Was. He could make a funny story out of anything, driving home from work or buying a loaf of bread. The gift of gab. I didn't inherit that. I take after my mother's side of the family."

"What kinds of stories?"

"I don't know. It was a long time ago. He's out of the picture, now."

I waited, not wanting to say the wrong thing. "So he's. . ."

"He lives in California," Damian said, cutting off the end of my sentence. I got the message, being well-trained in that particular protocol, but I'd had enough of that by now, so I pushed ahead.

"That's rough," I said.

"What?"

"Living without your Dad."

"We don't need him," Damian shrugged. I watched him closely.

"But it's got to hurt."

"He means nothing to me," Damian said. Everything in the relaxed swing of his arms and shoulders suggested he was telling the truth. But I pushed a little more.

"Aren't you angry?"

"Oh no, Julie Sykes. Don't turn those x-ray eyes on me. Keep your mind on our business. Besides," he bumped me with his shoulder, "I already told you once before, I don't do anger."

By then we'd arrived at Uncommon Grounds, where Maureen had agreed to meet us. Besides the fact that there is no public transportation between downtown Saratoga and the Wilton Town Hall, she didn't want her office mates to know she was digging up this material for us.

When we opened the door to Uncommon Grounds, the slightly burnt scent of roasted coffee rushed out and enveloped us like a wooly sweater. Maureen was already in line. She had permed her hair since we last saw her.

"Hey, kids," she said when she saw us. She winked a feline eye. "Have I got news for you." After we'd ordered coffee and bagels and found a table in the corner, she leaned toward us. "Don't ask me how I did it," she whispered loudly, "but I got a look at the police report from the day they found Jacob Johnson's body."

"Wow, how'd you—"

"I said, don't ask. It's *very* interesting. Normally, I'd keep it to myself, but justice needs to be done here, and I'm not in a position to do it."

"What is it?"

"Well first, the cause of death was a gunshot wound."

The red explosion.

"And second, there were signs of a struggle. I saw the picture. The kitchen table was broken, and chairs were scattered."

"Oh my god, that's—" Damian stiffened, and I stopped on cue, "so amazing." We couldn't tell her we were trespassing and that this information confirmed my vision to be true.

"Do you think he was murdered?" I asked.

"Could be." Maureen shrugged her shoulders, non-committal.

"Don't leap to conclusions," Damian cut in.

I glanced at him. "Don't get your panties in a twist," I said with a huge smile so he wouldn't mistake my tone. He didn't smile back. I sensed a slice of emptiness open and close inside him. Or was that me?

"Most likely he threw things around himself," Damian said quickly. His eyes had become those shiny gray shields like last time.

"Yeah," said Maureen, shrugging her shoulders again, widening her eyes. "Or, he could have fought with someone and then shot himself." I couldn't tell if she was being sarcastic or not.

"Or," I said, "someone could have shot him by accident in the struggle."

Damian's body stiffened next to me, and my heartbeat elevated a hair.

"Guns don't appear by accident," Maureen said.

"Do they know if someone else was there?" Damian asked.

"Get this. They didn't investigate."

"What? Isn't that illegal?" I said.

"No," she said noncommittally. "Police make judgment calls all the time on what to investigate and what not to investigate."

"Well, whose gun was it?" I asked.

"His own," Damian and Maureen said at the same time.

His eyes were steely gray, his was pale again, and fine beads of perspiration misted his upper lip. "How'd you know that?" I asked.

He shrugged. "It was obvious. That's why they didn't investigate, right?"

"I suppose," said Maureen. "But this is the most interesting part. Jacob Johnson had contacted a lawyer. He was going to sue the town of Wilton over property values, and that was going to hold up the whole thing in court for years."

"Wow."

"Did it give the time of death?"

"Sevenish," Maureen said. "And get this. Michael Wright was late to the town council meeting that night, which starts at 7:00 p.m."

If I knew how to whistle, I'd have done it. Damian said nothing and looked at his hands.

"Well. That's all I got," Maureen said. "Don't tell anyone you got it from me." She checked her watch and stood up. "Gotta go."

"Thanks," I said. "I hope we didn't get you into trouble."

"For what? Meeting an adorable young couple on my own time? She laughed and her voice bounced around the room like a tennis ball. I blushed and decided not to correct her about us being a couple.

"Yeah . . . Thanks," Damian said as if emerging from a dream.

"'Kay, doll," she said. "Toodles." She headed for the door.

As soon as she was gone, I pounced. "Damian, what happened?"

"What do you mean?"

"You got kinda—hostile."

He shook his head, thinking back. "Yeah, I guess I did. I'm sorry, I don't know why. All this anger came over me as Maureen was talking."

"But I thought you didn't do anger."

"Yeah. Weird."

I caught his eye. "I don't want to get all Amityville on you, but, what if an evil spirit was in that house and it—got into you."

"Jacob Johnson doesn't strike me as an evil guy," Damian said. He seemed way too cool about all this.

"Yeah, but what do we really know about him? We know he yelled a lot. We know he got into a fight with that Wright guy."

"Michael Wright."

"What if Michael Wright killed him, and Jacob's out for revenge, and you're his—vehicle."

"Well, first we have to figure out if it was murder, right? And then we can worry whether I'm possessed or not. What makes you so sure he was murdered?"

"It makes sense. I mean—I saw this red explosion in my mind just before the table broke. Someone put that table back together. That means someone was covering up something. And it makes sense that his spirit—if that's what we're dealing with—can't rest until the secret is known and justice is done. That's the plot of practically every ghost story on the planet."

"So, what next?" Damian said.

"Maybe we should talk to Michael Wright. He's the most likely suspect."

"I don't think that's a good idea," Damian said. "His family is very powerful. We don't want to get on the wrong side of the Wrights."

"No pun intended," I said, whacking his shoulder lightly.

"And you don't want to run straight at a thing like this. You've got to sneak up behind it."

"Yeah, zigzag. Turn left and then Wright," I said, grinning.

It was his turn to whack me.

"Anyway," I said, getting serious again, "Maureen said Michael Wright was in a nursing home."

"What needs to happen," Damian said, "is to get the police to open an investigation."

"Why not use *The Adirondacker*? It would be real investigative reporting."

"That would draw too much attention to us. The first thing they would do is tell us to stay out of it."

"We could send an anonymous tip to the police."

"They've already demonstrated they don't care," said Damian.

"True."

We stared at the table for a while in silence.

"We could post flyers around town with a headline like *Justice for Jacob* explaining the mysterious circumstances of his death," I said.

"Same problem, too much attention."

"We could do it at night, so no one would know who posted them."

"What good would it do?" asked Damian.

"Maybe his spirit would be satisfied knowing the truth was out."

"Or maybe," Damian said, "he wants us to stop this next round of development."

"How on earth could we do that?"

"Well, there's a group in town—Citizens for Responsible Economic Development, CRED. We could approach them. See if they could take this up."

"Let's do all three," I said. "Send an anonymous tip to the paper, post flyers, *and* call CRED."

"Deal," he said.

26

THANKSGIVING

NOVEMBER 22, 2016

My mom and I always had a quiet Thanksgiving without extended family. For one thing, my Dad didn't have family in the U.S. as far as we knew, and my mom's parents lived in Florida. My mom wasn't on great terms with them. We'd gone down there to visit once when I was little. Chubby angel-child statues adorned the shelves along with framed pictures of Jesus and embroidered religious homilies on the wall. We hadn't heard from Aunt Peg or Elisha in a long time. They were somewhere out west. Sometimes we shared Thanksgiving with my mom's friend Felicity. Other times we worked at the soup kitchen on Thanksgiving.

That's why I was intrigued when Mom asked me if I wanted to invite Damian's family to Thanksgiving. She'd been appropriately casual the first time she met him, but later she teased me. "Ooooh. I *like* him. So cute. And *polite*. You two make a nicely matched couple."

"Shut up, Mom," I said. "We're just friends." But I was smiling.

She nodded. "Sensible. Go into it slowly. But if you decide to have sex, birth control is a must. Are you all set up?"

"Mom! Ugh," I said in mock outrage.

"Minding my own business now," she called over her shoulder with tones of laughter as she walked away from me to her study.

I wanted to meet his family, though, and he always made excuses whenever I suggested we get together at his house. The next time I saw him, I asked, but unsurprisingly, he came up with another one of those vague excuses he was so good at.

So you can imagine my surprise when I answered my mother's cell phone one day when she was in the bathroom, and Damian's mother gushed, "We'd *love* to come. The boys will be so *pleased*, and I can't wait to meet you all." I wondered if Damian had changed his mind and forgotten to tell me, but my mother explained she'd sent them an invitation. Damian's mother had a low voice and a beautiful Puerto Rican accent.

November was continuing to do its drab November thing with brown grass, twisted weeds, and the sun going down impossibly soon. My energy surges had calmed down, miraculously. I had no idea why, but I wasn't complaining. My mom and I had a good time prepping the turkey and making all the usual sides. We spread the table with a silvery linen cloth and our best plates. Mom even bought some flowers. It was the first time we had ever entertained together. It felt festive and right.

Dolores Quinn swept in effusively, hugged and kissed us both, and handed us a pumpkin pie. She was quite beautiful with large eyes that slanted up in the corners, and high cheekbones. Now I saw what Damian meant about how he favored his mother's side of the family. Her skin was a shade darker than his, and she had that same slender build he did. Her full, black hair was pulled back into a loose ponytail. Sandy-colored Carl slunk in behind, stoop-shouldered and barely making eye contact. Sidney, who was only seven, had an attack of nerves and clung to his mother's hand and wouldn't come out from behind her for the first half-hour. Damian, who had met my mother a couple of times before, was curiously formal, shaking her hand somewhat sternly. He had an apple pie. "I'm sorry. I didn't realize my mother had sent an invitation," I said as I pulled him into the kitchen with the excuse of putting the pie into the oven to warm.

"It's okay," he said, but he said, but his shoulders were tight and his jaw set.

"What's up with Carl?" I said. "He looks subdued."

"Oh, he and my mother had a huge fight right before we came."

The first part of the meal went fine with introductions, small talk, dish passing, and compliments. The turkey was perfect, roasted red-brown and juicy. Carl ate like he was starving, and Sidney was in constant motion, hopping off his chair and back on. Once his shyness wore off, he wanted to show everyone his magnifying glass. Damian quietly gave him little tasks to do with it, like examining the tablecloth for grains of salt and crumbs, and that kept him entertained while we talked. But before too long, it became apparent that Mrs. Quinn was steering the conversation.

"Julie. It is so nice to have a chance to get to know you. I've been begging Damian to bring you home for months. He doesn't confide in me, but when he says your name, I can tell how he feels about you. A mother knows these things."

My face grew hot and I couldn't look up. Her rich energy was alluring but also sticky.

"Damian is quite a catch, you know," she said. "He's my hero. You'd better hang on to him." She pinched his cheek.

Damian tolerated the pinch and then leaned away from her to whisper in Sidney's ear, pointing to a bit of turkey on his plate. Sidney nodded his head eagerly and examined it with a magnifying glass.

"He was a *perfect* child. Oh, you wouldn't believe it." She talked like someone who was starved for a listener, and now that she had two, the dam had broken, and her words overflowed.

I glanced quickly from Damian to my mother. They were both busy pretending this was normal.

"We thought all children were that way because he was our first," his mother continued. She smiled at us and rolled her eyes. "He was so smart and well-behaved. He never cried. Never cried. He was like a little adult." She reached over and squeezed his knee.

Damian looked like he had heard it many times before.

The stickiness of her energy became cloying.

Carl, who had already devoured a second helping, was surreptitiously texting or playing some kind of game on his phone beneath the tablecloth.

"But things changed when Carl came along."

"Mother, why don't we—" Damian said.

"Don't interrupt me, dear," she pushed past him blithely. "Carl was the complete opposite. He came charging out of my womb like a bull, that one," she gestured with her hand toward him. "We couldn't control him. And he was so *strong*." She squeezed her fist in the air, seemingly proud of his strength. "You'd think it would be easy to control a toddler. But Carl was like Hercules."

I glanced nervously at Carl to see how he felt about being contrasted to Damian that way.

He kept playing his game, not looking up.

My mother shifted in her chair uncomfortably.

"Carl didn't respond to mild scolding as Damian did. Even a strong scolding." She laughed and then sighed and took a small sip of wine.

She had barely gotten through half a glass, so I knew she wasn't drunk.

"*No one* could control Carl except Damian. Damian has a way with Carl that no one else can master." She gazed at Damian fawningly. Then her face darkened, and she shook her head. "Carl brought out the worst in my husband. I never knew he had a temper until Carl was born. One time he whipped Carl so hard he couldn't sit for two days."

Carl turned sideways in his seat, away from us, no longer hiding the fact that he was deeply engrossed in his game. I understood, now, why Damian had refused our invitation and avoided letting me meet his mother. Sidney peered at us all through his magnifying glass.

"Mom," Damian said quietly, putting his hand on her knee.

"How terrible," I murmured.

"Dessert?" my mother asked too brightly.

"But Damian would try to protect Carl. There were some terrible scenes, everyone in the house shouting and crying, except Damian, of course. He never lost his temper. He'd stand in front of Carl when my husband started to unbuckle his belt, and he'd get such a determined look on his little face that even my husband would stop. A ten-year-old boy. Such a hero," she said admiringly. Damian was looking at a spot on the tablecloth, his Adam's apple flexing.

"Mom, can we have dessert now?" Sidney asked.

"Great idea," I said as I jumped up. Though I craved information on Damian's past, this was embarrassing everyone except his mother. My mother stood to clear the dishes.

"Where is your husband, Mrs. Sykes?" Damian's mother said, also standing, grabbing the leftover mashed potatoes and gravy, and following us to the kitchen.

"Audrey," my mother corrected her. "He passed away," she said. She was ahead of me, so I couldn't see her face or read her body energy, but her tone clearly said, this topic is a dead end.

"Oh, I'm sorry. How difficult for you, Audrey."

I grabbed Damian's apple pie and practically ran back to the dining room with it. Sidney hopped on tip-toe and stared at it with glossy eyes.

"Well. At least you know he didn't leave you by choice," Mrs. Quinn said, following me back out into the dining room. "*My husband turned his back on us all.*" She plunked the pumpkin pie and forks on the table. "Which is far worse. Left me alone without a penny to take care of these three kids. And three boys! It was so difficult." Tears saturated in her voice.

"Jesus, Mom," Carl said, shooting out of his seat. "Take a cue and shut up." He grabbed his coat and headed for the door. Sidney's face crumpled and he began to cry. Damian, also standing, pulled Sidney back against his legs, hugging him.

"I'm sorry," Damian said to me and my mom, "I better go after him." Then to Sidney, "Want to help?"

"Yes, but I want some pie."

"Here you go," I found a paper plate and cut him a slice.

"Got your magnifying glass?" Damian said.

Sidney held it up.

"We'll need it to see which way he went."

Sidney smiled now, excited.

I handed Damian Sidney's pie slice.

I tried to catch his eyes, but he avoided mine.

When the door closed behind him, Mrs. Quinn sat. "Why does this always happen to me? What did I do?"

27
OWNING THE NIGHT

NOVEMBER 29, 2016

Frost dazzled the ground. Cold air spiked our lungs, and the moon was so bright that tree branches drew charcoal lines across the ground. "Hey," I whispered as Damian emerged from behind a tree. "You got the flyers?" It was one o'clock in the morning, and we stood outside my house.

"No, I thought you had them," Damian said, his eyes glittering in the darkness.

"What?"

"I'm kidding, you dope," he said.

"Hey, no name-calling."

Off-season, by ten p.m., mostly everyone in Saratoga Springs was home in bed, and by one in the morning, the town was pretty much dead.

Damian, Sam, Jonathan, and I had spent the entire week after the *Thanksgiving Fiasco*, as we nicknamed it, making flyers and sending anonymous letters to both the police department and the *Saratogian* for good measure. Some were more political, like "Stop the Sprawl" and "Down with Big Box Stores." Others were more ominous, like, "Who Killed Jacob Johnson?" We didn't expect it would shake the world up, but it was deeply satisfying, and we hoped it would set an investigation in motion or at least satisfy Jacob's spirit. Besides his bartending job at Hamlet and Ghost, Damian also worked at FedEx, so he was able to make copies for free.

All Damian had said about Thanksgiving was, "Now you know why I don't invite you over. Drama central." He shrugged and smiled. There he was being too cool . . . and that was beginning to irritate me. But I was afraid to press further.

We had also contacted Citizens for Responsible Economic Development (CRED), and they said they were already working on stopping the project. They didn't have much hope, though, because the area was already so developed. If they could find an endangered plant or animal that lived there, they'd have a prayer. We didn't give our names so that we could do our flyer project without being discovered.

We walked toward town in silence. Most of the houses were dark. The cars were all parked and frosted. Occasionally we'd see the blue flickering light of television in someone's upstairs bedroom. Milky pools of light illuminated every gable and tree limb. As we neared the center of town, the Broadway street lamps diminished the moonlight. We had to walk close to the buildings and stay in the shadows to avoid the occasional police patrol. There was a bulletin board at the corner of Caroline and Broadway where bands advertised, which we hit first, but then we moved all over town, slipping flyers under doors and between handles. Jonathan and Samantha were covering their neighborhood. We sneaked into the brightly lit 24-hour Price Chopper lobby—called the "Ghetto Chopper" before the west side was gentrified— and hung a few there. Our silent laughter puffed into warm clouds in the cold air above us as we ran from the scene of our crimes. The world was like our own private snow globe, with us at the center.

By the time we were done, the moon had moved further west in the sky. Damian walked me all the way back to my house. My coat was too thin, and my sneakers held more cold in than they shut out, so as we walked, my teeth chattered. It was now 3:30 a.m.

"I remember once," I said, "when I was very little, I saw the moon at the top of the Saratoga Battlefield, and I thought if I ran to the top of the field, I'd be able to catch it. But I ran and ran and ran, and the moon kept backing up. When I got to the top of the field, it seemed to leap into the sky. I realized then that I'd never catch it."

"But now, look how it walks beside us, as we walk beside it," Damian said. With our eyes on the moon, he pulled me out into the street and back onto the sidewalk again, and the moon swooped through the sky with us, around the bare crown of the trees. We walked for some time in silence like that, eyes for the moon only, pulling it through the sky.

"That's so cool," I said.

"Like I've been walking beside you, Julie Sykes," he said, as we stopped in front of my house.

I was so cold and exhilarated that all my barriers were down, and I practically jumped at him to hug him goodbye. He opened his jacket, and I, desperate for warmth, slipped my freezing hands around his body—and it felt so good to finally feel *his* body, *his* ribs, to hear his heart, and the air in his lungs. All of who he was seemed written in every inch of his body. He hugged me back tightly, and I fit my head into the crook of his neck and shoulder to avoid that begging kiss, smelling the wool of his coat and a green, leafy scent that was uniquely his.

"That was fun," I whispered, leaping back from him as quickly as I'd hugged him. He held onto my hand and pulled me back a fraction. The valves of my heart began their painful squeezing action. His eyes were very dark, and in the moonlight, his face shone pale and still, as if every cell of his body was holding its breath, watching me.

"Julie Sykes," he said quietly. His energy swirled gently around me, warm, graceful. "What *about* . . . us?" finally verbalizing a long, silent conversation we had been having on and off since we met.

If this were a scene in a movie, I'd cut it out—it was all pumping heart, stomach rushing, and not being able to breathe right. But it wasn't a movie. For once I stood my ground and endured the urge to run without acting on it.

"Tell the truth," he said like the voice of my conscience, his breath a silver cloud rising into the branches above us. The trees' solid rootedness, their impossible uprightness, their utter calm settled around me. A piece of me that had been buzzing around inside clicked into place, and I was free.

I took a step closer. "For me, Damian," I said, not knowing what I would say next, "there is no other." The words carved a new reality out of all that was unspoken between us. I stopped, a little shocked at what I had brought into the world, a truth bigger than I'd expected and seemingly eternal. "But . . ." I added, able now to release the next truth that pressed as hard, "when it comes to all the other stuff—"

"Sex?" He said softly, laughing at me.

"I want to, but I'm afraid. I don't know why. Maybe it's because of what happened to my cousin Elisha," I said trailing off, thinking, "or maybe it's that my energy perception is already so tangled with the energy of others. I don't know what would—"

"It's okay," he said, his laughter brushing me, soothing me. "I'm a little afraid, too."

"It's not a little fear, but a big wall-in-the-middle-of-the-road kind of fear. I have to go with it until . . ."

"What," he said, pulling me one step closer, so that I was only inches from his face, standing in the heart of his energy which brushed me like velvet. "What . . . if it was . . . a kiss? No more?"

"What if we can't stop?" I said, unable to take my eyes off his mouth.

"We will," he said, looking at my mouth in a way that made the bottom drop out of my stomach. "I will." Had his eyelashes always been that long and dark?

"Promise?"

He pulled back a fraction, "You *know* me. You can trust me. Can't you see?"

"I think—" I said, beginning to swirl inside, "I know—" I relaxed against his body. "I can." When his lips touched mine, they were surprisingly soft, wet, and warm, and they slid over my lips like pillows. A part of my mind detached. This was such an odd thing to do. Why do humans do this, touch our speaking parts together, the place where we take in food and air?

He pulled back a fraction of an inch, his eyes sweeping over my face. I swear I could feel his gaze like an eyelash kiss. A tiny huff of vapor from his lips brushed my face like a hand. His lips pulled back into a smile, and tiny diamond-shaped indentations tucked inward deliciously above the corners of his mouth.

"Okay?" he whispered.

"Yeah, I think, hold on, my mind is whizzing all over the place."

I took a deep breath, cleared my mind, and pressed my lips against his, and kinda melted into the here and now. My energy dovetailed with his, and warmth spread through my body like whiskey in hot coffee, all the way down to my you-know-what. My lips parted and our tongues slid past each other like dolphins, a passing nudge, then, in primordial recognition, returning and pressing deeper. Then we were nothing but body, heat, and breath, defying winter's crystalline grasp, blending our energy in a paisley pattern like that Mandelbrot equation video, folding and unfolding into each other for what seemed like hours.

Finally, with effort, we dragged our bodies apart, because we knew we needed time before we went to the next step. We studied each other's faces and I'm sure we both saw the same thing, giddy love folded into fear folded into joy folded into embarrassment, folded into disbelief, folded into love again.

"Okay, good night," I said, firmly pushing him away.

"Yes, good night," he said, pulling his coat tightly around himself, and hopping from one foot to the other.

"Good night," I repeated savoring the lean figure he cut out of that cold night.

"*Good* night," he said, ruefully.

"Shut up," I said, laughing, as we backed away from each other, and turned our backs like we were getting ready to count out steps in a duel.

"Julie Sykes," he said as if to himself. When I glanced over my shoulder at him, he was looking back over his shoulder at me.

"Damian Quinn," I said, turning away and stepping toward my house.

"Yes," I thought I heard him say. But I didn't look back.

Feeling tipsy and beautiful inside and out, I staggered into my house and up to bed, where I fell into a deep and dreamless sleep.

28
THE DAY AFTER

NOVEMBER 30, 2016

I was almost relieved when Damian didn't come to school the next morning. Almost. I wasn't sure how the kiss had changed things, and without him, I could carry around this capsule of dizzy, unstable joy inside myself, safe from the taint of reality.

"You're never going to believe it," Samantha said as she pounced on me after class. She steered me over to one of the round tables in the corner, far away from the candy machines. Was my secret already out?

"My mom is home. And she's clean!" she said.

My haze dropped away, and I took Samantha in. She was luminous. Her white cheeks were rosy and her eyes were big, tastefully touched up instead of thickly corralled in eyeliner as they usually were.

"What happened? How'd she do it?"

"The Goddess answered my prayers and healed her."

"Wow. You must have a direct line," I said.

"No. The Goddess this time was a female judge. When my

mother was arrested, the judge ordered her into a new drug rehab program they have in Albany. It worked! My mom is home!" She jumped out of her seat, and I could see all her energy dancing inside her as clean and clear as the daylight that spilled over us through the picture windows. "And you know what? I knew it would happen! I did a tarot card reading last week, and I got the hanged man – upside down. That means something that is stuck becomes unstuck!"

"I'm so happy for you!" I said, sparing her my knee-jerk skepticism re "the Goddess."

"Yeah. I knew she'd come through. If you pray and put it out there, the universe provides." She finished the last of her Doritos. "And since she's been home, I've been on this new diet. You pick the food you love the most and eat it for lunch and dinner, after a balanced breakfast, of course. After a while, you get sick of it, and then you eat less. I eat one Doritos snack pack now for lunch and dinner. I've lost four pounds!"

"I've got news, too," I said.

"Spill it, girl!"

"Damian and I . . ." I leaned closer and said quieter, "kissed."

"Congratulations!" she shouted and clapped her hands together.

"Shhh!" I said and giggled.

"How was it?" she whispered, leaning toward me.

"It was . . . amazing. I mean, at first—it was weird—because my mind got all clinical . . . but then I let go, and . . ."

"I'm so proud of you!" She hugged me like she was my mother and I'd performed a double twist off the high dive.

"Geez, calm down," I said, struggling out of her embrace.

"When are you going to *do* it?" she said, rubbing her hands together.

"None of your goddamned business," I said, whacking her thigh with the back of my hand.

"Oh come on, what are best friends for?"

"We're going to take our time," I said.

"Oh, good," she nodded like this was a novel idea. "Nothing wrong with that."

"I'm glad you approve," I said.

"Well," she lowered her voice as she leaned toward me again, "If you need anything—advice, love lube, condoms, whatever, I'm your woman."

"Thanks," I said, knowing I'd never take her up on that.

"Anyway, where is the dude?" she said looking around.

"I don't know," I said. "He hasn't texted me."

"Haven't you texted him?"

"I don't want to be the first one."

"That's silly," she said. "I'll do it." She whipped out her phone. "I'll be like, Damian and Julie sitting in a tree . . ."

"Don't you dare!" I said, lunging for her phone.

"Just kidding."

My relief that he didn't show up that morning deflated into unease as the day wore on. Sam and Jonathan had both texted him, and he hadn't answered. Where was he? He was always such a gentleman that I thoroughly expected him to check in on me— and to be the first one. Could he be sick again?

I finally gave in and texted, "Hey," to him. Nothing came back.

I tried to focus on my other classes at Skidmore, but I missed most of what they said. Flashes of the heat of our lips, our tongues, and that terrible intimacy stabbed me intermittently, sometimes sending a current of electricity searing through me, other times a rush of shame.

My mother tried to get me to talk over vegan enchiladas at dinner, but a dark mist swaddled me—just an emotional mist, you understand—but it was smothering me. I struggled to open my lungs enough to get a full breath. Even though I looked at my mother as she talked, she seemed far away, and her words came to me as if through cotton batting. She was saying something about how it had come to light that there was a white nationalist group forming on the Skidmore campus. She and all the faculty were worried about it. They didn't want to stifle free speech, but this had never happened on the Skidmore campus before. Was the whole world infected? I wondered.

The kiss had killed all the safety between Damian and me. What if he turned out to be like all those other guys that girls cursed in school bathrooms? Ones who treated sex like a conquest. What if the kiss made him afraid of commitment and sent him running in the opposite direction? What if I was a lousy kisser and he didn't feel the connection I had, and he couldn't tell me? What if he hated the way I tasted? What if he was after the forbidden fruit, and now that he'd attained it, he'd lost interest? Shame like an ocean wave toppled me and ground my head into the metaphorical sand.

I couldn't let that happen. I wouldn't allow him to toy with me. Even though the Damian I had known would never do that in a million years, that kiss had knocked me off balance. It now seemed possible that he could do a 180. Hadn't he already changed that day at Uncommon Grounds? He had all these slick ways of covering things up. My own mother had lied to me about my father, for Christ's sake.

I couldn't live like that. So, ignoring common etiquette, I texted him again. "What's up?" I said. "Are you okay?"

Nothing. Then I called. He didn't pick up. I tried to be all smooth in the recorded message, like I was worried about him, but it was all I could do not to say, "Where the fuck are you? How dare you ignore me like this after—"

That was Friday.

29
CONFRONTATION

DECEMBER 1, 2016

When I awoke Saturday morning, the sun gleamed through the windows with a tinge of whiteness. The first snow. As Mom and I cleaned the house, I waited for Damian to call. But when even the snow didn't raise him, I became sure something was wrong. Finally, as I was wrestling the vacuum back into the hall closet, my phone rang. My heart sprang porcupine quills as I pulled the phone out of my back pocket. The caller I.D. made no sense: it was a jumble of random numbers and letters. I slid my finger across the answer symbol.

Static rasped and crackled, and a male voice cut through at random moments that could have been Damian's voice, but I couldn't tell. All I heard between my renewed heart attack was short, choppy syllables sliced by longer, static-filled silences. Then it went dead. I hadn't heard enough to know if it was Damian.

But that's what prompted me to track him down. What if he had gotten in a car accident and was trying to reach me? I knew he was sensitive about his family, but we had reached a new level of intimacy, after all, and I thought . . . I don't know what I thought. I just knew I needed to find him.

Saratoga is divided into East and West in the minds of its inhabitants. Everything east of Broadway was mostly upscale, beautiful houses with broad porches, turrets, and two or three-car garages. The west side used to be the territory of the marginalized—Black people, then Irish immigrants, then Italian immigrants. Just west of Broadway, but on the north side, close to campus, was mixed, with some outlandishly huge mansions on upper Broadway, and then houses like ours that had been divided into apartments on Woodlawn Ave. Jefferson Terrace, where Damian lived, was actually on the East side of Broadway, but south. Though I had memorized his address, I had never been there, and most people didn't even know the Terrace existed. It was more than a mile away.

"Mom, can I borrow the car?"

"I'm sorry, I need it for errands."

"Okay," I shouted over my shoulder as I raced out the door. "See you later." The cold clawed at my face, surprising me. My lungs pursed shut in reaction to the cold. I checked our porch thermometer. Twenty-three degrees. Not that cold for these parts, but it was a big drop from the day before. I had on my winter coat and thin gloves but didn't think I'd need a hat. I realized my mistake by the time I reached Broadway, where the wind numbed my ears and cheeks. Downtown, a surprising number of people were out—considering the cold. Christmas shopping, I guessed. But I lowered my head and stalked onward, determined to find Damian. I knew Jefferson Terrace was somewhere past the Greenridge Cemetery on Lincoln Street.

I walked all the way through town, past the stores and coffee shops. I knew I was getting close when I passed Stewart's and McDonald's and came to the Mobil gas station on Lincoln. By that time, the cold had numbed my brain and made me a little dizzy. My fingers were cold inside my gloves and I balled them up in my pocket where they remained frozen. The new snow barely whitened the ground.

I hadn't realized how beautiful the Greenridge cemetery was. Tall granite pillars adorned either side of both entrances, with a wrought-iron gate the size of an elephant which was chained shut, and a small side gate that hung open. Inside, cedars had grown tall along rolling pathways, their red-brown branches looping gracefully at the base, their dark crowns neatly pointed. Celtic crosses and statues of angels dotted the graves, and there were a few mausoleums like miniature castles and Greek temples burrowed into small hills.

Over in a flat section among rows of stones, a tall, thin man in a down parka with his hood up leaned against a tombstone, looking in my direction. Was that Damian? My heart developed teeth that bit me. I walked uncertainly toward him. He was definitely looking up at me. I checked my stride when I realized it wasn't Damian. His skin was a lot darker than Damian's, and Damian wore a Navy wool pea coat. Was that duct tape on its sleeve? The hairs rose on the back of my neck and my heart turned into a maniac shaking the bars of its prison. He was still too far away to make actual eye contact, but he gave me a quick man-nod and pointed to his right with his ashy hand. I took two more steps in his direction, passing behind a tree. When I emerged from the other side, he was gone. I inspected the area. He was nowhere. Had he ducked behind a stone? I stood stock-still for a few minutes trying to decide whether to approach or retreat. Quelling my crazy heart, I walked slowly past the plot where he had been to see if he was behind one of the stones. It was empty. Heart maniac calmed a fraction, but head maniac was darting all over the place, putting together the pieces. No one was in the cemetery but me. I took a deep breath and walked over to the stone he'd been leaning against.

You could have carved the name on that stone right into my heart and it would have hurt less. Jacob Johnson.

I ran out to the street. The frozen air scratched my lungs sore. Now, which way? To the right of the cemetery, a trailer park sat only one short block off Broadway.

To the left, the direction the man had pointed, was Jefferson Terrace. I strode toward a series of identical cement buildings, stucco on the first story and vinyl-sided on the second. A big sign in the middle of it all announced it was a Housing Authority Project. That had to make people feel real cozy. The cold was now unbearable. My eyes watered like crazy and my lips were numb. No one was around. Bikes, toys, and sun-bleached toddler slides were mounded beside back doors alongside rusty barbecue grills. The wind blew, and a pine branch screeched thinly against a metal street sign.

I slowed in front of number 14. A white plastic arbor curved over the door covered with faded plastic flowers. I was dizzy from the cold. My cheeks had turned to boot leather, totally without feeling. The muffled sound of a woman crying floated like a silk scarf in the frozen air. I was hesitant, but finally got up the courage to step onto the front stoop and knock. The crying stopped. Silence. I knocked again.

The door flew open and there stood Damian, his face cutting the air like a hatchet. "What do you want?" he asked sharply, his eyes like steel ball bearings.

I stumbled backward off the stoop. "What is *up* with you?" was all I managed to stammer.

"Who invited you here?"

"I didn't know I needed to be invited."

"Get lost."

"But D—" He slammed the door in my face. I stood there panting; my lungs strained to suck in more air, but I couldn't get enough. The cold had frozen them. Next, anger electrified me, wonderfully hot. How dare he? I didn't care if he was mentally ill, possessed by the devil, or by God himself. He had no right to treat me that way.

I hopped onto the stoop and pounded on the door. "Damian!" I called. "Damian!" I didn't care anymore who heard me or what kind of a scene I caused. "Don't you do this!"

He yanked the door open again and grabbed me by my collar. "Look, little girl," he said through gritted teeth. I was so surprised I went as limp as a kitten between her mother's jaws. "Who the hell do you think you are?" I stared at his white teeth and a small drop of spittle on his taut lips. "Get your snotty little butt outta my yard." He shoved me backward so hard that I stumbled and only managed not to fall by instinctively torquing my body and wheeling my arms. He slammed the door again.

I was stunned. All my electricity short-circuited. I might as well have been a clod of dirt. Ice dirt. I stood there a moment trying to understand what had happened. I couldn't believe it. Where was my best friend? Where was the guy I had kissed the other night? That dark, warm moment came swirling around me with an intimacy that was now so shocking it made my knees weak. "You *know* me," he had said.

But I didn't know him. At all. Maybe it had taken me this long to get to the core of who he was. Maybe he was bipolar or schizophrenic.

He might as well have raked my heart out through my intestines with his fingers. I tottered numbly along the sidewalk, reeling. Two men, walking toward me, loomed ominously. One in a plaid jacket carried an open beer can and stepped to one side of me. The other with long hair and all-black sunglasses stepped to the other side of me and said in mock politeness, "Well, hello there, young lady."

In a daze, I found my way to the center of town where the rest of the world was still shopping, clouds of vapor rising from their lips, brightly colored bags in their hands. Christmas wreaths with red bows haloed the lamp posts, absurdly cheerful.

Then, I'm not sure what happened. A wall of noise slammed into me and surged through me, riddling my body with holes. People blurred into clusters of whizzing atoms. Electrons jumped orbits, outward, inward, and all mixed. Their energy shot through my chest in all kinds of textures like wood and titanium bullets, sideways, upways, and downways. My legs, my chest, and my head became one inflamed neural net shot through with the energy of all those people coming, going, breathing, eating, talking, arguing, shitting, and thinking. It all mixed and vibrated at a pitch that fried the inside of my skull.

Nausea roiled inside me and every cell of my body bloated outward to the popping point. If I exploded, I'd spray the town with tiny bits of myself.

My brain lost its grip on my body. With each step, my feet slammed into the ground too soon, causing me to stumble and teeter. I grabbed onto the nearest thing that seemed even remotely solid—a lamp post. I tried to sling my arm around it, but the whole thing went rubber and sank with me as I succumbed to the herringbone-pressure-weave of noise-mash the world had become.

Then—mercifully—two warm and amazingly solid hands gripped my arms and anchored me in time. They muted the sound. They damped the vibrations. They solidified matter.

"Julie," a voice said. A woman's voice. The voice itself blew a warm, organizing wind over the mess I had become. Everything slowed, dried up, and receded. Saratogian shoppers had faces once more, the lamp post became rigid again, and sparse flakes of snow blew.

But next, exhaustion landed on me like a vulture, and all my energy spilled out onto the ground. So, when that voice said, "Come with me," I would have happily followed it to the far reaches of Siberia.

I don't remember clearly what happened next, only that the hands and the voice steered me to a car. I could only focus on my pain, like a dog licking its wounds, and was barely aware of anything external. I remember sinking with relief into a heated leather car seat, looking over at the person driving the car, and dimly recognizing her hawkish nose, strong eyes, and white hair.

30
ATHENA

DECEMBER 1, 2016

Bright, diffused light pricked my eyelids and woke me. I found myself in a greenhouse with a white marble floor, lying on a daybed, staring at the glass roof supported by Grecian marble columns. Fear skimmed my body like a blade under my skin, and I sat up. My head swirled and settled. Unpolished white marble floors resonated with light. Earthy vapors of fig and orange trees enriched the warm air. I zeroed in on a painting that glowed from an easel of a woman standing over a silver brazier, holding a cream-colored cloth out over her head to catch and inhale the rising smoke.

Finally, with a slight shock, my eyes found the flesh-and-blood woman sitting next to the painting, reading: the strange woman who had been following me, haunting my peripheral vision for weeks.

"Ah, you are awake," she said with a British accent. She closed her book. She was a handsome woman with a prominent sculpted nose and strong brows that contrasted strikingly with her gray-white hair. She appeared to be fifty or so. "I am Athena." Her low voice calmed me despite the surrounding strangeness.

"The goddess of wisdom?"

She laughed, a loud, cascading laugh. "I dare say I've accumulated a good store of wisdom, and I've been accused of arrogance, but I wouldn't go so far as to call myself a goddess."

"Have you been following me?" Clouds of outrage billowed.

"Yes." Her simple honesty surprised me and checked the build of emotion.

"Where am I?"

"Only blocks from your house. On upper Broadway. Worlds away, yet next door," she said, her smile shaping her words.

With the mention of my house, Damian's violation crashed in on me. I closed my eyes and the sickening tar of it filled my body.

"You've suffered a shock. A psychic slap in the face." I opened my eyes. She was holding up her hands as if to still and contain me. Her black eyes bore into me under her furrowed brow. The extraordinary turn of events pushed back the shock. "Waking up here only adds to your disorientation." She rounded her vowels and carved her consonants in that very British way.

Two frames of unreality wrestled back and forth through my body. I gave myself over into this frame, because strange as it was, it was preferable to the last one.

"Why have you been following me?" I leaned forward.

She hesitated a fraction of a second as if thinking it over. "I ascertained some time ago that you are a *sensitive*, but I had to make sure before I approached you."

"A *sensitive*?"

"Someone who senses what is beyond," she fanned her hand elegantly through the air.

"Beyond what?"

"Beyond sight, beyond sound, beyond the obvious. Your senses are extraordinarily developed for someone with no training. We've been watching you for a few months now."

"That's creepy. We?"

"I'm sorry. There is no smooth way to do this. We call ourselves the Order of the Anima Arcanum, the mystery of the spirit. We are an international society that acts as stewards to the mystery. We help the spirits of the deceased who are trapped in this realm to move on. We keep an eye out for sensitives and train them to become 'adepts.' I would like to train you."

"Train me to do what?"

"To become one who is adept at using her senses to usher spirits to the next realm."

I shook my head. "You're a ghost-buster and you want me to be one?"

She laughed with a trace of scorn, and laugh lines wreathed her face. "You've heard, then, of the International Paranormal Society, and perhaps even visited their website. No. We are not like them. For one thing, we are a *secret* society. I will have to ask you to keep all you learn here to yourself."

"Why is that?"

"Because naming spirits can summon them by accident. That is why we would never have a website such as the Paranormal Society. Another difference is they insist on using technology to record and prove the existence of spirits. We do not concern ourselves with proof. To sense spirits and communicate with them, you can't use anything as clumsy as a machine. You must use the infinite intelligence of your mind and your body. Work the energy. That is what you have been doing without realizing it. You see the spirit energy of people both alive and dead."

"How could you possibly know that?"

"Call it intuition," she said and close observation."

I absorbed all this in silence for a moment, both alarmed and relieved.

"That *was* you at the house on Gick Road, wasn't it?"

"Yes, and I'm aware that a partial spirit is trapped there."

"What's a partial spirit?"

"Sometimes when a person dies, only part of their energy moves on. That is why some spirits are visible, and some are not. Some can speak, and some cannot. It all depends on what circuit of energy, or chi, was left behind—which depends also on how they died. In some cases, I've had to use feng shui to deliver a spirit. In other cases, simple psychology does the job."

My pulse quickened. I was so relieved to have someone confirm my reality.

"I know who it is. It's a guy named Jacob Johnson." I leapt off the daybed and told her as fast as possible everything I had seen and felt at the house, what had happened to Damian, what I had seen in the cemetery. "I think he has possessed Damian. We've got to help him."

"Yes, yes." She caught my hands in both of hers. "You're right. But we don't know enough to help either Damian or this Jacob Johnson yet. We have to find out what part of this spirit is stuck and why." She explained the three main categories of reasons a spirit might get trapped in the physical realm: the manner of death, a previous condition before death, or a physical element in their environment keeping them there. "When someone gets infected or possessed, as Damian *may* or *may not* be," she paused here and made sustained eye contact, "there is always a pre-existing reason for that person's receptivity to the spirit. In other words, Damian's energy resonates with this spirit."

"But I already know how Jacob died. He was murdered by Michael Wright."

"You have a good hypothesis, but we have more investigation to do. We can make things much worse if we don't know what we're treating. Does this mean you will consider my invitation?"

"What does it involve?"

"At first, many hours of training. But later . . . encounters that could involve danger. Of course, I would not expose you to anything until you were ready, but since you have already tangled yourself with a partial spirit . . . I could protect and steer you."

I considered the possibility that she was some kind of con

woman, but nothing in me was tilting or swirling. Everything felt solid, and she also seemed oddly familiar.

"Can I change my mind and quit, if I don't like it?" I said.

"Of course," she smiled. "This is not the mafia."

"Then I accept. When can we get started?"

Her head jerked back and she stood holding my hands for a minute, her brows creased. When the light went out in her eyes, they looked like caves where much was hidden.

"No," she said. She dropped my hands and turned away to look out the window, then continued in a contemplative voice. "You must sleep on it. This is an enormous decision that comes with much responsibility and danger. We are considering a complete life change. And most importantly, you must talk to your mother."

"But I'm 19, and I can't talk to my mother! She's been trying to stop me from seeing my whole life. She won't believe me."

"You must make her believe. You can come back in the morning if the answer is still yes."

"But—"

"Come. I will take you home. Talk to your mother, but to no one else. And talk to no one about the partial spirit on Gick Road."

I know this seems pretty unbelievable, but everything she said to me reverberated so perfectly with what I had already experienced that it produced an energetic shift inside me when it matched, a burst of energy, like the clap of a bell. I knew in my body that everything she was telling me was completely true, more true than what most people experience as reality.

31
MISSING

WINTER, 1999-2000

The weather was particularly bitter the week after Peran stormed out of Athena's apartment, with nights going down to twenty below, and the days rising to barely above zero. His silence was as bitter as the weather, capable of chapping hands in seconds. At the end of the week, at two in the morning, Athena's phone rang.

"Is Peran with you?" Audrey's voice was tight.

"What do you mean?"

"We went to bed as usual, and—I don't know what woke me—but he's gone."

"Did you have a fight?"

"No, no, nothing like that. The car's still in the driveway, his coat is still on the hook with his wallet in his pocket, but he's not in the house. He's been sleepwalking more than ever, and last night I found him outside on the doorstep. It's so cold out, I'm worried. I can't leave the baby. Could you maybe drive around and look for him?"

"Absolutely. I'll keep you posted."

"Likewise," Audrey said, and then, *"Thank you."*

Athena knew exactly where to look first. She stumbled from her bed, dug out an extra pair of wool socks, and dressed in layers. She rolled up the feather quilt from her bed and raced down the wide stairs to the back door.

Sure enough, he was at the well in the North Woods, curled against the wall on the ground. Terror caught at her throat as she took in his stillness and his bare feet, but when she spotted the thin stream of vapor that rose from his mouth, her throat relaxed. "Peran!" she called.

The college had turned the area into a dig for their anthropology classes, so the hole in the ground had been shored up and turned into an entryway and crude staircase. A gate had been added to the fence, but it was padlocked. She threw the quilt over the chainlink fence and scaled it, the wire links clanging in the bitter cold. A loose wire caught on her coat sleeve and scraped her arm as she dropped beside him. She checked his pulse. It was weak and erratic. She called his name again and shook him. His body was stiff in hypothermic sleep. She wrapped the down quilt around him, pulled the extra wool socks from her coat pocket, and put them on his feet. She pulled a vial of dirt from her pocket, dusted her palms with it, rubbed them together until they were radiant with heat, and pressed both hot palms to his chest as she entered a trance. In minutes, his eyes flew open.

He blinked and smiled. "You've come," he said, putting his hand on her cheek as if she'd accepted an invitation. His hand felt like stone.

"Peran. It's me. Do you know who I am?"

"You belong here, with me," he said.

"Who am I speaking to?" she asked. She took a deep breath to enhance her energetic field. Peran's energy was tangled with a foreign entity. She breathed on her palms and rubbed them until they radiated again. She placed one palm on his forehead and the other over his heart. "Peran, return."

Peran gasped for air as if drowning.

"Peran, surface."

"Let go," he said, pushing her hands away and coughing. She pressed harder. Numb with cold, his hands were uncoordinated, his strength weak. "He's mine," a deeper voice came out of him.

Athena unfolded her power like massive black wings and surrounded them both within their sphere. "Release him," she commanded, her voice resonant with power. "He belongs to the living."

Peran sat up coughing, eyes open. "Athena," he said.

Athena got him back to her house and into a warm bath. It took a solid hour before he stopped shaking. When Athena reached for the phone, a drop of blood fell on it. She examined her hand and wrist and found the scratch from the fence. It was time to come clean with Audrey, she realized, wiping the blood away from the scrape and watching it bead again. It was all getting too dangerous. And she would ask Cavendish for help with a redirection of Hilton and Peran's spirits, which appeared to be hopelessly tangled.

32
SEER AND PUSHER

DECEMBER 1–15, 2016

"Hey, kid. You okay?" My mom caught sight of me as I tried to slip back into the house that evening.

"Yeah, fine," I said, edging toward my room.

"You look exhausted. Better take some Echinacea and vitamin C in case you're coming down with a cold."

"Okay," I said, heading toward the kitchen, hoping that my acquiescence would stop the probe.

"Dinner will be ready soon," she called through the pass-through.

I squeezed the vitamin C bottle in frustration.

"I'm really tired, Mom. Would you be offended if I went upstairs to lie down? My throat does feel kinda sore, now that you mention it."

She appeared at the kitchen door.

"I wish you wouldn't shut me out," she said gently, brushing my hair away from my forehead.

I wish you wouldn't freak out if I told you what was going on, I thought.

"I'm not, Mom. I'm just tired. Really."

"Okay, but you know you can always talk to me if something's on your mind."

Yeah, right, I thought as I retreated to my room. She'd commit me to the nuthouse if I talked about ghosts and a stranger named Athena who said I was a *sensitive* and wanted to mentor me to deliver my boyfriend from possession. I'd commit myself to a nuthouse.

I sank into bed, exhausted by so many world-shattering discoveries, not the least of which was that I was deeply angry at my mother and I finally knew why. I'd always known she loved me, but I'd also always felt this darkness and anger she had toward me. I could never figure out what I'd done to deserve it. But I understood that night that she was angry at me because of what I saw.

I could barely wait to meet Athena on Sunday morning. It was perfect that her house—mansion—was so close to mine. I could get there without needing a ride or being observed. She was a welcome distraction from the disaster with Damian, and at the same time, she was my road to gaining him back.

I told Mom I would be studying all day at the library, so I was all clear there. I stepped onto the back porch into a morning as bright and hopeful as I felt. In the absence of yesterday's vicious wind, twenty-three degrees felt downright balmy.

"First off," I said, as soon as Athena opened the door. "I accept, with all my heart."

She smiled and the light of many years emanated from her eyes. She gripped both my arms in an arm-length hug. Then she steered me into the library to a comfortable leather chair.

"How did the talk go with your mother?"

I avoided her eyes. "I didn't talk to her."

Athena started to speak and checked herself. "Why not?"

"She wouldn't give her blessing, anyway." People are dead wrong when they say it doesn't hurt to ask. When you know the answer is going to be no, it hurts *you* and pisses off *them*.

She walked over to the fireplace, leaned on the mantle, and said, "Tell me why you want to join us?"

"To save Damian, obviously."

She waited, her face impassive, her wavy white hair streaming out from her face and over her shoulders like it was permanently windblown.

"And," I stumbled onward searching for the answer she appeared to be waiting for, "because I've been hampered all my life by being—different. I like the idea that my weakness might be my strength."

"It is not a question of weakness and strength. You must remove that kind of judgmental language from your frame of reference. It is a question of identifying your attributes and finding the right application for them."

"Makes sense," I said. "I still want to join the Anima Arcanum and learn how to be a what-do-you-call-it."

"An adept."

"Yeah, that."

"Have you considered the danger?" she asked, her brows creasing sternly.

"It seems more dangerous for me not to be trained." I shrugged my shoulders.

"True." She studied me. "And of course, you have no idea what you are getting into."

"I guess."

I stood there uncertainly, waiting.

"Whatever it is, I believe you are up to it," she said, and her brows cleared, letting white light spill from her black glittering eyes. "Let's begin."

"Don't we do some sort of induction ceremony or something?"

She laughed. "You are so funny, Julie."

I didn't think so. She saw she had embarrassed me.

"We don't swear members of Anima Arcanum to absolute secrecy, but listen carefully to your intuition. It will tell you who is safe to share information with and who is not. Most importantly, don't talk about any of this unless you have to, and when you have to, set a containment circle first and do not refer to the spirit by name."

"Can I tell my friend, Samantha?"

"That is your best friend?"

"Yes."

"Is she good at keeping things to herself?"

"I think so. And she's into Wicca, so she wouldn't scoff at it. Speaking of Wicca, is there any validity to it?"

"We use knowledge gleaned from all over the world, all cultures. Every culture has its wisdom, and it's all part of the big picture."

"So, Wicca isn't bullshit?"

"No, but there are a lot of practitioners who don't know what they are doing. The ego has a way of inserting itself in all the wrong ways. If you are practicing magic from the wrong place, usually nothing will happen. But sometimes bad things can happen. That's why it's best to train with a skilled teacher and to be sure your intentions are pure."

I nodded.

"Have a seat." She pushed me gently in the direction of the living room. "I'm sure you have many more questions."

"Well, the first thing I want to know," I said, falling onto the leather couch, "is how much danger is Damian in?"

"I cannot be sure in this particular case. I don't know if he is merely infected or if he is possessed." She explained that when people are "infected," it means a spirit may have passed through the body and left a remnant of its energy behind. It might affect a person's chi or body energy, which might make them feel sick in various ways. I told her all the things Damian had touched in the house and how it had bothered me, and then he also had gotten sick. She explained that possession is when the spirit enters your body and tries to take over. You start to act more and more like that person. I explained how he would act weird one day and normal the next—how anger and physical violence were totally uncharacteristic of him.

"That could be possession," she said gravely. "There can be a battle between the host and the invading spirit, which would explain why he changes back to his true self sometimes."

"What will happen?"

"If we do not get it out, the invading spirit could banish his spirit forever. In one case I was intimately involved with," she hesitated, "the possessed person died."

"My God."

"But that is rare," she emphasized. "In this case, the man possessed was an adept. An incorporator. He was called in on the most difficult cases because he could willingly invite a spirit into his body, trap it there, and then redirect the spirit's energy to its proper domain. It can be dangerous if you don't know what you're doing. But we don't have to worry about that here. Damian is not a *sensitive,* and he is healthy. I've seen people endure possession for years and come out okay. But we'll solve this quicker than that."

"Can't you cure him?"

"My best shot at helping him is to help you. Spirits are shaped by their landscape. Those indigenous to the place where the problem occurred will have better luck interacting with the spirit in question. That's why we cultivate adepts all over the world. This," she waved her hand at our surroundings, "is only one of our many safe houses."

"But how can *I* do it?"

"With your vision."

"But what the hell is it that I'm seeing, exactly?"

"Tell me as much as you can, and I will tell you."

At first, I couldn't think of anything. You know how when a flavor, or gesture, or place is so familiar to you that you can't describe it because they are so much part of daily life? Like, you don't even know anything different? It was like that, but once I described some of the granules and spirals, and the streak of yellow I'd seen going through Damian and how his eyes changed, it got easier. When I was finished she said, "My dear, you inhabit the subatomic realm."

"The what?"

"Most people only see the largest aspects of reality, but you see the subatomic parts. And because you see those parts, you can affect them. Quantum physicists have established that the observer can change the observed."

"So why can't I bend pencils and spoons?"

"You do, in a manner of speaking, but the changes are smaller. Remember I said, *sub*atomic. This is smaller than the atoms, which cannot be seen with the human eye or even with our finest instruments. At the subatomic level, the spirit realm, you are changing things you cannot see. Everyone does. We do not see the chain of cause and effect until the ripple of action reaches the cellular level. Another word for it is chi."

She explained that chi is like life energy and that the Chinese do not distinguish between matter and energy.

"That's like what Dr. Fish taught us about atomic structure," I said.

"Scientists are only now able to prove things that Eastern cultures have been acting upon for thousands of years." She took me into the greenhouse where I had first awoken and pointed to the plants and the marble floor while she explained that chi was matter turning into energy and energy turning into matter. As I listened to the river water notes of her words, I absorbed the white light falling from the glass roof, the glossy oval leaves of the potted orange tree, and the marble floors. All of them were different kinds of chi. I had always thought that rocks were inanimate objects. But Athena said that chi is the thread that connects all things, mountains, plants, human emotions, even manmade objects. I thought of the clay horse in my room. Could I learn about my father by practicing these arts?

"The first thing we must do is teach you how to manage your vision."

"But why is my vision so weird? Is that really how things look deep down?"

"You may have a bit of synesthesia."

"That's what *I* thought!"

Full training took months and even years, but given the likelihood that Damian was possessed, she said she could speed things by performing an "energy weave" with me. She would merge her energy with mine and teach me how to meditate. Through meditation—complete relaxation—I could learn to manipulate my vision.

I lay on the massage table she'd placed in the atrium, conservatory—whatever it was called. She placed one of her hands on my forehead and the other on my sternum. Her hands felt like hot stones, and the heat worked through me instantly, like I was saturated with sun. Immediately, a wonderful stillness permeated me. My mind stopped leaping like a squirrel through branches, my heart slowed, and my lungs expanded like balloons that could double in size, filling and filling and filling with air.

"Now, remember this place. There are two triggers for your vision, extreme stress, and deep relaxation. I have created a path to deep relaxation. Everything works better from that place. You should now be able to return here with ease."

That helped me a lot in dealing with the changes in Damian who surfaced occasionally over the next few weeks but—unbelievably, ignored me and acted less and less like himself. Sometimes at night, the wound of our sudden estrangement felt like an actual stab wound in my chest. She warned me not to try energy weaves with anything but plants until I was fully trained and insisted that Damian would last until I was ready.

Over those final weeks of the semester, between exams and final papers, she taught me to melt into this wonderful clear place and open into the interior expanse of my cells. I came to recognize two different kinds of perceptions or presences. "Give them names," Athena said. "Naming calls things into existence and makes them real. The root of the word 'name' is *anima* or soul."

One energetic presence was thick and driving and emanated from my gut. I named this my Pusher. When my Pusher showed up, my ability to see energy was impaired, but my energy to act on what I saw was huge and explosive. That was the one that prompted me to scream and push my uncle away and pull Damian out of the house that first time. The second energetic presence was this very light, floating energy, which usually came out of my sternum. When I sat up very straight, it filled my lungs with air. It was a perceiving energy, a loose, permeable energy. I called this my Seer. When the Seer opened inside me, my ability to see into people was at its height.

As I honed my skills that December, I came to realize that these two energetic beings had always been with me, like guardian angels. "Are they real guides? Or just brain chemistry?" I asked.

"There is no difference in the subatomic realm," Athena said.

I don't know why I found that disappointing. I wanted to believe in a humanoid god or angel that had a particular fondness for *me*. The idea that God was galactic energy was so much more impersonal. It made me more of a spec in the universe, unimportant.

"Understanding that we are all a small piece of the same fabric is essential for those practicing these arts," Athena assured me. "Otherwise, there's too great a tendency to become a narcissist, sociopath, or megalomaniac. We are all equally important, all part of that fractal design your science teacher described to you. When pieces of the design get misdirected, that's when you get things like cancer."

The sun had gone down that particular day, and it was almost dinner time. I was exhausted.

"That's enough for today. We've covered months of training in two short weeks. Now you are ready to use your newly sharpened skills to help Damian. Later this week, see if you can bring him here."

33
MEANWHILE

DECEMBER 1-21, 2016

I need to back up a bit to the week I started training and tell you what was happening with my friends and with Damian.

"I always knew you were different," Samantha said when I confessed what I'd been withholding from her. We were lounging on my bed. "That's why I love you so much. But I'm sorry you didn't think you could trust me."

"It wasn't you I didn't trust. It was me," I said. "I was in denial."

"And you gave me so much shit about Wicca and my spells and charms."

I dropped my gaze to my lap, ashamed that I'd harbored this secret superiority complex over my best friend. "I know. That was unfair."

"That's okay," she said. "I bet it made you uncomfortable. You were trying to be all normal, and here I was bringing up supernatural powers all the time."

Warmth and admiration for her rushed through me. "That is such a generous interpretation, Sam. You're amazing."

"De nada," she said with the flap of a hand. "And now you have a mentor? I'm so jealous! Do you think she could mentor me, too?"

"I don't know, I'll ask," I said, feeling a bit possessive of Athena.

"But you *should* tell your mother all this," Sam said.

"I can't. I just can't."

"You don't give her enough credit. You're so lucky to have a mother who isn't an addict."

"Speaking of which, how are things going with your mother?" I asked.

"Good. I mean, we are all getting used to each other again. I find myself watching her for signs that she's secretly using. Then I feel guilty. And she's needy. Like, I have to mother *her*. I'm worried that if I don't, she'll start using again."

"You know it's not your fault, right?"

"I know, addiction is an illness and all that," Samantha said, her gaze turning inward.

"Only she can rescue herself," I said.

"Says the woman who is trying to rescue Damian," Samantha quipped.

———

Later that same week, I finally got up the nerve to go to Uncommon Grounds. I had been avoiding running into Damian. The shop's familiar red and ochre walls reminded me of so many good moments with Damian. I searched the tables quickly, heart pounding. He wasn't there.

As I stood in line spacing out, he came up behind me and said quietly into the pocket of air between my neck and shoulder, "Hey." That simple, short word lit every cell in my body on fire. I spun around to face him. One sight of the expression on my face and he stepped back.

"What's wrong?"

"You don't remember, do you?" I asked. The energy state that I named the Pusher hugged my waist like heavy lion paws, girding me.

"Thursday night? How could I forget?" he said, referring to the night of the kiss. His eyes were wide as he searched my face. I pulled him over to a secluded corner at the back of the coffee shop where the walls were painted deep orange, and we sank into worn leather armchairs. My lungs felt like they were cinched by a steel band. Athena had taught me that acceptance was the best route to disarming an emotion. I practiced allowing and staying with the steel band, breathing in for four and out for four rather than trying to get a whole breath.

I searched his night-blue eyes. It was all him again. The lion paws loosened, and I exhaled.

"No. Saturday. You don't remember anything that happened Saturday, do you?" Something flickered in his eyes, like a shutter closing.

"I waited for you to call," he said. "I didn't want to crowd you, so I didn't call."

"I came to your house."

"What?" The blood drained from his face, leaving his brown skin greenish gray.

I told him as quickly as I could what he had done, how he had behaved. He listened in silence, alternately searching my face as if to question whether I was telling the truth and looking grieved.

"That explains why my mother has been looking at me so strangely, and Sid has been keeping his distance," Damian said.

I told him about Athena, about being a *sensitive*, and about my training. As I talked the steel band loosened, and my lungs expanded, thin and elastic, becoming permeable so that I could breathe him in. First I sifted through his cool water energy, dark, fragrant as hemlock, yet clear and crisp as night stars. But as I related seeing Jacob in the cemetery, his cells rumbled, like thunder. Underneath the water energy, a dense snarl pulsed inside, deep red and as woody as overgrown beets, and it expanded as I talked. His eyes flashed.

"Why do you have to bring up Jacob Johnson all the time? Jacob Johnson this, Jacob Johnson that. Stay in the *real* world for once." The Pusher clutched my abdomen and my Seer shut down.

"Damian, stay with me. Tell me what's going on."

His eyes turned to metal shields. "Quit digging into me. It's none of your damn business." He reached out to grab my collar. I stepped back. His hand froze in the air and his eyes flashed again.

"Jesus," he said in disgust. He curled his fingers into his palm and dropped his hand. Then he leapt out of the chair, turned his back on me, and walked away.

I slumped back into my chair. The floor opened and I swirled down, down, down into a pit without bottom. But the Pusher hugged my hips again and cinched the pit closed.

That Pusher helped me through the rest of that day and, for that matter, the rest of the week, as Damian blew me off completely. Honestly, my Seer and Pusher got me through finals, too, allowing me to settle my mind when it was in tumult.

Meanwhile, Damian wore clothes that were alien to him, like polo shirts, and he began hanging out with Payton, of all people. Sometimes from afar, I'd see him in the parking lot with the jocks, joking loudly enough for everyone to hear. At one of our *Adiorondacker* meetings that Damian skipped, Payton was boasting about the best party he'd ever attended given by one of his Skidmore classmates.

"That was some crazy shit," Payton said. "They had, like, cases of Veuve Clicquot, if you know what that is," he said. "My dude, Damian, was the life of the party."

Samantha rolled her eyes at me. "We know what Veuve Clicquot is. Dude."

I sure didn't.

Later, I heard Damian got into a pushing match with someone

downtown. I felt acutely embarrassed for him, but he seemed to have no shame.

That whole time, I lived for those afternoons with Athena. She used her energy weaves to remind me how to relax on command, and by the end of that period, I discovered a third being, the Changer. This was the hardest to connect with, but when I did, it began with prickling around the crown of my head, like the top of my skull was a cold cantaloupe cut open to the sky. Whereas the Pusher and the Seer felt like they emanated from my own body, this third energy felt like it breezed through me from somewhere high above.

I called it the Changer because when this energy was present, I could affect the energy of others.

I discovered how it worked one day in the greenhouse as I stared at a wilted philodendron. The conservatory, as it was called, was one of my favorite spots. It formed the central courtyard to the house with balconies all around. It was at least twenty feet wide, with plants all around the edge and a round raised garden bed with a retaining wall at the center crowded with tropical trees and flowering vines. Athena had me practice on plants a lot because their energy was more stable and consistent than animal energy, and human energy was the most snarled. My Seer was open, and as I breathed in the plant's greenness, its heart-shaped, slotted leaves, and its clean coolness, I could feel the irritation at its center. I breathed this in, getting closer to it until the disorder expanded and filled my senses. At first, I tried to send the plant the message to smooth itself out, to sand off the irritation. But this felt like a lot of work, and it shut down the whole "energy weave" as Athena called it. Then one day, I gave myself over to the plant completely and asked it to do what was best for it. My scalp tingled. The crown of my head opened to the sky, and this cool column of air siphoned down through me into the plant. Each time I inhaled and exhaled, the column of air moved through the plant, sifting and soothing it until it was ordered again.

When I opened my eyes, the plant was exactly the same, deflated and slumped. But two hours later it had completely recovered.

Athena was proud.

Naturally, I was bursting to share my accomplishment with Damian, but I couldn't get near him. He was utterly changed; everyone noticed it. Whenever I saw him around town or at the SUNY ADK extension, my heart felt like a rusty hunk of metal scratching the inside of my ribs. I could never catch his eye or catch up to him in the halls. If I raised the courage to sit next to him, he'd get up and move, so I stopped trying. From where I sat in class, several rows behind him, I would try to open my Seer to see if I could figure out what the problem was, but my Pusher refused to cooperate. He continued to hang out with Payton, and hoot and holler in the parking lot. By the end of the week, he was driving a brand-new car. Until now, he had given most of his earnings to his mother.

"Whoa," Samantha whispered as he stalked past us on the way to our biology final. "The dude is seriously possessed. You better speed up your training. I'll do what I can from my side, but..."

Samantha called me a few days later, "Did you hear the news?"

"What?"

"Damian was arrested last night for getting into a fight on Caroline Street, outside Gaffney's."

Caroline Street was a place we always avoided at night. It had a lot of bars, and people came from all over to drink excessively. In the morning, you always found vomit on the sidewalk. Until now Damian had always disliked alcohol.

"Shit, Sam, this is out of hand. I gotta talk to Athena."

"You go, girl," she said. "Let me know if there's anything I can do."

"Just stay away from him, for your own safety. Maybe do some peace spells or something."

"You got it," Samantha said.

I hung up the phone and ran as fast as I could to Athena's house.

I'm no track star, and the cold air hurt my lungs as I ran. I was wheezing badly when I got there.

"We've got to move faster," I said. "He's completely out of his mind. I don't know who he is anymore."

Athena's brows furrowed and her lips tightened. "Let's go to the house on Gick Road, and see what we find," she said.

"Can't we go find him right now and do an energy weave?"

"We still don't know what's possessing him or why."

"But I told you—"

"I'm not convinced."

34
AT JACOB'S HOUSE

DECEMBER 21, 2016

What should have been a five-minute car ride was fifteen because of traffic and stoplights. Like someone looking through the wrong end of a telescope, I realized the rest of the world was Christmas shopping. Athena had instructed me to wear boots with rubber bottoms to help insulate against unwanted energy transfer. As it was the solstice, the darkest day of the year, spirit energies would be stronger than usual.

With my heightened sensitivity, I was jarred by the energy of the shopping district, of people encapsulated in metal and glass, wide traffic lanes with no sidewalks, identical bushes all in a row, and artificially cheery signs over gray box stores. The energy was fast-slow, packed-empty, cheery-soulless, busy-flat. I hated it. We parked unobtrusively in the All-Mart parking lot and headed for the brush behind it. People streamed out of the mouth of the store with full carts. None of those things would fill the void, I thought, dimly.

Once we were past the dumpsters and the drainage ditches and into the weeds and brush, the land energy ironed out my jangled nerves. The sun was nearing the horizon, and daylight was half-assed.

When the house came into view with its mansard roof and curved front door, I had mixed emotions of anticipation and fear. Athena, who had changed into jeans and a jacket, scrambled under the fence like she was no stranger to rough living. We skirted the rotten front porch and headed to the back door, as I had done before. I checked my watch. Only four o'clock. When I reached for the door handle, Athena stopped me, pulled out a silk handkerchief, and grasped the doorknob with it.

"Neither of us is prone to possession, but let's take precautions." She explained that the chi of silkworms doesn't let psychic energy pass through. "That's why I asked you to change your boots. Limiting input sharpens perception."

The house seemed to sigh as we opened the door. I expected the scent of coffee and licorice, but it was too cold for that. We crept through the gray light, absorbing the house's energetic vibrations. We finally stopped in the kitchen. "Now," she said. "We are here to find clues to what has gotten a hold of Damian, whether it's a whole spirit or a partial spirit, whether it's rational or simply emotional. What part of Jacob was left behind? What is keeping it? Is it Jacob? Whatever we find, you must stay resolute. A spirit can only affect you if you allow it."

"Surely Damian didn't *allow* this to happen to him."

"When we are unaware of ourselves, as are most of us, we allow many things in without knowing it." Athena's eyes glittered darkly as if remembering past mistakes. "Prepare yourself as we have practiced." She straightened and took a deep breath.

My lungs filled with hers automatically. I closed my eyes and became aware of my body. I was freezing, so all my muscles were tense. Athena put her hands on my shoulders and her warmth radiated through my shoulders and lungs. My body relaxed.

"That's it," she said.

I breathed again and my lungs loosened their weave. My mind loosened with them.

We began in the living room. As soon as I warmed, I could smell the coffee-licorice scent. I breathed it in. Everything in the house felt calm, steady, and solid, nothing like the growling, tangled energy I had felt in Damian. We creaked up the stairs, and I examined Jacob's four-poster bed. Athena opened the closet door with her silk handkerchief.

"Now," Athena said, "Before you touch his shirt, I want you to summon your Pusher."

"But my Pusher shuts down my Seer."

"Your Pusher and Seer are symbiotic. I will help you hold the Seer open. You need the Pusher present to guard yourself from Jacob's energy. It will make your body surfaces impermeable so that you will feel the energy as it slides against yours, but it won't stick."

She reminded me of the steps we had practiced so many times: concentrate on my gut, clench my abdominal muscles, and remind myself of what the Pusher energy feels like. "Meanwhile, I will place my hands here," she pressed her palms against my shoulder blades, "and that will help to keep the Seer open. Ready?"

In a moment or two, the heavy muscular energy of the Pusher saddled my abdomen and hips while at the same time, the Seer energy opened inside my lungs. Following her directions, I held the two opposing energies together yet apart as I touched Jacob's flannel shirt.

"I don't feel anything. It's just a shirt."

"Relax the Pusher, a hair. Imagine it melting a bit, shifting."

I focused on my stomach muscles and imagined the lion paws hugging my hips.

"Good," Athena said. "Now breathe in through your chest. Tell me what you feel." I inhaled the particles of the house and my whole body vibrated. The light changed to liquid amber, and my inner ear clicked from the new air pressure. Everything swished like the ocean inside a seashell.

"That's perfect. You're weaving, now," Athena said, her voice coming to me as if through water. "Don't lose yourself in it. Use your peripheral senses to feel my hands on your back, but stay open to whatever you see."

I blinked and scanned the room. "Let's go down to the kitchen," I said, my own voice sounding muffled and interior as if my ears were blocked.

As we approached the kitchen, the tingling and amber light intensified. When I stepped through the doorway, a swarm of multi-colored light particles dazzled me. I blinked. "Steady," Athena said. "Remember to breathe."

I stayed with the moment. The particles coalesced into a human form that clarified itself by the millisecond. The interior of my body itched slightly all over like when a wound is healing. The shape of a man emerged, but the particles were missing in his neck and chest region. His hand felt around the hole. His face concretized, and his eyes, which were a paler brown than his skin, came into focus, shallow as saucers, with white rings, filled with despair. His eyes darted back and forth between me and his own body, still checking the patch where the particles seethed. Then he reached out and stepped toward me, moving his mouth as if talking, but I heard no sound except for the swishing of my clogged ears. The Pusher clenched, my heart jumped, and the vision collapsed. I was standing in gray light in an ordinary room again, breathless.

"He's here," I said, falling back into Athena's hands. Amazement overwhelmed me. It was *all real?* The afterlife? Spirits? It was simultaneously thrilling and horrifying. My mind jumped to the possibility of contacting my father but recoiled from Pandora's box.

"Tell me what you saw."

Her grip grounded me.

"Are you sure it's safe to be here?" I asked.

She nodded curtly. "You can answer that question yourself."

I reviewed. He had calm, woody energy. A quiet, deeply sad energy. It didn't feel dangerous, I told her.

"That's what I felt through you. Rest assured, I never lost contact with you. All the channels are clean. Tell me what else you saw."

I described a tall, light-skinned black man with his hair cropped close. When he coalesced, he looked both solid and immaterial, though all his colors were faded. Around him floated a sort of shroud, a transparent memory of clothing. I closed my eyes to remember better. He was wearing that blue parka with the silver duct tape across a shoulder rip. A piece of tape had come loose off his elbow and hung down as he checked the empty spot at his neck. His legs were long and skinny and stuck into big, mud-caked work boots. His hands were calloused and dirty. Athena explained that a spirit can remember what it looked like alive and project that image. The presence of a living person helps them to remember and thus organize their remaining energies better. But the hole in him was clearly where he had been shot. His chi had been catastrophically disorganized there or had even passed on.

"Jacob's spirit could be trapped in a traumatic pattern," Athena said. She explained that post-traumatic stress syndrome was energy caught in a repeating pattern. Just as in life, where a small event can trigger the body's fear response to the original traumatizing event, so a person's chi could get trapped in a traumatic cycle when they die violently.

"This might be what the Chinese call zhi—the part of the spirit that governs Jacob's will, stuck in a mindless loop, like a tape playing over and over."

It didn't seem mindless to me. He seemed completely there, reaching out to me, asking me to do something. Athena said we would try a redirection for Jacob right then and there.

"You mean an exorcism?"

Athena wrapped her arm around my shoulders and gave me a gentle squeeze. "It is much kinder than an exorcism. In an exorcism, the spirit is simply cast out. We try to help the spirit achieve balance and guide it to its proper realm."

"What realm is that?"

"Well, that depends."

"Then how do you know when you get it there?"

"We have faith that once balance is achieved, it knows what to do. No one has to tell a seed which way is down and which way is up. That knowledge is written within the DNA, and when all elements are balanced, the tree grows."

She said we should start with the simplest redirection ceremony first. She pulled out a pouch from her coat, unfolded it, and set out objects that represented the five elements or "phases of chi": a tiny green plant in a jar of dirt to represent wood and earth, a candle for fire, a piece of metal, and a vial of water. She laid the objects in a circle. Then she adjusted the furniture in the kitchen, making sure that no windows were obstructed by furniture. She also cracked one window open.

As she arranged things, she explained that Chinese astrology deals with the chi of the sky, acupuncture and Chinese medicine deal with the chi of the body, but feng shui deals with the chi of earth. She showed me a diagram of the five elements arranged in a circle and explained that if you followed the circle clockwise, each element helped produce the next one, so wood produces fire, and fire produces earth. If you follow the circle counter-clockwise, that's the reductive cycle, earth reduces fire, and fire reduces wood. The elements also dominate elements they are opposite of, so fire dominates metal. But you never use domination to achieve balance, because it only increases the imbalance.

She said Jacob's house was already very balanced in all the elements, so she doubted the environment was keeping him here. But if he was trapped in a traumatic cycle by the metal of the bullet, water might help to bring him in balance. She opened the vial of water and set it in front of the others. If the whole spirit was present, the redirection might be a simple matter of talking to Jacob.

"Prepare yourself as before," she said. "I will be your anchor to this realm." She placed her hands on my back. "I'll tell you what to say. If he's trapped in a cycle, he won't answer your questions, he'll merely repeat his gestures."

This time I moved easily into the Seer mode and opened my chest to my surroundings while keeping my Pusher active in the gut. The tingling began all over my body, the light went amber and the air around me hummed. Jacob stood right in front of me, watching me intently, gray-colored, both there and not there. The tingling turned to an itch. Athena seemed to feel that and told me to use more of my Pusher. When I clenched my abdominal muscles, a balm to the itch spread through my body.

"Are you Jacob Johnson?" I asked.

He nodded.

"We honor you and your home," I said as Athena instructed. "We come in peace and we want to help. We humbly ask that you move on to the next realm. Your journey here is done. Your physical body has dispersed. We will care for your things so that you can move on."

The particles that comprised him loosened and reassembled, like static fraying a picture. He shook his head and pointed to his right where the kitchen table lay in pieces on the floor.

"Did Michael Wright shoot you?" He nodded his head, looking relieved. "Do you need justice?" He shook his head, fingered the hole in his upper chest and neck area, and pointed again.

"You are worried developers are going to destroy your house?" He shook his head again. My eyes got blurry and my whole body went heavy. I rubbed my eyes. The darkness felt so good. "Do you need Michael Wright to confess?" He shook his head and wrung his hands. He didn't seem to know what he needed, and neither did I.

"That's enough," Athena said. "Thank him and tell him we'll do our best to rectify the situation." I did this and closed my eyes, letting the Pusher take over. My hearing returned to normal. When I opened my eyes, it was dark. The sun had sunk, with only the candle flame providing light. "Your energy is flagging. We mustn't overdo it. That's when spirits can attach themselves to us."

When I told her what Jacob had indicated, she pondered in silence. "Something else is keeping him here," she said. "Whatever it is, it's not in the house. And it seems that he has most of his faculties." We walked out of the house. There was nothing in the immediate surroundings that he could have been pointing to, just an open field and the highway going back toward town.

"Sometimes family members hold onto their loved ones without knowing it," she said when we got outside.

"But he was the last of his family," I said.

A realization hit me so hard that I stopped in my tracks. "If Jacob is here, then what is inside Damian?"

"Right," she said. We walked back to the car in silence, turning things over. Something very small was scurrying around in circles in the parking lot ahead of us. A mouse? Two cars passed by, and I held my breath thinking they'd flatten it. Miraculously they missed. As we got closer we saw that it *was* a mouse. Its eyes were huge, and the tip of its tail was bloody.

"What's wrong with it?" I asked. I was afraid to catch it in my hands, so I tried to use my feet to steer it off the pavement, but it ran into my feet, stopped for a second as if stunned, then circled and ran into my feet again.

Athena shook her head, pulled out her silk handkerchief, scooped it up, and let it go into the grass. It dove into the darkness between the brown blades. I imagined how the darkness soothed its nerves.

"That was weird," I said.

Athena nodded and looked back at the house.

"What about Michael Wright?" I asked. "Could he be holding onto J?"

"That's an excellent possibility," Athena said with a lilt of excitement. "We must pay him a visit as soon as possible. I'll track him down and make the arrangements."

She dropped me off at my house and hugged me goodbye. "You

did an excellent job. Now get some sleep and call me in the morning."

Up in my room, I pulled the blue horse out of the cigar box on my shelf where I'd hidden it, and held it in my hand. I was not imagining it: the horse vibrated with energy that could be none other than my father's.

35
MISTAKE

DECEMBER 22, 2016

But when I called Athena the next morning, she told me she had to leave for a day or two. "One of our initiates in New York City is experiencing a crisis. I have to help resolve it."

"You're leaving?" A sense of betrayal snagged at my gut.

"I'm sorry. It's unavoidable."

Was that alarm I sensed in her voice?

"I'll get back as soon as possible," she added, her voice warmer.

"But—"

"Keep practicing the management of your vision and studying those books I lent you. Damian will be okay. And don't do anything with him before I return. Under no circumstances are you to attempt a redirection without me."

"I wouldn't dream of it," I said.

I called Samantha to tell her what we'd found at the house behind All-Mart. She would be so psyched. But she didn't answer my texts or phone calls. With Athena gone, Sam unavailable, and Damian unapproachable, I was in limbo. I hate limbo, especially on snowless winter days when clouds seamlessly wad the sky and the sun is only a murky suggestion of light. I decided it wouldn't hurt if I visited the house alone. I could protect myself using the silk, my boots, and my Pusher. Maybe Jacob had left behind some physical clues.

My mom wanted me to do errands, so she lent me the car. After a smattering of snow in early December, it hadn't snowed in weeks. The promise of a white Christmas was as distant as the sun, and the ground was hard and bare. Winter was always dark, but without snow, the darkness was relentless, and summer's abundance was now as choppy and tangled as a bad haircut. Around Jacob's house, spindly trunks of fallen sumac trees snarled in the twisted brown grass, and the limbs of the lone oak next to the house curled like arthritic hands with thick knuckles. But the house itself almost welcomed me, or I welcomed it. Moss at the lower corners of the house was the only spot of green in the otherwise dead landscape. How could moss stay green in all this cold? The windows of the house reflected the colorless sky.

Using a silk scarf, I pushed open the rattling door, surprised to find it colder inside than outside.

As soon as the door opened, mumbling reached my ear. Synapses all over my body shot from forty watts to a thousand. Someone or something was here. Whispered syllables tripped over themselves, rasping the velveteen coils of my inner ears. I checked my Pusher and Seer. They were inactive, so I knew I wasn't causing the noise. Erratic brushing sounds, like someone sweeping the floor, emanated from the kitchen. My heart clenched, and a shot of pain zigzagged through my body. I took a deep breath and tried to calm myself. With the next breath, my Pusher filled my belly and lungs, those warm lion paws embracing my hips. Inside their embrace, fear modulated itself into a pleasant vibration of—was it? Yes. Excitement.

I snuck toward the kitchen, rolling my feet from outside to inside to keep the noise down while my Seer opened as airy as artisanal bread. When I rounded the corner into the kitchen, I was stunned to find Damian on his hands and knees, running his hands back and forth over the floor as if looking for something.

"Damian!" I cried before I thought better of it. My Pusher evaporated for an instant, leaving me a frail husk, and then returned with a growl of hostility.

He looked up from the floor with those hematite eyes, then stood wiping his hands on his back pockets. He was decked out in brand name clothes I didn't recognize, and—loafers? That was almost scarier than a ghost, as far as I was concerned. The huge black screen of an Apple watch bulged from his delicate wrist. The Damian I knew could tell time without needing to look at a watch, and he never would have spent the money on an Apple watch.

"*Why* do you keep following me *around?*" A note of sorrow rang through his open hostility.

Mentally I put a hand on my Pusher, stroking it as if it were indeed a large cat. I took a deep breath, trying to remember what I was supposed to do. My mind whirred mechanistically through what I had learned, but that seemed to be sending me further out of the room, away from reality. *Right—I can't solve this with my intention or my rational mind*, I reminded myself. I must use the Seer. My body. My whole complex web of chi already contained the knowledge of the universe, Athena had said. I needed to get my ego out of the way and trust my chi.

"I'm going to help you," I said, skirting him and keeping to the periphery of the kitchen until I stood near the cast-iron sink that hulked on a two-by-four frame.

He seemed to forget me and he knelt back to the floor, muttering again, rubbing his hands, blue from cold, across it.

Athena said I should not attempt a redirection by myself, but she hadn't said anything about trying to summon Damian back to the surface. Whatever was inside him seemed to have taken over. If I could help Damian get back on top again, maybe that would give us the time and information we needed to find out what possessed him.

The cold of the house had been penetrating my bones, and now it shook my core. I watched my breath puff upwards before me. I held my breath a moment, warming it in my lungs, and, when I exhaled, I imagined the warmth radiating through my body. My Pusher came back, heavy paws embracing my abdomen. Athena said I needed an anchor. It would protect me.

I took another deep breath and sent my own warmth back to myself. I stroked my Pusher and felt it hug me tighter. I thanked the Pusher for its warmth and stability as I breathed again. The lion's stony claws glowed like iron in the fire. I breathed again; the claws melted. My lungs ballooned outward, more elastic and expansive with each breath. What a wonderfully easy feeling it was. My spirit expanded and unfolded its filmy arms to encompass the muttering figure who groped the floor between the scattered limbs of the broken table.

First I felt the grinding inside him like rocks being pressed together by a massive force. It was a terrible pressure, an angry, dominating pressure that approached the level of sound, a guttural growl as if a giant straight out of Norse myth was grinding his stony teeth with an insatiable hunger. My Pusher grabbed my gut again, and I stroked it down.

Go into the mouth of it, between the teeth, a calm voice in my mind said. The rocks ground and grit fell hard and fast, bits of quartz, granite, and mica piling below. I breathed again, and when I exhaled, I tried to send a small spike of breath between the grinding rocks, and there!—a glimpse—the scent of green river, a hint of hemlock—a fragment of Damian!—but it was gone as fast as I perceived it, ground out by that gritty force.

My scalp prickled. Ah—the Changer was coming online. *Go into the heart of it, through the teeth of it*, that voice said again. I inhaled deeply, but this time, I sent my exhalation upward, through the crown of my head. My spine adjusted itself, found its perfect balance, and elongated. I inhaled again, drawing a cool tongue of blue down from the heavens through my scalp, and when I exhaled, I sent myself up through the atmosphere to the stars.

There I was, in outer space, breathing in the blackness of the universe and the silvery light of the stars. I was no longer Julie Sykes, but the stuff of stars and clay, a river of energy that had flowed for more than nineteen years through a particular set of riverbanks called my body. I expanded with silvery, connective energy. It was joy. So this was what they meant when they said, *God is love*: the creative energy of the universe is akin to human joy. Joy holds it all together. Joy powers it. Joy *is* stars, galaxies, and infinite space.

My hands reached out and grabbed Damian's hands, and a lightning bolt of joy arced through my body straight between the teeth of his juggernaut, pushing the rocks apart. Damian's spirit came gushing through, a great living flood of green, hemlock-tinged water, pouring glassily and abundantly over the dam. In the next instant, Pusher, Changer, and Seer folded and vanished. And there I was sitting on the linoleum floor, my hands grasping Damian's forearms and his grasping mine. When I looked into his eyes, I fell into their dark blue night, that starry expansiveness where I'd discovered that creative energy is the same as joy.

"Julie Sykes," he hugged me to him as if we'd been separated for years, holding me hard, fully present.

I clamped my arms around him and fit my body into his like we were two interlocking gears.

He grasped my shoulders and pushed me back to look into my face. "I don't know where I've been. I've been caught under the most oppressive weight."

"You're back," I said.

He exhaled heavily as he hugged me again. "But I've been trying to reach you, trying to reach anything. It was so tangled and heavy. I was so lost. And I've been watching this other part of me do— terrible things. I couldn't stop it." His body shook. I rubbed his arms and back vigorously. "I've been full of this huge anger, and at the same time I felt so cocky."

"Let's get out of here. So much has happened since you've been —gone." I helped him to his feet, and we staggered down the hallway. Outside, watery sunlight pricked my eyes, surprising me. How could it be the same day? How could the sun be in the same place when the universe had shifted?

I pulled him toward my mother's car as fast as our legs could carry us, but he seemed as weak as I felt. My limbs were loose and shaky from the energy weave I had unintentionally performed. He fell into the passenger seat, and I slammed the door and ran around to the driver's side. As I drove, heat blasting, I tried to explain everything to him as quickly as possible, how I had met Athena, what she said about my visions. He smiled weakly when I told him that.

"See, I knew you were something special," he said.

I told him how she was training me, and what we'd found only yesterday at Jacob's house. Yesterday seemed miles and months distant. I explained how I had originally thought that Jacob's spirit was possessing him, but that Jacob's spirit was still in the house, and that Jacob's energy was calm and tree-like, not at all like the hot rocks I had found grinding inside Damian.

He told me how he'd watched himself buy that car and new clothes, and hang out with people he didn't like, how he found himself picking fights. He said he'd been cruel to his mother and brothers. A part of him was so aggrieved and ashamed at his behavior, that it made him weaker, less able to fight this thing that possessed him.

"Do you have any clue what it is?" I asked. "It's definitely not Jacob." I glanced over at him quickly, not wanting to take my eyes off the road. He was leaning back in exhaustion, chin tilted upward, eyes closed. "And I don't know why it picked you," I said, "and not me or Jonathan or Sam. I'm not sure where it is now, or if I expelled it."

Damian looked over at me. "It's not gone," he said, "I can feel it inside—in the background. I'm glad I know what's going on now because I can fight it better." He bowed his head as if concentrating.

I clutched his arm. "Don't talk anymore, Damian. Don't exhaust yourself."

Damian's eyes took on the unfocused look of someone scanning their interior.

"Oh Jesus," he curled forward like he had a massive stomach cramp. "I don't know how long I can keep it—" Then he went limp, his head knocking against the side window. I pulled over.

"Help," I screamed at the air. I shook him and pushed him upright in his seat. But his eyes slid back under his eyelids.

"Wake up," I screamed, pulling uselessly at his arm, "Damian, you've got to wake up! Help!" I fumbled with my phone, but my fingers were shaking too badly. I threw it down, started the car, and drove as fast as I could without killing anyone to the hospital.

36
EMERGENCY ROOM

DECEMBER 22, 2016

At the emergency room they pumped me for information as they laid him on a gurney and rolled him into the hospital —was he on drugs, did he eat anything? What was I going to say, *No, he's possessed*?

I sat in the waiting room for a few minutes, buffeted by a storm of self-blame for having gone against Athena's instructions, wondering what I had done wrong. I hadn't meant to do a redirection. One thing just led to another. The hospital's cheery wallpaper, framed pictures of flowers, and brightly upholstered chairs seemed alien, as if made without the human touch. A great gulf had opened between me and the rest of the world.

There were so many delicate choices and perceptions during an energy weave. It was so confusing. How could I have thought I could do it on my own? I *hadn't* been thinking. That was the problem. I had seen Damian was in danger, and instinct took over.

I remembered some of Athena's advice on cultivating mindfulness. "Don't try to change yourself or quiet your mind. Domination increases resistance. Simply observe what is going on. It will shrink to its proper size if you look at it and stay present."

I looked at it—the fear, the guilt. I stopped trying to analyze my motives and my moves. I had made a mistake. *Accept it*, I told myself. Athena was right. My guilt quivered and shrank as I became aware that I was essentially okay. A few minutes later I got over myself long enough to remember to call Damian's mother, my mother, and Sam.

Dolores Quinn arrived in a panic, still wearing her house slippers and a large, nubbly sweater, towing Carl and Sid behind.

"Oh, my God," she said, hugging me tearfully. The enormous weight of her need engulfed me also. "Thank God someone was with him. I knew something was terribly wrong, but I didn't know what to do."

Carl slouched toward the vending machine and stared at the lighted snacks, hands in pockets, his face illuminated green in the glow. Sidney clung to his mother's hand.

"Oh, I wish his father were here," she said, wringing her hands. "But he doesn't care." Her voice turned acidic. I shifted uncomfortably. Was she going to get way too personal again?

"I'm sorry," was all I could think to say. I steered her over to the front desk. "This is Mrs. Quinn."

The receptionist checked her computer. "They will be moving your son out of intensive care into critical care shortly, and then you will be able to see him."

"Critical care?" Mrs. Quinn gasped.

"That's good news. It means they still need to keep a close eye on him, but the immediate crisis is over," the receptionist said.

"Oh, thank you," Mrs. Quinn said, beginning to cry. "I had to bring my other boys with me. I've got no one else to look after them."

"That's fine," the receptionist said. "You may all have a seat in the waiting room. We'll call you. The children can't come into your son's room, though, until we know what the problem is."

"Oh, dear. Will you stay with them?" she said, looking at me.

"Of course."

She linked her arm through mine as if we were old friends. Sid, after glancing across the room at a box of toys in the corner a few times, decided it was worth letting go of his mother's hand to check it out. He sat beside the box and lifted one toy out after the other, laying them in neat rows on the carpet, as if taking inventory.

"It has been so hard on Damian since his father left. He has had to be the man of the house. I'm afraid I have depended on him too much. Maybe that's why he got sick. Too much responsibility." She pulled a rosary out of her bag and began fingering it, whispering a prayer.

"Don't blame yourself."

"What's gotten into him? That car! How could he spend money on that car when we need so much? He has always been my golden child. My jewel. And now the fights and arrests? I would expect that of Carl. Not Damian. Never Damian."

I glanced nervously at Carl. He pretended to ignore her as usual.

"He has been so cruel to me lately." Her eyes watered and she rummaged in her purse for a tissue. "Tell me honestly, Julie. Is he doing drugs?"

"No! Damian? Never." But then, he wasn't fully Damian right now, I thought.

"If something happens to him, I'll be lost. Who will handle Carl?" She fingered her rosary again and dabbed her eyes with a balled-up tissue. "He was only ten when his father left, poor boy. Do you think that's what it is?" She eyed me eagerly, her sticky energy making it hard for me to breathe.

"I really don't know," I said.

"It's all their father's fault. All the boys have problems because of him. Sid wets the bed. Carl fails at school. Do you think their father cares?" She spoke rapidly as if anger was a place made safe by its familiarity, a conveyer belt that pulled her mindlessly along. "Do you think he ever visits? So what if he lives in California? He makes enough money to fly here. But no. He's too busy. New wife. New business. No wonder Damian won't take his calls. Serves him right."

But in the blink of an eye, she switched from aggressor to victim. "I should call him right now. But I can't. Will you call him for me?"

"Me?"

"Please, I can't talk to him. He won't believe me. He'll think I'm trying to get more money from him. Here's his number," she scribbled on a scrap of paper and pressed it into my palm.

"Mrs. Quinn," called the receptionist. "You can see your son now."

"Julie," my mother said like my name weighed a ton as she rushed into the waiting room. She practically pounced on me. Inexplicably irritated, I looked up from the worn picture book I was reading to Sidney. He had brought it to me and asked me to read, and as we plowed through the pages, he had surreptitiously climbed into my lap, smelling slightly of unwashed hair and dirty socks. Carl slumped in a chair across from us, secretly listening.

"How is he?"

"Well, he has stabilized, so that's good news," I said, putting on a smile intended to keep the boys calm.

"Hello, boys," my mother smiled and patted Carl's knee.

Mrs. Quinn came back into the reception area. When they shook hands, I was struck by the contrast between them. My mother was older, lighter-colored, and stronger, but also more privileged-looking. Damian's mother was frail and needy, but somehow, more worldly and looked to be not quite forty. She must have had Damian as a teenager. Mrs. Quinn explained to the boys that Damian was stable and sleeping, so there was nothing more to do but go home and return in the morning. She pulled me aside and filled me in on what was really going on, that he was in a coma and the doctors were mystified. The automatic doors of the emergency room parted for us as we all walked out into the parking lot together, tensing against the cold.

"Please," Mrs. Quinn whispered, as she hugged me goodbye, "Call Damian's father. Do me this one favor. He should be here."

My mom and I stood by our car watching the Quinn family pull out of the parking lot in their rusty car.

"Oh, honey," my mother said, leaning toward me with arms outstretched. I accepted her hug and hugged her back. The solidity of our bodies felt good. She might not accept me or understand me, she might be rigid and stand between me and the memory of my father, but she had clothed me, cared for me, and loved me. She had been a good mother. After we got into the car my mother asked, "How is he really?"

"Not well—they said his white blood count is through the roof, that his body is fighting something, but they don't know what. He's in some kind of coma. They're going to test him for flu, pneumonia, mono, epilepsy—even cancer and keep him in the hospital until they know what it is."

"I'm so sorry, sweetheart." She patted my knee as we pulled out of the parking lot. We drove silently the rest of the way home. A thick dusting of snow had fallen since we'd entered the hospital. All the houses slept peacefully, most strung with white lights, a few with old-fashioned colored lights, and one with a large electric menorah in the front yard. They looked so normal, so happy. I wished I lived in one of them.

"I'll make you a snack," she said, as we pulled into the driveway.

"I'm not hungry," I said, slogging up the stairs behind her.

"When was the last time you ate?" she asked.

I threw my coat over the coat tree by the front door and headed for my room.

"Julie, wait," she said.

I turned back in irritation.

"Come, sit here for a second." She gestured to the kitchen table.

"What?" I said, sitting down into one of the creaky chairs.

"I'm worried about you. This is a hard time in any kid's life, but with Damian ill and all your questions about your father—" she cut herself short and paused. "I'd like you to see a therapist."

I snorted. "I don't need a therapist."

"Well, I think you do. You haven't been sleeping well or eating well, and I think you're taking on too much responsibility for Damian's well-being."

Rage flared up, warming my neck and back, but I squeezed it still.

"Mom, you really don't understand."

"Well, help me to understand, then."

"I've got to help Damian."

"He needs doctors."

"He needs me!"

"He needs you to be sane," she shot back.

I ran my thumbnail along the crack in the table where the additional leaves could be added. If she and I were going to have a real relationship, and if I was going to do what was necessary to help Damian, there was only one good option: tell her the truth. Tell her that the situation was dire, tell her all about Athena and learning to be an adept, and tell her that Damian was possessed.

"Tell me what's going on," she said.

"You won't believe me," I said.

"I'll try."

Where was a good place to start? I mean, how do you tell someone something like this? Someone who doesn't believe?

"Mom, remember that time when Aunt Peggy came to our house with her husband?"

"Yes."

"Remember how I freaked because I said he had worms?"

"Yes."

"Remember that time I asked you why you had lines around your head?"

"What does this have to do with—"

"I've been trying to tell you that I've been seeing things all my life."

"I don't want to talk about this. I don't see what this has to do with—"

"It has everything to do with what's wrong with Damian. He's possessed and if I don't help him, he will die."

She dropped her head into her hands and shook it. "This can't be happening again."

"Mom, you said you wanted me to tell you. I'm trying to, but you won't listen."

"Look, I don't know where you got all these ideas, but it's all nonsense!"

"It's not nonsense. It's my life. It's my whole life. It's the core of who I am." The words came fast, fluid, now. "Why can't you accept that? For once?"

"Because it's not healthy."

"You tell me you want me to let you in, and when I do, you say, I'm not healthy."

"I'm trying to support you."

"If you want to support me, listen to me," I said, jumping out of my chair. "See me, goddamn it." I was bent over, forcing the words straight from my gut. "See me for who I really am."

"I do, but I can't do it blindly. If you're making bad decisions or going to jump off a cliff, I have an obligation to stop you."

"Do you have any idea what it was like growing up with this message—this unspoken message—that you totally don't accept me as I am?"

"Julie, I love you. I accept you, but—"

"I give up. You're the one who needs therapy," I said.

I turned on my heel and ran to my room.

37
FATHERS

DECEMBER 23, 2016

In the morning, my body was heavy, like my blood had been replaced with sand. My bed was no comfort at all. Instead of a warm safe place, it was tangled and empty. I'd had dreams that my father was walled into a stone tower. At least, I think that's what it was. All I could see were his hands pounding on the rock walls. But I knew it was him. When I awoke, the cigar box that held his blue ceramic horse was on the floor, and the horse had tumbled out. Maybe the sound of it falling is what had made me dream of my father pounding the walls of a tower. But what had made it fall?

Afraid it was broken, I leapt out of bed and picked it up. Its solid weight was a comfort to my hand. It was intact. Also inert. No vibrations whatsoever. When I set it back into its box on the shelf, a wrinkled piece of paper caught my attention, shoved into the crack between the shelf and wall, right behind it. No way was it there before. I pulled it out. It was a black-and-white photograph—a portrait of a man, but mildew mottled the image of the face so much that I couldn't make out who it was.

Wonder and fear lifted me and set me down like an ocean wave. Could this be a picture of my father? How had it gotten here?

Once I was fully awake, only two things mattered. Damian was in the hospital, and I had put him there. Next to that, everything—the heaviness of my body, the horse on the floor, this crumpled picture, were all meaningless.

The thought that Athena would be gone for a few days made my head ache. In the kitchen, the cereal clinked hollowly into the bowl. I stared at it, not hungry at all. When my mother entered the room, she snapped the light on, surprising me. I hadn't realized I was sitting in the darkness. She brushed her hand lightly across my back as she passed me to get to the electric kettle. I loved her for not giving up on me even when I was angry.

Damian's mother called me to give me the update. He was on monitors. His white blood cell count was still elevated, but all his other vitals were normal. They didn't know why he hadn't regained consciousness. They did all the tests, including an MRI to see if there was a tumor in his brain but found nothing. The doctors were mystified.

I called Samantha and we met at Uncommon. When she arrived with Jonathan behind, she looked gray and listless. The eyeliner was on thick again making her eyes look like black holes from across the room.

"What's up?" I asked.

"My mom's using," she said. "She says she's not, but she is."

"My God. How do you know?"

"Her pupils are dilated all the time, and she talks too long and does this little junky dance. You can tell."

"She's twitching," Jonathan said by way of explanation.

"I'm really sorry," I said.

"Enough about me, tell me what happened to Damian."

I explained how I'd found him at Jacob's house—how I'd seen Jacob's spirit with Athena the day before— how it couldn't be Jacob possessing Damian.

"It *must* be Jacob's murderer," Sam said.

"Shh! Don't say his name," I said. "In any case, Michael Wright is still alive."

"Then maybe it's another spirit," Sam said.

"This is turning out to be the nightmare before Christmas," Jonathan said.

No one smiled.

Damian's mother called later that day to say that the doctors had determined that he didn't have anything contagious, and they encouraged visitors to keep him company.

"The doctors believe that it helps to talk to him, even though he's unconscious. But I can't be there the whole time. Will you visit him as much as possible?" she asked.

"Absolutely," I said, glad to have a purpose.

Winter had finally dumped twelve inches of snow during the night. It swaddled the world, muting traffic noise, and filling our apartment with its bright light. The hospital had polished floors, textured wallpaper, and no smell of the disinfectant that you might expect. A tabletop Christmas tree and string of cards adorned the nurses' station. With my 'Totally Normal' Julie Sykes mask firmly in place, I walked into Damian's room. But the sight of Damian in bed made me want to run. His body was too flat under the blanket, and his olive skin tone looked like a surface color applied to a pasty patient, contrasting with the white and blue print of his hospital gown. His right hand was bruised greenish-blue where the IV needle had been attached. He had four wires attached to his chest by suction cups, and an oxygen and pulse monitor attached to the index finger of his left hand.

I inhaled deeply.

"Damian." I took his right hand. "It's Julie."

He didn't stir.

"I miss you."

Nothing. His eyelids didn't flicker. He was all wires, IV bags, and monitors.

Awkwardly at first, I began talking to him. I told him about Samantha's mother and the snowstorm. I'd never been good at small talk. I held his hand in silence for a while.

"Damian," I whispered, finally. "Your mother told me about your father. She wants me to call him. She says he won't listen to her, but that if I called, he might come. Should I?"

He gave no indication that he heard me.

When I closed my eyes and opened my chest to breathe him in, all I felt was something black and viscous, like tar bubbling in a pit. It burned my lungs and shut out all air.

It had been so long since we had talked about normal things. I missed his grace and subtlety. I missed how the sound of his voice reverberated in my chest. I missed the urge to tell him my deepest secrets, my weirdest and most whimsical thoughts. A hundred invisible strings of memory pulled at me. Then, for some reason, the crinkled, mildewed picture I'd found that morning popped into my head. I told Damian how strange it was that the box had fallen off the shelf, and how I thought the picture might be of my father. His eyes moved under their lids. That decided me. If I was sick, I'd want my father by my side. If I called Damian's father, it put the ball in his father's court. It gave him the opportunity to do the right thing. The rest was up to him. On the way out of the hospital, I stopped in a quiet alcove, fished out the paper Damian's mother had written the number on, and dialed. I was relieved when he didn't pick up.

"You know what to do," a male voice with an Irish accent said before the beep.

"Mr. Quinn," I said as firmly as I could, "this is Julie Sykes. I'm a good friend of your son, Damian. He is very ill. He's in the hospital here in Saratoga Springs in a coma. *You* know what to do."

38
ATHENA RETURNS

DECEMBER 23, 2016

Within minutes of when Athena called to say she'd returned, I was on her doorstep. It was only 4 o'clock, but the sun was nearly down. She opened the door immediately. She was different. The lines on her face, which I'd never particularly noticed before, were deeper. Her eyes sank into her eye sockets which had a bluish hue. All this time, she had been the strong teacher and I the overwhelmed student. I forgot my concerns about Damian in my alarm for her. I was embarrassed that this was the first time I wondered how *she* was.

"Are you okay?" I asked.

"I'm fine. I'll explain another time. But you," she said, registering what must have been my own frazzled appearance and reaching for both my hands with hers, "you look like you have had a great shock. What happened?" She pulled me into the high-ceilinged foyer. Her staccato consonants cut through my wall of frozen emotions, and set things slowly, painfully, in motion.

Different feelings struggled for dominance. I couldn't name

them, only feel their texture and weight—sawdust and beef bone. How could I tell her what I had done? Would she be angry? Or worse, disappointed?

She ushered me out into the conservatory. The humid air enveloped us, rich with the scent of peat moss and jasmine, gentling my frayed emotions.

"When you find yourself at the bottom, and can sink no farther, turn to the earth," she said, pressing my hands into the garden bed at the center of the conservatory out of which surged a jungle of trees and vines. The soil was loose, black, warm, and just the right level of moist. "The earth can withstand all your grief and anger. I learned this from the Mohawk elder Tom Porter," she said. "Its balance of order and disorder, its genius for variation from lichen to mountain ranges will always ground and restore you. Depend on it."

I stood there absorbing the soil's rich messages. Crystalline light refracted from the snow outside and intensified the greens and browns. Broad banana tree leaves curved overhead, taupe tree trunks restored my vertical depth perception, and lime sprays of maidenhair fern speckled the horizontal planes. Life, which had become so flat, popped open into three dimensions. The plants' sheer physicality and full occupation of geometric space opened a corresponding spaciousness inside my own body. I could breathe freely again.

With the loam surrounding my hands, a realization popped. I didn't know where my father was buried. My mother had never taken me to his grave. But also, I had never asked.

"Athena, if my father is dead, and I can see ghosts, why can't I sense him?"

She looked stricken for a moment, then recovered. "Most people pass over."

"Can a spirit choose to stay?"

"Only adepts who have attained the highest level." She tucked a strand of my hair behind my ear.

"If he was here, could I feel him?"

"With your skill? Most likely. Unless something was blocking him."

"Do you know anything about him? You said the Anima Arcanum was keeping an eye on me—did you know about me before my father died?"

"I can't say that we did," she said quietly.

"Do you sense him?"

"I'm sorry," she said, her eyes big and full of pain for me.

I was silent again. Droplets of water fell randomly to the ground throughout the greenhouse punctuating the low hum of the fan that was keeping it all warm.

"What happened?" Athena asked quietly.

"It's Damian," I finally said, a judder starting at my core. "I made a mistake." Athena gently pressed me onto a bench.

"You tried a redirection without me?"

"No—I didn't mean to—I—he showed up at the farmhouse at the same time I did. I thought it would be okay if I tried to find him in all that mess. I just wanted to touch him—to make sure he was still there." My words twisted and toppled over each other as I told her as precisely as possible what happened, the voice that told me to go through the teeth, seeing the stars, the arc of joy, how his spirit emerged, and then how he collapsed.

She was silent for a long few seconds, looking hard at one of the paving stones.

"It's alright. It's not your fault," she said at last.

I held my breath, wanting to believe her, but needing evidence.

She grasped my forearm. "You did a very good job. I am impressed by how quickly you have come along. You are well on your way to being an adept. Your intuition is powerful and accurate. Unexpected things occur routinely in these pursuits, and we must learn from them. Do not waste time blaming yourself. Blame is merely a distraction. Instead, let us carefully examine what occurred and deduce the cause."

I swallowed and nodded.

"Now, you say he was weak but okay when he first emerged."

"I think so."

"Did he touch anything on the way out of the house?"

"Well, we had to crawl under the chain-link fence." She sat silent for a moment. A drop of water from an overarching branch splattered on a paving stone near my foot. Sweat prickled my shoulders. I shrugged my coat off.

"And was it raining or snowing?"

"Neither," I said.

She was silent again. "What were you talking about right before he collapsed?"

"He said he thought he could fight it."

A light went on in her eyes as she pondered. "It's possible," she muttered.

"What's possible?"

"That he is a *sensitive*, too." She leapt up and paced back and forth. "It would make sense that you two were drawn together and that he became so easily possessed."

"Damian?" But even as I said it, I remembered how we instantly understood each other, how connected I felt even across the hallways before I knew him, how he seemed to sense more than could be seen, and finally, how he believed me.

"But he doesn't have visions like I do," I said.

"There are all different kinds of sensitivity and conductivity. Do you remember that incorporator I knew who lost his life? Damian may be an incorporator. That is, he perceives by taking the whole spirit into his body."

"But isn't that what I do?"

"No, because of your access to the Seer, the Pusher, and the Changer, you have some detachment. The energy flows through you and you spin it all together and let it pass through. Incorporators are," she paused looking for the word, "stickier inside. They physically absorb and become the spirit, rather than perceive it, and when the procedure is done correctly, they achieve balance internally.

Incorporators can often solve the most difficult cases, but at great risks to themselves, as was the case with the person who died saving my life." She gripped a carved stone that hung on a cord around her neck.

"But why didn't you know Damian was a *sensitive* when you knew I was?"

"Because I wasn't looking for it." She shook her head ruefully.

"What does this mean?" I asked.

"It complicates things. An ordinary person wouldn't know how to fight a possession. But if Damian is an incorporator, it means his body can perceive the spirit and is treating it like an infection, hence the elevated white blood cell count." The knuckles of her fists turned white. "But of course, his body can't fight the spirit on that plane, and the effort to dominate only feeds the bad energy." She stopped pacing, thinking hard, then took a deep breath and said, "This is both good and bad. If we don't redirect it, his body will fight itself to the death."

The thought nauseated me. "That's not going to happen, because we're going to stop it," I said, "right?"

"If we can solve the puzzle fast enough." She strode toward the foyer and snapped up her car keys from the side table. I followed her. "We've got to talk to Michael Wright. Come. I made the arrangements before I left. You can fill me in on your energy weave on the way over."

39
THE NURSING HOME

DECEMBER 23, 2016

Michael Wright's nursing home was a cream-colored Queen Anne mansion with mustard and red details and a round tower off to one side crowned by a red-shingled onion top. Its front porch swept from the front door to the opposite side in a curve. It had been converted for super-wealthy seniors in need of assistance. Athena had convinced them that we were distant relatives visiting him for Christmas. I loved how Athena smoothed her way into the trust of the nursing home so that they would do things they normally wouldn't do. It was the kind of thing Damian might do. Love for him pulsed through me, but my heart quickly bit down on it. It's not safe to go there, my Pusher said as we mounted broad porch stairs.

The sun had set, and the white Christmas lights between the evergreen balls with red ribbons stood out against the blue-gray dusk. We pushed open the carved wood door, but an electrical device took over, and it swung wide. A middle-aged woman in a blazer and skirt greeted us from behind a polished wooden counter with elaborate scrollwork. I paused for a moment to take in the expansive living room to my right through the arched opening, with floral couches, a million throw pillows, and bronze statuettes that held aloft lit glass globes. Fresh flower arrangements sat on myriad side tables. It was astonishing but fussy.

After we introduced ourselves, the receptionist steered us into an old-fashioned elevator with curly gold-painted grillwork. Instead of clanking and groaning like in the movies, it rose soundlessly to the second floor.

"He's been particularly agitated for the last month," the woman confided. "We put him on tranquilizers. If he seems groggy, that's why. Other than that, he's in excellent shape. Heart like a horse and the blood pressure of a teenager." *Not a teenager trying to save her boyfriend's life,* I thought.

We followed her down a wide, floral-carpeted hallway with a window at the end, ensconced in curtains, sheers, and valence. She knocked on a heavy wood door, announced us, and held the door for us.

She smiled apologetically. "He can't make sense of anything you say, but talk to him as though he does."

"We so appreciate your excellent care," Athena said as she patted her arm.

The woman left.

The only nursing home I'd ever seen was the flat, beige public one with gray linoleum that we had visited for a school community service project. It hadn't prepared me for the high four-poster bed and tasseled drapes. He had one of the tower rooms, with a circular alcove off to the side, complete with cushioned window seats. A man in his sixties or so sat in a wheelchair in the tower alcove. He was portly but still had a full head of hair and was staring out the window through sheers and mumbling to himself.

"Mr. Wright?" Athena spoke. He didn't look around, but his mumbling grew louder.

Athena moved between him and the window and put her hand

on his shoulder. "We have come to help you, if we can." He rocked from one side to the other, as if she were obstructing his view of a horse race upon which his future depended. "Come over here." Athena held out her hand to me. I stood next to her. Michael Wright's eyes seemed unable to find us. He looked at points to the right and left of us and all around the edges of us as a newborn does, and he kept straining to see out the window.

Athena put her hand on my shoulder. "Use your Seer to collect what information you can."

I examined him. His skin was dry and flaking, giving him an ashy look, but other than that, he appeared healthy.

"All my gut is telling me is that I should get out of the room."

"Practice acceptance."

I closed my eyes and let my worries rise to the surface. I didn't like treating him like a science project. I was stressed over Damian. I tried to breathe in, but that steel band cinched my lungs closed. She placed her hands on my back, and their warmth radiated to my core. After a few false starts, I was able to let all my worries fall away and take in a wonderful, loose, life-filling breath. My Seer opened, and I pulled the surroundings through the sieve of my lungs: the twirl of fibers in the heavy curtains, the spray of light, the jagged contours of Michael Wright's babble, and finally the vast space inside Michael Wright's cells. My crown tingled and opened to the sky. Love poured down through me from those silver stars and embraced the man before me. Now I understood. No matter who he was, he was a thread in the fabric of life. He served some sacred purpose. We all did. My mind spun euphorically. Pixels of light and dark buzzed, filling up my mental screen.

"What do you see?" Athena's voice was far away.

"All I get is dots, like snow on a TV screen."

"Good. Keep breathing with it. Keep your focus general and relaxed."

A line or a shape wiggled through the snow, but it dissolved before I could tell what it was.

"Does everything seem to belong together?"

"Ye-es," I said uncertainly, breathing through him again. I was starting to feel tired and my focus wavered.

"It's okay to rest," Athena said. I waited until my focus became clear again.

"Something is missing inside him—everything is missing; there's no organizing entity—no self here. It's this gritty, sandy static."

"Good. Keep at it for a few more minutes. Make sure." My body filled with pity then, and love, and the dots in his mind seemed to feel this and cohered into a blob in front of me like a school of fish. A loud sob jerked me to the surface, jolting my eyes wide open. It was Michael Wright.

"There, there, dear," Athena patted Wright's shoulder, but he was back to babbling again and looking out the window.

Athena checked his pulse. That was when I noticed his hands. They were large, with thick fingers and so dry that his fingertips were cracked. Nausea rose and fell inside me like when you drive fast over a hump.

I barely noticed her thanking him and steering me out of the room. My legs wobbled, and she assured me it was a reaction to the energy weave I had performed. "You will build more stamina with time."

We said goodbye to the woman in the lobby and went out to Athena's car. "Can a person sometimes survive when his spirit leaves his body?" I asked as I slipped into the leather passenger seat.

"It all depends on which part leaves and which part stays. From now on, we should avoid using W's whole name, until we know whether his conscious spirit is abroad. At the very least, W's body needs its physical energy to keep on living. We call that the 'corporeal spirit.' But there's another kind of energy—the part of the spirit that forms his consciousness—that appears to have left his body."

I glanced back at the house as we drove away. The Christmas

lights outlined the porch and the tower so prettily against the dark. "J isn't haunting Damian." I said. "W is."

Athena pressed the brakes. "What makes you so sure?"

"His hands. They were big and rough like the ones I felt in the Gick Road house. And I sensed no organizing entity inside the man in the hospital. Now it all makes sense. W was rich. Damian is all of a sudden acting like he's rich, his clothes, his car, who he hangs out with."

Athena nodded her head. "People can lose a piece of their souls in a traumatic event. W's pulse was floating and short, which indicates a shocking deficiency in chi."

"So his spirit could have gotten stuck in the house when he shot J?"

"At the point of death, the spirits of the living and dead *do* mingle. That's why people feel so dead when a loved one dies." The hum of the tires on wet pavement turned to a high-pitched whir as we crossed a bridge over a creek that hadn't frozen down the middle. I craned my neck to look up the dark finger of water that pressed into the snowy woods.

Athena continued: "If W shot J—"

"I'm sure he did," I said.

"—a part of his spirit might have attached itself to the bullet and bound itself with J's body. That part of the spirit which governs compassion and which produces good works might have been so at war with the rest of his spirit that it left his body. It could also be a simple case of guilt. His mind keeps returning to the scene of the crime and is trapped there."

I imagined Michael Wright struggling with Jacob Johnson in the kitchen, the explosion of the gun, the shock on both men's faces, and Jacob falling into the table.

"But what caused it to enter Damian's body?" I asked as I hugged my legs to my chest.

"Well, Damian might have incorporated it unconsciously, or his repressed anger energy was so familiar that W's spirit thought it was returning to its own body. Remember, a pre-existing imbalance in the living can draw out the dead. My guess is that W couldn't face the truth. The more he fought it, the more imbalanced his spirit got. Or maybe this part of his spirit doesn't want to be bodiless anymore, but it can't bear to return to W, so it sought out a new entity. It might work if we do an energy weave with Damian, and see if you can contact W and help him accept his guilt, then direct him back to his own body."

"Would we have to have Damian and W in the same room?"

"No, the spirit is still attached to the body."

Like those split atoms that continued to mirror each other's actions, I thought.

"If we can get Damian to stop fighting W's spirit with his body, and get W to accept his guilt, Damian will recover, and W's spirit will find its way back to his body or move on. We'll try it first thing in the morning."

"But—"

"No buts. You need to be well-rested to pull this off," Athena said as she dropped me off.

40
AT THE HOSPITAL

DECEMBER 24, 2016

It was going to be tricky performing a redirection in the hospital in the first place, but on Christmas Eve? There was no way to do it totally unobserved, and there was no way to know how long it would take. The plan was that while I was in the room with Damian, Athena would quietly keep watch and head off any hospital staff that might interfere. She'd also keep an eye on me to help me when I got into trouble. We would have to be quiet, no chanting or anything earthy-crunchy-new-agey that would call attention to ourselves. And the only feng shui we could perform would have to be in our minds. No furniture rearranging.

But when we got to his room, it was empty and the mattress was stripped. The nurses wouldn't tell us anything because we weren't family. I called home and my mother told me Mrs. Quinn had called with the good news. Damian had regained consciousness and had been moved to the regular inpatient ward. She gave me the room number and we rushed over.

He looked exhausted, and he was still hooked to an IV and a

blood oxygen monitor. But he was awake. I ran to him and clasped his hand before I had time to think.

"Damian," I whispered.

He smiled faintly. His returning grip was weak. But at least it wasn't rejection. Lava seared my heart as I grasped how depleted he was. But also, it was Damian looking out of those eyes, not Wright, not anything else.

He opened his mouth, but no sound came out. I fed him an ice cube from a paper cup on his bedside table.

"How are you feeling?" I asked.

"There was this terrible speed—everything was spinning and shaking."

"You had a fever and your white blood cells were fighting like crazy," I said.

He scanned the room and his eyes rested worriedly on the bathroom door. "Can you close that door?" he asked, as if the open door was related to the spinning.

He relaxed somewhat when I did it. He scanned the room again. His eyes came to rest on his bedside table where the top drawer was jutting an inch. I pushed it shut. He raised his arm to examine the IV bruise on his hand, looked at the ceiling, pressed his other arm to his chest, and sighed, closing his eyes. "I don't want it to start spinning again."

Athena came up behind me and put her hand on my shoulder. His eyes flickered to her and back to me questioningly.

"This is Athena, who I told you about. Remember? Anima Arcanum?"

He looked confused.

"When I found you at the house on Gick Road and drove you to the hospital?"

"It's so vague."

"I know. It's hard to believe. That was only two days ago." I reminded him how I'd found him on the floor of Jacob's house, and how he'd come back to himself, and we rushed to the car. "Athena knows how to help you."

He nodded and attempted to smile, but he was too tired to fake it.

"Hello, Damian," Athena smiled warmly. Her dry, hot energy flowed through me and into him.

"You must stop fighting the spirit inside you, Damian," Athena added. "Leave it to Julie and me."

The lines of his face tensed. "I can't stop. It's taking over," he rasped.

"Fighting it only locks you in the battle and depletes your energy."

"I don't know how to stop." His eyes were dull and washed out.

"Will you let us help you?" Athena asked.

He regarded her silently.

"She can help you relax," I told him. "It's the greatest thing. When she lays her hands on you, it radiates right to the core."

As gently and as quickly as we could, we described our visit to Michael Wright and why we thought it was Michael Wright who had possessed his body, not Jacob. His face and eyes regained some color as we talked.

"So what do I do?" he asked after we filled him in. His voice was clearer. I remembered the day we made fairy houses in the woods, how he had quietly set lichen and moss around my structure. That world was so far away and yet so close.

"Just close your eyes and let me do it," I said.

"Remember to pace yourself," Athena said to me. "This is more work than you've ever done before."

Just then, a man in street clothes walked into the room.

"Pardon me," the man said loudly, beginning to back out of the room. "I must have the wrong room." He had a pronounced Irish accent. Damian's breath caught and he coughed.

"Mr. Quinn?" I asked, my heart tripling its beat.

"That's right." I stood aside so he could see Damian. His eyes locked on Damian and he froze for an instant then forced a grin. I saw his resemblance to Carl, wide shoulders, broad face, reddish-brown hair, and freckles.

"D'you mind if I come in?" he asked Damian.

Damian eyed his father in silence and then closed his eyes for a second and reopened them.

"It's up to you," he said tonelessly.

"You've every right to toss me out, but I caught the first red-eye I could as soon as I heard."

"I don't care one way or the other," Damian said.

"I'll leave you two alone," I said, backing out of the room.

"I'd be glad if you and your mother want to stay," Damian's father said.

"She's not my—"

"Pardon. You two look so alike."

"You both need your privacy," Athena said, and left.

I was halfway through the door after her when Mr. Quinn called out, "So you're his bird, then?"

"His what?" I said.

"His mot. His girlfriend."

I blushed.

"Say no more," he grinned. "Have a seat. Your secret's safe with me. Besides, the boy looks like he needs a good, strong girl at his side. You look knackered, Damian."

Damian said nothing. I filled a cup of water for Damian and took a seat on the other side of his bed where I could watch them both.

"It's alright to hate me, lad. I know I've let you down. But that's no reason to die, now is it? Buck up, so you can give me a clatter in the jaw, at the very least. It'll do you a world of good." He picked up Damian's limp hand, curled it into a fist, and leaned his chin into it, pretending the force of it jolted his head back.

Damian pulled his hand away swiftly. "I'm not going to punch you, Dad," Damian said with a hard edge to his voice.

"Come on, I deserve it. It would make *me* feel better. To hell with you." He grinned.

"Look, I'm tired. Thanks for coming by."

Mr. Quinn's smile dropped, and his shoulders sagged.

"Seriously, though," Mr. Quinn's tone quieted and dropped a few pitches. "I *am* sorry. It scared the life out of me when I heard you were in the hospital. I didn't realize I could lose you permanently. I'd like to make it up to you, if I could."

A rumble of thunder plugged my ears and stuffed the spaces between the atoms, then died away.

"Make it up?" Damian's eyes flashed open darkly and his face turned as pale and as hard as his voice, "Make it up? You can't change the past, Dad." Moments ago he had been wasted, but now anger animated him.

"There you go. Let me have it. A little anger'll do you good."

"I'm not friggin' angry," he said as he pulled himself onto his elbows. My heart sped up. Was this Damian or Michael Wright?

"Damian," I stood and put my hand on his shoulder. An idea had begun to work itself out at the back of my mind concerning Damian's anger and Wright's spirit. "You *are* angry. Maybe if you could forgive—"

"I'd have to give a shit, to be angry," Damian said in a voice that was somehow toneless and tight at the same time. He threw back his covers and swung his legs out of bed, his eyes flashing sapphire. "And I don't. I don't give a flying fuck whether you come or go." He stood unsteadily, and his father stepped back. "You mean nothing to me." Spittle flecked his lips. All my training flew right out the window. I circled the bed and grabbed Damian's arm.

"Damian, try to stay cool," I said.

"I am cool," he snapped at me, shrugging me off. "I'm so cool I could freeze a fucking ice cube." Then, to my horror, Damian's eyes slid up under his lids and his whole body convulsed. The vitals on his monitor flashed and beeped at high speed as he fell backward into the bed.

"Christ!" Mr Quinn said. "Nurse!" He dashed out of the room.

Damian's body convulsed, rattling the bed fiercely. A voice came over the hospital monitor, "Code Blue."

People raced toward the room from all directions. I clamped onto his hand. Someone pushed me aside, but I wouldn't let go.

"I'm sorry, you've got to go."

The nurses and doctors crowded around him in their blue and green scrubs, pushing me aside more roughly this time. Knowing I was clueless, I let go and backed out of the room. A nurse pulled Mr. Quinn down the hall to the nurse's station.

My phone rang. I fished it out of my pocket. Unknown Caller. I swiped the green phone icon, and static crackled loudly over the speakerphone into the empty hall. A male voice stuttered in and out through the static. I tried to hit the audio button to get it off the speakerphone. Athena, who was standing only a few feet away, stared at the phone in alarm, her face as taut as a sheet across a hospital bed.

"What is that?" she asked.

"I don't know," I said, still jabbing the audio button, accidentally muting it, and then blasting it into the hall again. Athena grabbed my phone and stared at it. I couldn't make out the words. Then it hung up.

"Has this happened before?" she shouted at me. I was already so rattled by Damian that I froze, trying to make sense of her sudden agitation. I'd never seen this side of her before.

"Yes, once, a few weeks ago," I stuttered.

"Come with me. Right now." She pulled me toward the exit without waiting for a by-your-leave.

41
REVELATION

DECEMBER 24, 2016

"There's something you need to know," she said as she drove toward my house. "I thought it could wait, but I had no idea that it had gone this far."

"What are you talking about?"

"I've been investigating another matter—to do with the North Woods and the Skidmore property. It was once part of the estate of an ancestor of mine. Its owner has been haunting it for some time. He is dangerous and gathering strength. I have tried to redirect him many times before, but I was unsuccessful. I have managed to trap his spirit in an old well, but he has been testing the boundaries. That's what I was doing yesterday, trying to reinforce his restraints, but it's draining me, and now . . ." she tore her eyes off the Christmas-lit streets for a second to look at me, "I think he's reaching out to you."

"Me? Why me?"

"It's time for you and your mother to have that talk I wanted you to have."

She pulled into our drive and swung out of the car, slamming the door behind in one fluid movement, and strode toward our door.

I jumped out after her. "You're going to tell my mother?" My gloves fell out of my lap into the snow, but I was in too much of a rush to pick them up.

"No, she's going to tell you."

I unlocked the lower door and led her up the stairs to our apartment.

My mother, who was standing at the kitchen table over a mess of wrinkled papers, looked up as I entered.

"Julie," she said, holding up what appeared to be a wrinkled photograph, "Did you put these here?" As soon as Athena entered behind me, my mother's whole body went rigid. "You," she said as if accusing a murderer.

"Audrey," Athena said.

"You two know each other?" I asked.

My mother exhaled so sharply her breath hissed.

"It's time for the truth, Audrey. Your daughter needs the truth."

"Ha! That's a laugh, you charging into my house talking about truth," my mother sneered. I didn't know she could sound so mean.

"Julie is a *sensitive*. There is nothing you can do to change that reality," Athena said.

"Reality?" my mother spat. My head snapped back and forth between them. Anger had chiseled my mother's face to stone.

"Tell her, Audrey, about her father."

That word paralyzed me, sent me out of my body. For a fraction of a second I was standing next to myself, looking at the three of us bound by sizzling lines into a fraught triangle, thinking, *Now here's a moment I will never, ever forget.*

"Tell me what?" I said, snapping back into my body and driving my words like a spear into my mother—this Audrey— I'd never known, apparently. She glanced at me in panic, then fixed her eyes with hatred on Athena.

"How dare you tell me what to do with my only child?"

"Julie has agreed to train to be an adept," Athena said.

"What?" My mother turned on me, but Athena kept talking.

"She's talented, but she can't achieve balance unless she knows all the elements she's dealing with."

"How long has this been going on, Julie?"

"A couple of—" I started to say.

"You're hurting her by keeping the truth from her," Athena bulldozed on.

"What truth?" I asked, looking back and forth between the two of them.

"Hurting her! I'm trying to protect her," my mother said.

"But it's having the opposite effect." Athena focused now on the kitchen table and rushed over to it for a closer look. "He's back, then." Six black-and-white photos lay wrinkled across the table, some looking as if a person had wadded them up, and others were rippled with water damage.

"I don't—that's what I was going to—Did you put these here?" my mother asked Athena accusingly.

I crowded in behind Athena. One was the same photo I'd found wedged behind the cigar box on my shelf, a black-and-white portrait of a man in a suit, his face occluded by mist or mildew. Another photo was of a little girl in the arms of a man whose face was only a blur of light. Another was a photo of a sepia-toned portrait of a man with white hair.

"Mom?" I turned to her in disbelief. "Will you please tell me what's going on?"

"I have no idea," she said. "I thought you—"

"He's back, Audrey," Athena said. "You know who is back, and he's trying to get to Julie. I've been holding him back, but he's getting stronger. I need her help. And to do that, she needs to—"

"Do you know who this lunatic is?" my mother said to me. "She killed your father."

"What?" I said, reeling backward like I'd been slapped in the face.

Ice, burning as it froze, rushed up to my head and down to my feet as I stood motionless, waiting for Athena to deny or affirm.

"It's not true," Athena said quietly. "He was my brother. I loved him. He was an incorporator. But the owner of that estate," she was careful not to say his name, "was too powerful. He siphoned off your father's energy and now, he appears to be reaching beyond. There's no way of knowing, but I wouldn't be surprised if the new white supremacy club on the Skidmore campus and the new trend of ostentatious parties off campus is a result of his energy getting out."

I thought of Payton's boasting and the Trump virus that seemed to have swept the country. Could they be connected?

"Your father became obsessed with this ancestor, and it was clear that the spirit was making him sick. Then I felt it trying to pull me in, as well. So, I called in two other experts from Anima Arcanum. On the night we performed the redirection, something went wrong. Your father attacked me. He was choking me, but then—I don't know what happened," she halted. "He died. And that's what saved me."

"It was an aneurysm," Audrey said.

"That was the medical diagnosis. But I think he willed it. I think it was the only way he could get the spirit to let go of me. If we don't face the cause of the aneurysm, more people will get hurt. That spirit wants all of his family back, and that's why I *had* to get in touch with you," she turned to my mother. "He is still coming after me, he's still holding onto Peran's spirit, and I just found out he's been trying to contact Julie. These pictures confirm it."

My mind tumbled through a razor patch of questions shooting in all directions. "So *he* was the incorporator you told me about who died? And you're my—aunt?"

"Yes."

"But how come your last name is Todd?"

"I was married briefly and," she paused, "disastrously."

"Why didn't you tell me this before?" I shouted.

"I didn't want to overstep—"

Betrayal is like a tidal wave that knocks you over, grinds your head in the sand, and lets you go. When it recedes, it pulls all the love and connection you ever had out of you. The next wave that comes in to replace it is a bitter knowledge that goes all the way back to the first man: people are not to be trusted and you have been a fool for ignoring what you have wordlessly known all along, and that you would never let anyone in ever again.

"Ha!" my mother exclaimed. "You contact my daughter, fill her head with all kinds of crap, start training her to become some kind of exorcist, and you don't want to *overstep*? Julie, these people are crazy. The stuff they teach has absolutely *no basis* in fact. Your father was mentally ill. He suffered from schizophrenia and bouts of psychosis." She was seething.

"That is not true," Athena shouted and stamped her foot. Where was the cool, calm master?

"Yes, it *is* true. He was on medication, and you know it," my mother shot back.

"Sure, he was on medication. Sensitives often have what Western culture calls mental illness. These powers are hard to handle, and they often take a toll. I do not claim to have a monopoly on truth. But you are betraying your daughter when you refuse to listen to her and validate her version of life and keep her from knowing her father."

That much was true. I glared at my mother.

"*They* say he was possessed, but to me, it looked like he had a psychotic break. He needed psychiatric help, medication, and institutionalization. *They* wouldn't let him go to the hospital."

"You saw the pictures, Audrey, how they changed. Tell her what really happened. Tell her why you destroyed them all."

"God damn it!" My mother shouted and swept the pictures off the table, turning her back to me.

We all stood in silence, panting with spent emotion.

Then my mother slumped. She sat heavily at the kitchen table and rubbed the spot between her brows.

"Please," I said.

She thought in silence for what seemed like forever, then finally spoke in a monotone.

"After he died, all the pictures of him changed. At first, I thought they had somehow gotten mildewed. But it was every single one, all the ones in picture frames, all the ones in storage. Even the pictures online. It was bizarre. Then one night, I found one of the pictures in your bed, and it wasn't mildewed. It was a different face. White hair, white handlebar mustache. That's when I decided to destroy them all. I took them all out back and set them on fire. And for good measure, I tossed in everything your father owned, his ties, his socks, his wallet, everything. I'm not saying I believe anything he or Athena told me, but the safest thing to do was destroy anything that might connect you to this—thing. I vowed to raise you so that you couldn't be influenced."

Anger swelled in me and warmed my body, shutting out the shock. "You both betrayed me," I said, my voice shaking with the effort not to shout. "I asked you if you knew my father and you said—"

"I said I couldn't say," interrupted Athena, "which is technically the truth. I wasn't allowed to. I had to wait for your mother to tell you. It's protocol."

"Technically?" I said sarcastically. "I can't believe this. How could you keep this from me?" I glared at my mother, at them both.

"I was trying to stop this from happening—all this. I was trying to protect you," my mother said.

"More like manage me and manipulate me!" I shouted. I looked at Athena, whom I had so idealized. What if she was crazy? What if the Animus Arcanum was a figment of her imagination? Or some kind of cult, and she was taking advantage of what turned out to be my mental illness. Cults did that kind of thing. And my father had been mentally ill, too. Schizophrenic, my mother said. The whole world teetered out of balance. Everyone I knew had turned out to be someone else. The only thing saving me from despair and keeping all the pieces together was anger as black and as sticky as tar.

"God, you two make me sick!" I shouted. I slammed out the front door and down the stairs, but when I stepped from the porch to the walkway, I tripped and went flying face-first onto the snow. I fell so hard on my chest that my lungs collapsed and wouldn't open for a few long moments. I wheezed and croaked as I tried to suck air back in. I crawled over to the huge maple tree in our backyard and sat with my back to the trunk. I gazed into its branches. Whoa. Take a breath, I said to myself, standing outside myself again. I breathed and kept looking at the branches of the tree. They injected me with calm. My lungs relaxed. That's when it hit me—a realization like a silver axe in a frozen sea—anger. Damian was filled with anger, the kind of sticky, long-enduring anger that develops way underground, a tar baby that won't let you go. Michael Wright wasn't possessing Damian. Damian was possessing Wright.

42
AT THE WELL

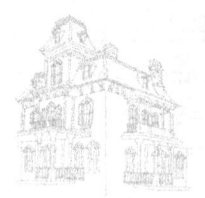

DECEMBER 24, 2016

How do you reconcile four irreconcilable facts: that your mother lied to you your entire life, the mentor you idealized deliberately misled you, she was also the indirect cause of your father's death, and that the person you love best in the world is possessed by his own anger?

Well, I wasn't going to take it sitting down; the ground was much too cold, for one thing. Weirdly, it was liberating. If the world was truly this mixed up, I wasn't that far off track. The most important fact was that Damian still needed my help and I had discovered the key.

The street lamps illuminated the cloudy night sky, making it pink. Parallelograms of light from the downstairs apartment windows stretched across the snow to my feet, crystals of snow sparkling in their path. My body seemed to be enacting Newton's law: to every action, there is an equal and opposite reaction. As hard as these revelations had thrown me, they also buoyed me. Both my mother and my aunt had lied, yes, but that didn't mean everything

I'd learned from Athena was wrong. I had a lifetime of visions, and I knew how my body felt when I did an energy weave, particularly at Jacob's house.

The snow's glister massaged my eyes, and my ego fell away as I simplified and expanded myself to be the physical materials of the universe, a wonderful "we." It was all a pattern, the reason my mother had hidden my father's powers from me, the crumpled photographs. Damian's face flashed before me from that distant afternoon in the library, his fingers tapping *the gathering place of the sun*. "You know," he had said, "because it resonates. What's in here matches what's out there." I patted the tree. Its dormant energy radiated clear through me. The answer was in the physical. In the earth. It balanced me. When I ignored my intuition, I was paralyzed. When I followed it, I knew what to do. I got off my butt to galvanize Athena and Audrey into action.

That's when the phone rang.

The caller ID showed random numbers and letters. My heart burned like the coil of an electric stove on high. I pressed the talk button. Static. A male voice cutting in and out of static. Then the static cleared.

"Julie!" His voice was weak but urgent.

"Damian?"

"Help me."

"Where are you?" I said, my heart seizing.

"I'm at the well."

"The well?"

"The North Woods."

"What are you doing *there*?"

"He's got me."

"Who?"

"*Hurry!*"

"Hold on. I'll be right there. I'll get—"

"*No.* Come alone!"

"But—"

The phone went dead.

It wasn't far from our house to campus. I ran as fast as I could, the frigid air knuckling over my lungs like a washboard. By the time I got to the trailhead, my lungs burned. It was darker in the woods, but the pink-clouded sky made it possible to see. The path was a wiggly line of packed snow drawing me onward. I slipped and slid down toward the well. If I'd been thinking straight, I would have noticed there were no footprints. Damian stood on the path facing away from me. He was wearing a hoodie with the hood up, but I could tell it was him by his height and lean build.

"Damian!" I called. He didn't turn. I ran up behind him. "Damian." Still, he didn't turn. My foot slipped as I neared, and I slid right into him. He startled, turned, and steadied me, his arms on my arms.

It was someone else. A stranger. He smiled, and his teeth gleamed in the darkness—they were just like mine, with accentuated canines, front teeth a little longer than the rest, a little crooked. I was looking at myself in the mirror but older and male.

"Dad?" Fog, like the pink sky, clouded my brain. I swayed.

"Julie!" he said, his grip on my arms reaffirming itself, his voice lower, gruffer than Damian's. "I've been trying to reach you for so long!" His accent was faintly British, but Americanized.

This was wrong. It was all I had ever wanted, but it was terribly wrong. I pushed away from him. My mind cleared a bit. "You're dead." His body was definitely solid.

"Not dead, trapped. I've freed myself. Come. It's me. Remember."

I took another step back and swayed but regained my balance. I mean—this was crazy. Even though he resembled me and felt solid to the touch, it was twisted. He was speaking so sweetly, acting like this was so normal. And where was Damian? I was so sure that was his voice on the phone, the slight breathiness, the suede notes.

"Damian is hurt," he said as if reading my mind. "I'll bring you to him."

I knew this was a bad idea, but the tug in my chest when he said

Damian's name was impossible to resist. The thought that he was alone, that he was hurting, that he needed me, made my chest cave in. I threw a glance over my shoulder, thinking vaguely that I should contact my mother and Athena.

But again, as if reading my mind, he said, "You can't trust them. They're the ones who have been keeping me captive." That should have been the red flag. But Athena's words came back to me, *I have managed to trap his spirit on the property in an old well, but he has been testing the boundaries.* What else was she lying about? And then there was my dream.

"Mom and Athena trapped you?"

"*Yes.* They think I'm crazy, but I hold the key to this whole place."

I rummaged through the mess that had become my thoughts. My mother had lied, too, after all. *He needed psychiatric help, medication, and institutionalization.* It fit. Anything was possible. He could be alive, I supposed dimly.

"They've been keeping you in a hospital?" I said, fog filling my legs and arms. I couldn't remember the name of the place where people went when they were having a breakdown. It was nearby, down Route 9. Everyone knew the name. What was it?

He hesitated for half a second. "That's right."

"Four Winds?" I asked.

"We don't have time for this. Damian is in danger." His eyes flared when he said that. Or at least, I thought I saw a glimmer. But eyes don't actually emit light, do they? My pulse pounded in my ears like they were plugged. "Follow me," he said, motioning me toward a path that veered downhill past the well.

I slipped and slid after him down the hill, keeping a good ten feet away, so there was no way he could touch me or push me into a hole in the ground. I was lightheaded, my vision was slipping, and my inner ear was thrown off balance. It could have been the cold. It could have been that I hadn't eaten for forever, and it could have been that I was in shock. I hadn't dressed warmly enough. As I tumbled after him, my feet lost feeling, and my eyeballs felt like stone. He led me on a path I'd never encountered in all my runs through the North Woods, but I was only peripherally aware of this, as if he were also leading me down paths through my mind.

He led me to a cabin I didn't know was there. Maybe it was a dormitory, I thought, fuzzily. When he opened the door, warmth and light beckoned. "He's in here. I found him wandering in the woods," he said.

For some reason, when we opened the cabin door, there were stone stairs going down, but I immediately accepted this. We descended to a narrow hallway, then up wooden stairs. When we got to the top, he opened the door and light spilled over us. We weren't in a cabin at all, but an Adirondack great camp, with wood beams across the high ceiling, buck heads on the walls, and a huge carved stone fireplace in which a fire roared. A rose velvet settee with a camel back faced the fire, its curved arms rolling outward elegantly. It sat on a royal blue Persian rug bordered with roses.

I rounded the corner of the settee, and there Damian lay, asleep on the couch, one arm raised to cradle his head, his jaw carving an angular line against it. "Damian!" I ran to him and shook him.

"Shh, he's resting," my father said.

Damian didn't stir.

"Where are we?" I asked.

"We are home," he said. "I have waited for you so long." My head floated away from my body, but I managed to check my phone. No service.

He was now dressed in a wine-colored silk smoking jacket, and his hair was white. When had he changed? He turned his broad back to me and crossed the great room to a crystal decanter on a silver tray. Where was the lean figure in the hoodie?

"This will warm you," he said, pouring deep red liquid into a cut crystal glass. He brought it over to me, and I could smell the wine wafting toward me. "Drink," he said.

I did not want to take the glass, but my hands reached for it, oddly eager, and my mouth watered as if I'd been thirsting for this elixir my entire life. I stared into his puffy face with a white handlebar mustache, and my eyes stung as if from a bright light as I raised the glass to my lips to sniff it. Someone knocked it from my hand. It crashed to the ground and the house vanished.

I was sitting in what appeared to be the remains of a cellar. Athena stood panting before me, shining a flashlight through the darkness at me. I shook my head and looked at my feet. The thick, cut crystal goblet lay on its side, crusted with dirt. A puddle of wine still remained in it, the rest spilled on the packed dirt floor. I opened my mouth to ask her how she had found me, when a great force, like a swarm of shouting voices, rushed Athena and pushed her to the ground. The force took on a vaguely human shape and straddled her, hands at her throat. It doesn't matter how prepared for or unafraid you are of spirits. When you encounter one, it sends a shock of horror through your body. But my Pusher's lion paws gripped my gut and I scrambled to my feet.

"Get off her!" I screamed, pushing at the vague bulk of it, but of course, my hands went through it, and the current of its energy grabbed onto me like a riptide of electricity. For a second, I couldn't let go of it, like when you grab onto an electrified fence. It seemed to turn its head toward me, and then a great force threw me to the cellar floor. A scrabbling noise behind me drew my attention. The beam of another flashlight bounced down the stairs, and my mother came tumbling after, stumbling on the uneven wood steps, her breath rising in clouds above her.

"Mom, help!"

"What's going on?" my mother cried. By the confused way her eyes darted around the scene, I could tell that she couldn't see the force. She saw me sprawled on my back and Athena wrestling with nothing. Athena's voice rasped but couldn't form words because the force was choking off her air.

As my mother knelt at my side, the figure looked up. When it saw my mother, its seething molecules slowed to a momentary standstill. Athena seized the moment to roll clear of it.

The mass coalesced into the form of my father, thin, in the hoodie again, but I could see the walls of the cellar faintly behind him, illuminated by his own light. "Audrey?" he said, his voice and face flickering and frayed like a damaged hologram.

My energy calmed, my head cleared, and my chest warmed like whiskey as my father's love radiated through me.

As she stood, Athena's stern features cycled rapidly from concern to assessment to recognition to love. She pushed her long white hair back from her face, straightened, and smiled.

"What's going on?" my mother repeated again, now looking from me to Athena. It must have looked odd to her, the two of us scruffy-maned and panting, staring at the same spot.

"He's here," I said to her. "Dad."

"What?" she sucked in her breath sharply, all her features hardening with fear and resistance. Athena came to her side, and we both put our hands on her shoulders.

"Blimey, I've been so dense," Athena whispered behind my mother's back. "You and your mother are the missing elements. *This* is how we can free your father from the other's grasp," she said, referring to Hilton.

She turned to my mother. "Audrey. We need you to see him. Are you willing to try?"

"Audrey," my father said again, but the flickering grew more violent, his outline expanded and the other face, the old man with the white sideburns filtered through, his face gray and mottled like mildew. Mildew's sour scent emanated from him.

"I—," my mother said, shaking down to her bones under my hands. "I don't—"

"He needs you," Athena said. "He needs you to see him and to let him go. Your anger—"

A dry sob raked my mother's vocal cords, and her face crumpled.

"It's okay," I said to her, "We're here. We've got you. Please, Mom."

She nodded silently, her throat muscles tightening, the tendons standing out in a pronounced V in the beam of Athena's flashlight.

"Breathe with us," Athena said.

Together we all inhaled deeply, held our breath, then exhaled. Warmth radiated down my arms into my hands and into my mother's shoulders. Her neck and face smoothed like a lake after a storm. We all breathed together a few more times. Hilton's pixels continued to wrestle with my father's.

"Close your eyes," Athena said to my mother. "Julie, stand here," she motioned for me to stand behind my mother and put both my hands on her shoulders. Then Athena stood before my mother, rubbed her palms together, and placed one on my mother's forehead in the region of her third eye, and one on her heart as she whispered further instructions. Meanwhile, my father's spirit, which had been struggling with Hilton's, coalesced again.

My mother's eyes opened, and she gasped. "Peran?" She stepped toward him. She peered at me and Athena, her face a mask of shock and disbelief. "How is this possible?"

"Audrey," he said. And the tenderest expression softened his face.

My mother took another unsteady step toward him, but Athena barred her way. "Hold on. Don't touch him. It's both of them."

"Audrey," he said again, his voice cutting in and out like a bad cell phone connection. "I'm so sorry."

My mother's face softened, "Peran," she said, "I can't believe it's you."

"It is," he seemed to say, but there was no sound.

"I'm the one who should be sorry," she said.

My eyes stung and my throat throbbed as if lacerated.

My father's face flickered like a flame in strong wind. The image of the white-haired man took over, then my father's face again.

"Julie, I will need your Changer to reinforce me," Athena said. "Pull the energy down from the sky and send it through your mother to me."

I nodded.

Athena turned toward the grappling spirits, pressed her palms together, and bowed her head. With my Pusher's warm hug at my hips, a thin blue line of ice etched a circle at my crown and opened a path to the sky. The connected presence of the towering trees beyond the cellar stairs made themselves known, a network of calm. Reality filled out into four dimensions. It's hard to describe, but it's like there was an up, down, forward, back, and space in between. Something that felt like starlight shot down through my skull, out my hands, through my mother's chest, and into Athena. Cool energy unfolded from her like wings, surrounding me and my mother, as well as my father's spirit. It was the kind of cool you find on a summer's morning, dewy and easily warmed. Only after I felt it did I realize we were all feverish.

"Peran," Athena said. "We love you. We've come to free you."

His image stabilized, and he smiled at her. His mouth moved, but the words did not come through.

"Audrey, you need to forgive him," Athena said. "Your anger has been helping to hold him here and contributing to why he doesn't have the strength to free himself from you-know- who."

"Forgive him?" my mother said. "I need *him* to forgive *me*. I need you all to forgive me."

My father's lips seemed to form the words "For what?" but still we couldn't hear him.

"It's okay, Mom. We understand," I said, noticing that my cheeks were wet—was I crying? Or was it melted snow on my cheeks? The wintry air wasn't touching us. We stood in a pocket of summer's dawn.

"For not believing you," my mother spoke now directly to my father. "For trying to erase you. For keeping you from our daughter."

My father looked over my mother's shoulder at me, and bubbling energy like a whitecap foamed around me.

"Say the words, and say his name often. It strengthens him. Peran," Athena said. My mother reached down inside herself and straightened as if pulling a bucket up from a well. "I forgive you,

Peran, for taking so many risks, for dying. Yes. Peran. I have been angry, so terribly, angry at you for dying. I forgive you, and I'm sorry. I know you were just being who you are. Peran. My Peran."

He smiled and his image crisped at the edges.

"Dad," I said. That fragmented memory of sitting on someone's knee while he chanted *"This is the way the lady went,"* fused together, and I remembered this face laughing down at me, and me grinning up at him so hard my cheeks hurt. "I re-member you," I said, pausing between the syllables to emphasize how memory puts things back together.

Energy came from his eyes and connected to mine, warming them as he touched his hand to his heart. He opened his mouth to speak, but his face guttered like a flame in wind, and Henry Hilton's distorted face split through his like a fire shrieking through the cracks, burning into our chests, infusing our nostrils with the stench of mildew and rot, melting away Athena's envelope of cool. My energy faltered.

"Peran," Athena said, "Peran Sykes. Stay with us."

A high-pitched, undignified, "Oh!" escaped from my mother's lips as she backed up. Athena swayed.

Hilton's image churned into lines that twisted, exploded, condensed, and tangled. The smell of burnt hair filled our nostrils as the heat intensified, roasting our faces.

I must have whimpered or lost my grip. "Hold on," Athena said, but her cool wasn't reaching me.

Then it began to snow. Great, huge flakes, four or five adhering to each other at a time, came floating down the cellar stair like someone had torn open a down pillow and was dropping fistfuls of feathers.

Athena saw them and waved the snowflakes forward into the cellar, their energy cooling us.

The swirling mass of Hilton's lines lost energy. Athena's wings of summer cool flared back out, great pockets of dewy summer the exact same temperature as our bodies, and the snow-filled sky streamed down through me, through my mother, and through Athena, cooling the seething mass until it slowed, and as it slowed, shrank. My father's image reemerged, filled with light, though at his belly a tangle of worms writhed as if he'd swallowed Hilton.

"Peran, I love you," my mother said "I never stopped loving you. The depth of my anger is the measure of my pain, the measure of my love."

"We all love you, Peran Sykes," Athena said.

"Yes, Dad," I added. My father turned and put his hand against the cellar wall. We followed his gesture. There was a rectangle of some sort cemented all the way around the edges. That's when I realized, with a burn of adrenaline up my forearms, that we weren't in a cellar, but a secret mausoleum. "This?" Athena said, touching it. She directed her flashlight beam at it.

He nodded.

"Stewart," he said, his voice spattered with gaps of silence.

"We'll take care of it," Athena said.

He smiled and pressed his hands to his heart, but the wormy tangle at his center still seethed.

"Rest now," she said.

His smile grew strained and he spoke again, but the only word that made it through was "love".

He wrapped his arms around himself, pressing himself inward around the tangled mass at his core. Then his energy condensed into a ball of light that vanished into the rectangle on the wall. He was gone.

The air became just air, empty in contrast to what we had endured.

We, the living, stood, breathing hard, in the cold small room underground, without the dead. No one said anything. I felt like I could cry for days. My mother and Athena looked like they felt the same, and the feathery flakes kept drifting down through the stairwell. We mounted the stairs, and once outside among the trees, we wrapped our arms around each other and hugged each other tightly, feeling the solid flesh and bone of us, the heat of our breath at the center while snowflakes settled in our hair at the periphery. The enormity of the night's events buffeted us like gusts of storm winds. Collectively, our teeth chattered, and we realized we were frozen to the bone.

43
POCKETFUL OF DIRT

DECEMBER 25, 2016

We didn't want to separate, so we agreed to sleep at Athena's house. Also, if the redirection hadn't worked, her house, bolstered by Anima Arcanum safeguards, had the best protection from unwanted spirits. We called the hospital to see if Damian was there. He was. It had been Hilton's spirit that had lured me out and had taken on the appearance of my father on the path. Once we knew Damian was okay, we sank into Athena's beds which were deep, soft, and piled with heavy down comforters as thick as snow. I slept like—well—I won't say the dead—because—obviously they didn't always sleep that well, but it was a heavy, dreamless sleep.

The next morning, I stumbled into Athena's ridiculously opulent kitchen, with acres of glass-fronted cabinets, tile floors, high stools, and granite countertops. I felt like I had a hangover, with an achy head, tired body, and slight nausea. My mother looked like I felt, what with her pallor, smeared eyeliner, and the stiff way she moved. Athena's cappuccino machine gurgled and spit, and she placed a new cup before my mother, who wrapped her hands around it appreciatively.

"Merry Christmas," Athena said to me. "Coffee?"

"Wow. It *is* Christmas, isn't it? This has got to be the weirdest Christmas I've ever had," I said, pulling up a stool to the granite island where my mother sat.

We were all silent, each immersed in our memories of the night before. I was still in the *wow-that-just-happened* stage of things where I couldn't tell what I felt or how it had changed me. The hot infusion of coffee was divine. I'd woken with a revelation.

"I know what the problem is with Damian," I said. They both set their coffee on the counter and stilled. "He is angry at his father. But we didn't recognize it because it's not that ascending kind of anger-chi. It's anger mixed with grief and obstinacy, and it's been cooped up and pressed down because he could never admit it to himself because he's so busy being his mother's perfect son. So it's sticky and hot like tar. When Michael Wright—"

Athena shot me a warning look and I corrected myself. "When W killed J, he was consumed with anger and guilt, and a part of him must have kept returning to the house. That's when W had what everyone thought was a stroke. His spirit became obsessed with the place and couldn't let go."

"Go on," Athena said.

"When Damian showed up, W's spirit must have recognized his anger and, thinking it was returning to its own body, entered Damian and got stuck, like Br'er Rabbit to the tar baby. That's why Damian went back to the house that day I found him. W's spirit was trying to get home by taking Damian to the last place it remembered. When I pulled him to the surface," I looked at Athena, "Damian started to fight off W with his body—hence the elevated white blood cell count. Then his Dad came in and was trying to force Damian's anger to come out. I was trying to calm him down, trying to get him to forgive his father before he'd even acknowledged his anger.

Domination increases the imbalance. That's why he went into convulsions."

"That's brilliant. I think you've got it," said Athena, her dark eyes looking particularly sharp when the crease between her brows deepened.

"We need to do another redirection. Right away," I said. The phone rang.

"He's gone," Damian's mother wept into the phone.

"What do you mean? We checked on him last night!" I said, shooting a warning look at my mother and Athena. They stood up. I put the phone on speaker.

"The police are here. No one knows where he is, but they are focused on the fact that his father visited him yesterday," she said, her rich accent bending the vowels and accentuating the consonants.

"Oh, I don't think his father—"

"Kidnapping happens all the time," she said emphatically.

"I'll look for him," I said.

"Thank you."

I hung up. "He's at the Gick Road house. I know it."

"You should have told the police that," my mother said.

"No, she did the right thing," Athena said. "We need to get to him first."

"But—he needs medical care," my mother said.

"He could die if we don't perform a redirection right away," Athena said.

"Please, Mom. After what you saw last night . . ."

"No, you're right. I won't get in your way. I let your father down by not believing him, and I'll make it up to you."

"Meanwhile, we could really use your help," Athena said. "We might need Damian's father present to perform a full redirection."

"This is his phone number," I said, whipping out my phone.

"No," my mother grabbed my arm. "I'm staying with my daughter. You go get Damain's father."

"But she needs me," Athena said, "To keep her anchored."

"No, she needs *me*," my mother said, stepping in close to me. My right knee shook for a second as I realized how true that was. "I'll be her anchor." Athena searched our faces. Doubt and worry tumbled over her face like shadows from wind-tossed trees.

"Very well. If I don't find him right away, I'm coming without him."

"I'll call Samantha and Jonathan, too," I said. "We can use all the help we can get."

Athena grabbed my mother by the arm. "Keep your hands on her as she performs the ritual. Don't fight what you see. Stay neutral and hold on. Can you do that?"

My mother nodded. Athena grabbed her car keys and phone and headed for the door, then stopped. "If anything seems like it's more than you can handle," she said to me, "wait for me."

"I can do this," I said.

I called Samantha and Jonathan, and they were eager to join me. I figured it could only help to have a few more anchors—a few more safe people to call Damian home. I told them to meet me at the All-Mart parking lot but not to go into the house. My mom and I headed for the car.

It had snowed at least eight more inches since we'd gone to bed, muting the world. The bitter cold of the air shocked our lungs. The sky was so thick with clouds you couldn't see the sun. Our breath all but fell in chunks of ice to the ground as my mother cracked the doors and buckled up.

The plows hadn't gotten to Route 50 yet, and our tires rolled silently over the snow, sliding here and there. My mother drove grimly as I filled her in on everything that had been happening. "I don't know what we are going to find when we get there, Mom. But I will need you to listen to me and do what I say, okay?"

She absorbed this in silence for a moment. "It's very hard to force yourself to believe in something you've never believed in," she said, "even when you've seen it with your own eyes."

"Would you rather believe I'm crazy?"

She glanced over at me, her brows deeply creased. Then they cleared. "I know you're not crazy. And I know your father wasn't either."

My throat ached and my eyes pricked with tears at that. Seeing him made the loss fresher. But I had to push that from my mind to concentrate on Damian.

I described my Seer, Pusher, and Changer, and how I needed to relax and concentrate at the same time.

A couple of small trucks were plowing the All-Mart parking lot at the far end, the sound of the blades scraping against pavement muted by winter's swaddling. Jonathan's rusty clunker was already parked at the far end, exhaust billowing blue. The cloud cover had thinned somewhat, and the sun shone through milkily, but the earth was still cocooned.

"Julie!" Samantha said, as she hopped out of the car and ran toward me. Jonathan cut the engine and emerged more slowly. "So what's the deal? Are we going to perform an exorcism?"

"No, it's not called that. It's called a *redirection*."

"Tell me what to do."

Her energy was so vibrant and grounding that I grinned and hugged her. "God, I love you."

"I love you, too," she laughed and hugged me back.

"First off," I said, coming out of the hug, "we have to see if he's there."

"Oh, he is! Look."

A solitary line of footprints led toward the house.

"Mostly, I need you to be there. Your presence alone will help balance things and fortify my energy. I feel like a million bucks already because of you," I said.

"Aw!" she said. "I can do a calming prayer."

"Yes, whatever happens. I need you to stay as calm as possible."

"I can do that," she said.

I took a moment to focus on her. She had always had high,

bubbly energy, but something new was shining through, some older, more sober part of herself.

"Come on," I said.

We all zipped up, buttoned up, tucked our pants into our boots, and put on our mittens and gloves with the seriousness of a swat team of snow bunnies. I led the way, stepping in Damian's footprints and trying to open my Seer to collect information. It was hard going because I had to lift my feet high to get over the snow, and my foot kept slipping off the hard pack print at the bottom of Damian's footwells, throwing me off balance. The mottled brown and gray house rose with its mansard roof and side balconies, the spiky weather vane on top of the square tower barely surmounting the foot of snow contained by the iron railing. Eyebrows of white outlined the curved tops of the windows. Each branch of the lone oak beside it was outlined in white. The snow gave me hope because of how it had balanced the feng shui at my father's redirection the night before. As we neared the chain-link fence, that stone-grinding, hot tar energy reached me.

Damian had dug out the snow from the spot where we slipped under the fence. As I shimmied through the place his body had been, I picked up a skim coat of his body energy. It had reached a crisis point. "Hurry," I said, panic rising.

I held the fence as my mother, Jonathan and Sam slipped under. When we got to the back porch, I stopped and said, "Hold up." They all waited.

I needed something before I entered. I glanced around, closed my eyes, and breathed, staying with my uneasiness. Nothing. Then a craving for *earth*.

"I need a handful of dirt," I said. We all stared stupidly at the snow-covered ground surrounding us.

"Under there," Jonathan said, hands thrust deep into his army-green canvas parka, pointing with the tip of his boot at the rotting latticework at the edge of the porch. "I used to play under our porch in all weather, and the dirt was always loose under there."

"Brilliant," I said, admiring how Jonathan was stepping up. He was actually into this.

I dug through the snow and pulled off a few thin boards. Under the porch, as Jonathan had predicted, the dirt was gray, fine, and loose. I took off my gloves and rubbed it all over my hands as if it was soap. My hands were stiff with cold as I put a handful of dirt in each pocket. My mother stood on the porch steps, holding her collar closed.

"Stay behind me," I said, as we entered the house.

As soon as I opened the door, the volatile rotten egg smell of gasoline hit me. I ran to the kitchen. Damian was splashing gasoline out of a red plastic jug all around the kitchen. He stopped and tried to strike a match.

"Wait!" I cried. My mother, Sam, and Jonathan crowded in behind me. As soon as she saw Damian, Samantha started muttering, "Gracious Lady, Mother of all, we call on you to . . ."

I smiled gratefully and then tuned her out as I focused inward. Damian seemed not to hear us. His hands were bluish and wouldn't cooperate. He was so thin that his black jeans draped hollowly around his legs. His cheek and jaw bones jutted under a tinge of black stubble, and his skin was gray. His body was dying, I realized with a stab.

I took a deep breath. I had been too direct, too willful at the hospital. When you run at the moon, it backs up. I needed to walk beside the moon the way Damian had shown me and try to pretend it wasn't a ticking bomb.

"Damian," I said.

When he turned and saw me, he yelled, "You," dropped the gas can, and lunged at me. The shock and instantaneousness of it stole my breath away. He grabbed me by the collar and swung me around. My mother and Samantha screamed, my mother grabbed his arms, and I fought back. So much for staying calm. "You did this to me!" he yelled as he shook me.

All my senses slammed into hyper-drive at once, and I was

surrounded by the burning hot tar of his fury. Hot stones ground in my ears. The scene turned amber, and behind him, Jacob surfaced and reached out to us in alarm, but he was unable to touch us. I struggled to get free, yelling I don't know what.

"You brought me to this!" Damian said. I tried to look into his eyes to see who it was, but it seemed like both of them. We slammed around the room, knocking things to the floor, surrounded by that growling force. "You won't go away. I'll kill you as many times as it takes. I'll tear this house apart with my teeth if I have to."

"Let her go," my mother screamed, still pulling at him. I could barely hear her above the roar of fury. His hands closed around my neck. I pulled on his wrists.

"Precious Mother, guide us . . ." Samantha's voice reached my ears.

"Damian!" Jonathan yelled sharply, with command summoned from some secret source.

I used the weight of my body to fall backward away from Damian. Damian lost his grip and I twisted and began to crawl away, but he caught me by the feet. My mind turned animal—wordless and afraid.

". . .Bless our hands, that they may heal, not harm," Samantha's voice beat like a drum. "Bless our feet, that we may walk beside each other in peace . . ." Then it came to me. *Stop resisting.*

I slowed down. Damian dragged me backward by the feet toward the gasoline can.

"Mom. Let go of him. Hold onto *me*."

"He'll kill you!" Fear stretched her features so she was unrecognizable.

"Hold onto *me*," I commanded. I curled up, grabbed hold of Damian's arms, and pulled myself to my feet. "I need your anchor," I shouted.

Dimly, I was aware that Samantha was still chanting, pressed against the wall, eyes closed, "Great Goddess, mother of birth, death and rebirth, Goddess of the Earth that holds us, hold us *now* . . ."

My mother grabbed onto my coat and pulled in the opposite direction, ripping my jacket pocket open. Dirt flew out in an arc. Time caught and slowed. We were all transfixed as the gray-brown dust fell in slow motion around us and the finer parts drifted upward. *Dirt reduces fire.* I whipped off my mittens and wrapped my arms around Damian and let gravity pull me to the ground bringing us all down together. As we tumbled, I dove for the dirt, swiped my palm through it, then twisted and clamped my hand around Damian's wrist.

The rumbling noise lowered a decibel. I swiped my other palm through the dirt and caught his other wrist. The roaring lessened again. "*Hold* me, Mom, don't pull me," I said, as my calm mounted. I turned back to Damian. "I am your anger. Embrace me." He stopped moving and fixated on my hands clenched around his wrists as if he'd never seen them before. My Pusher helped me cast my energy around him. My Seer opened inside the circle, and the Changer came online as the crown of my head sliced open to the sky, opening the path. A clean, cool tongue of blue slid down into our bodies, filling us both with the height of the highest sky, the reach of the farthest, most invisible stars. "Damian," I said, whether aloud or in my mind, I don't know. "Come to the surface. Use the anger to pull yourself up." The right kind of anger could be a galvanizing energy, I realized, as I heard myself speak.

I reached inside of him, my lungs opening like wings of air, breathing it all in. A hot creosote smell filled my nostrils and singed my lungs, but instead of pulling back from it, I breathed into the burn. *It's okay. It's just pain. Embrace it.* A sliver of Damian writhed like an eel in darkness, deep down in the depths. Then anger became a ladder and he grabbed hold of the rungs and pulled himself up hand over hand by the very thing that had held him down, until he burst to the surface like a swimmer. He gasped and his eyes went dark blue. "I'm furious at him," he panted. "At my father. He lost control. He beat Carl. I couldn't stop him. And then he left us. He made me ashamed to be a man."

I hugged him tightly. "Hold onto that anger. Don't stop it. Don't become it. Walk beside it like we walked beside the moon. Remember the night we—kissed?" The kiss broke upon me as it broke upon him.

His breath caught as if he were about to cry, or hiccup, or cough. "I'll help you hold it," I said. "It's too much for one person to hold alone."

I don't know if it happened in our minds or outside of us, but I felt us holding hands and opening our arms into a big circle around a column of heat. At some point, Jonathan and Samantha joined the circle. The grinding stones, the growling energy, the creosote smell, we held it all between us for I don't know how long like the maid who held onto Tam Lin as he metamorphosed from snake to bear to hot poker. When you're in a sailboat and the wind gets too strong, you turn into the wind instead of away from it to stop, but at the first part of the turn, the wind bears down harder and the boat heels more dangerously than ever, and then it slides out of the sail and the boat becalms. That's just how it was. The anger billowed high above us and between us, but we stayed with it and held on as it frothed and bubbled and jammed. All the while I could feel my mother's hands pressing on my back, as Athena had done, reminding me that I was okay, that I was connected to the earth, that I was loved.

At some point, the anger reached its limit and gradually weakened and transformed to all the different colors of grief, love, beauty, and change. We held on until it had completely rearranged itself and achieved balance, whereupon it settled back into Damian like scattered tools returned to all their proper places. Damian took a deep breath. His skin turned pink. We embraced and I could feel his body was clear of Michael Wright and had begun to shake.

The change of air pressure clicked in my ears. I felt a scuffle in the air. My Seer opened. Michael Wright, now free of Damian's body, lunged for Jacob in what looked like liquid amber. "Let go of me," he yelled. Jacob raised both his hands and stepped back like a man under arrest, his brows wide, his face open, silently bespeaking his innocence.

"Michael," I said. He stopped, and looked at me, still grasping Jacob. "He's not holding onto you. You're holding onto *him*. Let go. Forgive yourself." His grip on Jacob loosened and his chest caved inward.. "It was an accident," he said.

"I know."

He paused, while anger and grief wrestled across his face. Then his face crumpled.

"I was greedy," he said.

"I know. But you're also sorry."

He looked like someone hearing distant music.

"Is that all it takes?" he asked.

"That's all it takes," I said, only dimly aware of the living bodies behind me, hovering in confusion. Samantha was chanting again.

Slowly Wright relinquished Jacob. Tension spilled out of Jacob's spirit in a long sigh. Then the two of them shimmered like the dying embers of fireworks and burnt out.

"Julie?" Damian said.

I locked eyes with Damian. There it was, that old look I loved so much, starry sky, deep compassion, wise love. Damian took in all our faces, and Samantha and Jonathan panted and smiled up at him.

The back door slammed, and in came Athena and Mr. Quinn at a trot. Damian's eyes widened when he saw his father, but they didn't lose their depth.

When Mr. Quinn's eyes met Damian's, I saw that familiar shock of surprise for one suspended second, and then he fell into Damian's eyes as I had done a million times before.

"My God, you're alright," he said, as he closed the distance between them, taking off his coat. He wrapped it around Damian, and Damian allowed his father to take care of him.

EPILOGUE

SPRING, 2017

That spring, Blue Karner butterflies mysteriously appeared all over Jacob Johnson's property. They are tiny, innocuous, periwinkle butterflies. It turns out that they are endangered, so the Wilton town council dropped the land quest. The area was turned into a preserve. A pocket park, they called it, and the house was scheduled for restoration for a small business incubator and environmental center.

Athena alerted Skidmore College to the location of the mausoleum, Stewart's body was exhumed, and the DNA was compared to his living descendants. It was, as far as could be ascertained, him. His body was restored to its proper resting place, and there was a new interment ceremony.

Not long after that, we learned from Maureen that Michael Wright had experienced a "miraculous" recovery and confessed to the accidental manslaughter of Jacob Johnson. She confirmed what we already knew: Wright had gone out to Jacob's house to convince him to drop the lawsuit. Jacob had threatened him with a gun, they had struggled, and the gun had gone off. Because it was so long ago and there were no witnesses and no proof, the matter was dropped. There are two kinds of justice in this country. One for the wealthy and one for the poor. Nevertheless, I was glad. Wright had been through enough.

I visited the mausoleum site many times, hoping to find a trace of my father's spirit. I was disappointed, even though I knew it was for the best.

My mother and I started to get to know each other again. Over a few months of therapy, she realized that she had unconsciously believed she was the indirect cause of my father's death. She had been so unable to deal with that possibility that she covered it with anger and devoted herself to denying every aspect of the spirit world. But Athena explained that even though my mother's anger had been part of what hampered my father's ability to extricate himself from Hilton after death, the truth was that Peran's shame and trauma over how he grew up had made him vulnerable to Hilton.

My mother agreed to let me continue to train with Athena, and sometimes she sat in on sessions so she could understand better. Damian began to train with Athena, too. Samantha would have joined us, but she discovered she was pregnant, and she and Jonathan decided to keep the child. I thought age 19 was crazy early to start a family, but then, Samantha has big mother energy, so, more power to her. She intuited what Athena confirmed. You don't want to mess with energy weaves when you're pregnant, because that's a particular weave of its own.

Samantha's mother didn't return, but Samantha learned that heroin blocks the part of the brain that feels a connection to other human beings. Her mother didn't leave her because she didn't love her, but because heroin had destroyed her ability to love. Samantha hoped that if she found her mother again, we could perform some sort of soul retrieval for her, and the thought of future training for that time gave her comfort.

No one but me saw the interaction between Wright and Jacob, by the way. But it was clear that Wright's spirit had been preventing Jacob's spirit from moving on. Like my mother, he was stuck in his anger, but his anger was actually covering the thing he was more afraid of, his guilt. When he was inside Damian, his anger got free reign, and mixing with Damian's repressed anger, began to build. Anger is supposed to have an ascending chi, but when it was mixed with his fear, his grief, and the stickiness of his mother's energy, his chi became sticky and overly intense. Wright was literally stuck inside Damian. That minor feng shui adjustment I had made by touching Damian with dirt had helped to contain the anger enough for Damian and me to do the rest of the work. Jonathan and Samantha's energy had helped guide him back to where he was supposed to be. The pull of community is huge, something humanity used to understand, and now something our generation is beginning to understand. The dirt had also, perhaps, helped to reduce Wright's anger enough for him to be ready to hear what I said. Anger isn't the enemy, Athena said. It was a tool being used in the wrong way.

"So, our greatest weakness is also our greatest strength?" I said.

"Not strengths. Not weaknesses. Attributes. Our greatest challenge in life is to discover our abilities and their limits, and then find the most productive application for each one," Athena said.

Those phone calls were from Hilton. He had been trying to collect all his descendants and bring them to the site of his once-opulent compound. His spirit was bound by his murder of Stewart, but it had been largely insentient until it began to siphon my father's energy off of him. The more powerful Hilton grew, the more his spirit infected the campus, and he was probably at least part of what fueled the rise in Trumpism on the Skidmore campus.

As for Trump . . . he hasn't gone away. He is the manifestation of our collective evil, our repressed past and disguised violence surfacing and squeezing out like pus from a subterranean pimple. Humanity is a haunted giant destroying everyone in its path as we march inexorably toward our own extinction.

But at least there are butterflies, at least the Nazi clubs at

Skidmore were addressed, and at least I had all my friends, a loving mother, and an aunt. I have faith in our collective energy to find beauty no matter what happens.

Damian's father hung around for a few weeks after Damian's deliverance, and he got to know all his children better.

"He's a funny guy," Damian told me one day. "He and Carl are nearly identical. They have a blast together until they get into a fight. But my Dad's in a better place now, and Carl can take care of himself. I stay out of it. They're like two cats. They get into a spat, ignore each other for a while, and then act like nothing happened."

Speaking of Damian, he recovered completely, and I got over my fear of intimacy. But gentlewomen don't kiss and tell, so I'm not gonna share that part. Use your imagination.

Spring came as never before. Or maybe with my arms around Damian and his around me, I saw it for the first time. I had forgotten what the earth smelled like when it was warmed by the sun, how you walk through clouds of flower scent before you see the flowers, and how black the hemlocks look when backlit by sun-filled beech trees. In winter, you can see the lay of the land, but when the leaves return, each step of the path is new. Damian and I spent every moment we could together, far off the path where all was sacred and private, floating a haze of pollen and cottonwood fluff, mesmerized by how each cell of our bodies contains the universe. Sure, our energy sometimes gets too enmeshed as I had feared, but Athena says that happens even with normal people, and we'd figure it out in time.

I dreamt of my father the other night. He was stepping out of a ruined tower, the stones of which had recently tumbled. He smiled at me and walked away. Instead of grieving, I felt happy.

BOOK CLUB QUESTIONS

1. What are the main themes of the book? How are those themes brought to life?
2. How many ghosts are in this story? Who are they, what keeps them here, and how are they different?
3. What other things haunt people and places in this book?
4. What part does the location of the book play in the characters' lives and the plot?
5. Did your opinion of the book change as you read it?
6. What was your favorite passage or part? Why?
7. What motivates the main character's actions in the book?
8. Which plot twists did you love?
9. Which scenes were pivotal in the book?
10. Have you read other books by this author? How do they compare?

ABOUT THE AUTHOR

Lâle Davidson is a distinguished professor of writing at SUNY Adirondack and winner of the SUNY Chancellor's Award for Creative Activities. Emperor Books, an imprint of Red Penguin Books, published her fabulist fiction collection *Strange Appetites* including winner of the *Wigleaf* top 50 of Very Short Fiction award, "The Opal Maker" in 2021. Her debut novel, *Blue Woman Burning*, was released in 2021, and *Against the Grain*, an environmental thriller with a mystical twist, was released in 2022. She lives in Saratoga Springs, NY, with her husband and two cats. Her adult kid, an artist, graduated from The School of the Museum of Fine Arts at Tufts in 2023.